# Praise for the Amish Quilt novels

### *The Wounded Heart*

"This relatable story, which launches Senft's Amish Quilt series, shows that while waiting to see God's plan can be difficult, remembering to put Jesus first, others next and yourself last ('JOY') is necessary."

—*Romantic Times*, four stars

"With this quaint, gentle read, Senft's promising series is off to a good start and will make a nice alternative for Jerry S. Eicher readers who want to try a new author."

—*Library Journal*

"Senft perfectly captures the Amish setting of the novel. Amelia is an endearing character, and there were a few laugh-out-loud moments for me that I wasn't even expecting. Although this is the first book I have read by the author, she has been added to my 'must read' list. If you are a fan of Amish fiction, then plan on reading *The Wounded Heart* soon!"

—Christian Fiction Addiction

### The Hidden Life

"I absolutely loved *The Hidden Life*! Nothing is as enjoyable as feeling the same way the characters do throughout the story and believing that you are mixed into the same world.... *The Hidden Life* is full of conflict, romance, and drama! Overall I felt Adina captured the Amish way of life with fine detail. Be prepared to become an even bigger fan of Adina's after you read this book and you will be eagerly anticipating the next installment *The Tempted Soul* just like me!"

—Destination Amish

### The Tempted Soul

"I do declare that Adina has saved the best story for last. I loved this book! Saying that it is a heartfelt story just doesn't seem like it does the book justice."

—Destination Amish

# HERB *of* GRACE

# HERB *of* GRACE

## A HEALING GRACE NOVEL

## ADINA SENFT

New York Boston Nashville

Copyright © 2014 by Shelley Bates
Excerpt from *Keys of Heaven* © 2014 by Shelley Bates

FaithWords
Hachette Book Group
237 Park Avenue
New York, NY 10017

www.faithwords.com

Printed in the United States of America

RRD-C

First Edition: August 2014
10 9 8 7 6 5 4 3 2 1

FaithWords is a division of Hachette Book Group, Inc.
The FaithWords name and logo are trademarks of Hachette Book Group, Inc.

The Hachette Speakers Bureau provides a wide range of authors for speaking events. To find out more, go to www.hachettespeakersbureau.com or call (866) 376-6591.

The publisher is not responsible for websites (or their content) that are not owned by the publisher.

Library of Congress Cataloging-in-Publication Data

Senft, Adina.
  Herb of grace : a healing grace novel / Adina Senft. — First edition.
      pages cm
  ISBN 978-1-4555-4862-0 (trade pbk.) — ISBN 978-1-4555-4861-3 (ebook)
  1. Herbs—Therapeutic use—Fiction. I. Title.
  PS3602.A875H48 2014
  813'.6—dc23
                                        2013043015

*For Molly*

# ACKNOWLEDGMENTS

While writing a book may be a solitary endeavor, researching and producing one takes the help and skill of many talented people. With deep gratitude I acknowledge the time and generosity of my Amish friend and reader, whose only goal in helping me is to be a light to others. My thanks also go to potters Heidi Hess and Anne Lewis, who introduced me to the art of pottery, and to herbalists Paula Grainger and Darren Huckle, who, with good humor and patience, diagnosed and prescribed for my imaginary people as though they were real. My thanks to my editor, Christina Boys, whose enthusiasm and good ideas never fail me, and to Jennifer Jackson, always the voice of reason. And last but never least, thanks go to my husband, Jeff, who treats living with a writer as though it's actually normal. I love you.

But the manifestation of the Spirit is given to every man to profit withal. For to one is given by the Spirit the word of wisdom; to another the word of knowledge by the same Spirit; to another faith by the same Spirit; to another the gifts of healing by the same Spirit.

—I Cor. 12:7–9, KJV

# AUTHOR'S NOTE

Medicinal herbs have been part of the human experience for thousands of years, as evidenced by the multitude of folk names some of them have collected. When I was researching the Healing Grace novels, I realized that people often summed up some spiritual property in certain herbs through the names they gave them, and the idea for this series was born. In each novel, the folk name reflects a healing property in the herb itself. But going a little further, God can effect a similar healing process in the spirit if we only allow Him the time and the room to do it.

So, in Book 1, "herb of grace" is the folk name for rue, a bitter and astringent herb used in small quantities for ailments of the digestive system. And as we know, *rue* is also a verb meaning to be sorry for something one has done in the past…but there is a world of difference between ruing one's mistake and coming to that place of repentance where God's grace can begin its healing work…

# HERB *of* GRACE

# CHAPTER 1

When Sarah Yoder ran the quilting needle into her finger—again—the women of her family who were gathered for sisters' day exchanged glances of sympathy, and her sister-in-law Amanda got up to fetch a Band-Aid and some cold water. Everyone in her own family and that of her in-laws knew that God had not given her a gift with needle and thread. But Sarah knew they'd never say a word—except perhaps for Ruth Lehman, who had come down from Whinburg on this windy March day to visit. Ruth was blessed with the happy conviction that when God put a thought into her mind, it was His will that she pass it along.

"Sarah, you were gripping that needle too hard. Stop fighting the thimble and it will go easier. You don't need ten stitches to the inch. Seven or eight will be just fine."

Sarah took the cloth from Amanda and dabbed carefully at the droplets of blood that she'd got on the blue border of the quilt. "I'm just grateful you include me in your quilting frolics. I'm a terrible quilter—whether the tourists at the quilt shop know it or not."

"You're a good piecer, though." Corinne's voice was gentle where Ruth's had been gruff. "Look at these pinwheels you made for the border, all color coordinated and so pretty.

My section looks as though it came straight out of the ragbag."

Corinne clearly had an obedient, color-coordinated ragbag. But Sarah appreciated the encouragement from her mother-in-law all the same. Amanda wrapped her finger as tenderly as if she were three years old, and took the cloth back to the sink.

"I like piecing," Sarah admitted, picking up the needle. Maybe she ought to put Band-Aid strips on all her fingers, just in case. "I like putting colors together and making designs. But colors and designs don't keep the boys warm at night—or *Englisch* tourists, either."

"Do they put them on their beds?" Amanda wondered aloud as she took her place and picked up her own needle. "Or do they hang them on their walls instead of using them?"

"As long as they're able to buy them, it doesn't matter to me," said Barbara Byler, who was Corinne's oldest daughter and married to one of the three Byler boys, who were now in their forties but who were still referred to as *boys*. "It's nearly time to plant the peas, and I don't know about you, but the seed catalogs eat more of my money at this time of year than I do the vegetables at harvest time. I need the money the quilts bring in."

Now here was a topic where, unlike quilting, Sarah felt right at home. But even the idea of her garden was edged with anxiety about money, because while the garden was a big one even by Amish standards, it still wasn't enough to support her and the boys. Despite the fact that they both worked hard and Simon gave her nearly all his wages, they still could not completely make ends meet. Somehow she had to come up with a plan to keep body and soul together before her house payments to her in-laws got any further in arrears.

Involuntarily, her hands tightened on the needle, she rammed it against her thimble, and it slipped down and into her knuckle. Tears welled in her eyes. With a mumble of apology, she left the needle stuck halfway through the top, batting, and backing, and fled Corinne's big front room.

When discouragement found its way past her defenses, there was only one thing to do—go outside into God's creation and look for His comfort.

On the back porch, the wind was every bit as cross and confused as she felt. It tugged the strings of her white, heart-shaped *Kapp* off her shoulders and tossed them around her face. Sarah corralled them and tied them together on her chest, the way they should have been in the first place, to signify her submission to God. Then she hugged her black, hand-knitted sweater around herself and breathed deeply of the familiar scents of an Amish farm—dairy cows; dark, fertile soil; and some indefinable sweetness—she looked down, and sure enough, in the sheltered nook by the stairs, crocuses had pushed up. Something loosened in her chest at the tiny purple blessing. Corinne's Red Star hens pecked contentedly in the cleared ground under their raised movable coop, heedless of the fact that the wind blew their feathers up the wrong way, like a woman's skirts turning inside out. And overhead, clouds scudded across the hard sky ahead of the wind, Sarah's skin prickling with the chill as they passed in front of the early afternoon sun. But despite the clouds, the sun was still there, and would come out again. All it took was patience.

When the kitchen door opened, she had almost regained her self-control, soothed by the living, growing things that reminded her of God's promise of life after a long winter. Just as the sun would not fail the plants and creatures that depended on the lengthening days for growth and harvest, He would not fail His own. She turned with a smile, expecting Corinne, and felt a spark of surprise as Ruth Lehman folded her arms and leaned on the wide porch rail.

"I hope I didn't offend you," Ruth said.

To say *ja* would be proud; to say *neh* would not quite be the truth. So Sarah merely gave her a smile as unsteady as the weather.

"How long has it been since your *Mann* died?"

That was not the trouble—or at least, not all of it. But Sarah had never confided in Ruth, though they were related by marriage and she saw the other woman fairly often. Ruth Lehman was a *Dokterfraa*—an herbal healer whose informal practice encompassed most of their district, as near as Sarah could figure out. Whenever she passed through Willow Creek to treat someone who could not come to her, Ruth stopped to visit her brother Jacob Yoder and his wife, Corinne.

During the summer and autumn, Ruth often came to the market up at the intersection of the county highway and Willow Creek Road to buy bunches of the herbs Sarah grew in her garden. Sarah tied up cooking herbs and the scented ones with raffia in pretty arrangements for the *Englisch* tourists, with recipe labels so they would know how to use them. The tourists liked her lavender, comfrey, thyme, and rosemary because they traveled well.

Ruth bought other things from her—coneflower, rue, mint, and lemon balm—because her own garden couldn't keep up with the demand. Different things than you usually found in an Amish garden, which Sarah grew because her mother had. The smell of them was all she had of her now.

"Michael passed away five years ago," she said, coming back to herself as Ruth moved impatiently. "When Caleb was nine, Simon twelve."

"Simon is a man grown now. I hope he's not one of those who use *Rumspringe* as an excuse to go wild?"

Ruth made it sound as if everyone over the age of sixteen was jumping into *Englisch* clothes and *Englisch* cars and moving to the city in droves. But not her Simon.

"We might not have as strict a bishop as you folk do up in Whinburg, but our young folks don't *all* go wild," she said, smiling. "Simon is a steady boy. He hasn't had the chance to run around much—I couldn't afford to give him his own buggy, but last fall some of the men put their heads together and gave him one. We got a nice horse for him at the auction this spring." Or rather, Jacob had.

Ruth nodded. "And the younger boy? Your own son?"

Sarah bit back a swift correction. Ruth was older, and enjoyed a position of respect in several communities—both very good reasons for Sarah to school her tongue to a soft answer. Simon may have been born to another woman, but when she had fallen in love with his widowed father, she had loved the little boy with every cell of her being and been the very best mother she had known how to be, mistakes and all.

"Caleb would do everything Simon does if I let him. But he still has to finish up his year of vocational school. Simon's apprenticing with Oran Yost at the buggy shop." She turned toward the door. "It's chilly, Ruth. They'll be missing us inside."

Ruth put out a hand to stop her. "Just a minute. I wanted to ask you something."

There was only one subject Sarah could imagine Ruth wanting to talk with her about. "Are you getting low on dried herbs? I am, too. This time of year holds so much hope, doesn't it—but it's also when I start running out of everything we put by last year."

"Corinne has told me a little about your financial situation."

Sarah felt her jaw sag. Why would Corinne, whom she trusted, have spoken about her private affairs to anyone? "It was not her place to do that," she finally managed.

But then, everyone knew everything in a district as small and tightly knit as Willow Creek. Sometimes—when she was the subject of talk—Sarah despaired of her fellow man. But other times, she was far more interested than she should be in what people said about one another. Folks did some strange things for reasons that weren't so strange at all. Love. Disappointment. Rebellion. She was guilty of letting all those things affect her actions, too, so she was certainly in no position to judge.

"It only confirmed in my mind something I've been thinking about for a long time," Ruth said. "Sarah, have you ever thought about doing more with the things you grow than simply selling them at the market?"

Sarah stared at her, lost. "What do you mean?"

Ruth settled her angular figure on the railing, and Sarah began to wish she'd taken the time to grab a jacket or a shawl on her way out the door. The wind was blowing over the rolling Pennsylvania hills and right through her sweater.

"I mean you could make some of the things that I do out of them, and charge more. I think you have a talent from God—you're just keeping it wrapped in a napkin, and not using it yet."

Sarah stared at Ruth. "Are you saying…make cures out of them? Tinctures and teas and such? As you do?"

The older woman nodded. "It's getting more and more difficult to find a healer in the districts around here, with the young folks going off to work in the towns and factories instead of finding a trade they can do around home." Ruth gazed over at Corinne's herbaceous border, where daffodils had already begun to poke through. "People are going in and out of our place day and night, and I'm in my buggy seeing to the infirm instead of to my own responsibilities at home. And now with my son and his family moving from Smicksburg to the farm this month to take over, Isaac and I will be moving into the *Daadi Haus,* and then I'm going to be helping them settle in and looking after the *Bobblin.* Things are going to change, as they tend to do."

"And you think I should...what, exactly?"

"I'd like you to consider apprenticing with me. Not in the sense that Simon does with Oran Yost, but...well, I need to pass on what I know. My daughter, Amelia, is busy with her home and the new baby, and doesn't have the knack. I think you do. Why else grow herbs and flowers that most people don't have in their practical vegetable gardens? Who else has coneflower and lemon balm tucked beside her porch when she can't pickle or can either one?"

*Because they bring Mamm back to me.* "Because I have a customer named Ruth who buys them?"

"I think there's more to it than that. I think God has been leading you in this direction. To this calling. Because it is a calling, Sarah."

She, Sarah Yoder, who couldn't quilt to save her life—and who was such an inexperienced provider that her payments to her in-laws were nearly six months in arrears—called to be a healer? To be responsible for the sick? She, in a position where people would trust her with their bodies when, no matter what she did, she had not been able to make Mamm or Michael one bit more comfortable in their last days? *Ach, neh.*

"Ruth, I couldn't." She was freezing now. She would say her say as quickly as she could and get back inside to warm up. "I'd be more likely to put people in the county hospital than keep them out of it. It's not my place."

Ruth gave her a long look. "You might pray about it. I have."

She might. Or she might take the denial of her entire body as a pretty good authority, as she backed toward the kitchen door and laid her hand on the knob.

"Sarah?"

"*Ja.* Sure, I'll pray about it." Anything to bring this conversation to an end. "*Kumme mit*, we don't want someone else to do our work for us."

That granite-gray gaze didn't move from hers. "I couldn't have said it better myself."

Someone had dabbed away any signs of her accidents on the quilt border, but Sarah didn't have the heart to sit and quilt anymore. This was unusual, since she and Corinne were close and she usually drew so much strength from the women of her family that sisters' day was like a balm to her spirit. She and the boys probably ate more meals in Corinne's kitchen than they did in their own.

So instead of endangering the quilt any further, she busied herself in the kitchen, taking the plastic wrap off trays of cake and squares and getting them ready for the snack that everyone enjoyed after their work was done. She emptied a jar or two of peaches, cherries, and canned pineapple into a big glass bowl to make a fruit salad, squeezed a lime over it, and snipped a few mint leaves that were hardy enough to survive the cold beside the back steps into tiny pieces to sprinkle on the top.

The scent of mint in her hands wafted her twenty years back into the past, into a different county, a different farmhouse. She must have been only fourteen, in her first summer out of school, learning how to cook properly for the noon meal for half a dozen hungry men, instead of merely amusing herself with cookies and pies and jam. Mamm had shown her how to pick the best mint leaves and dry them for tea, and it seemed as though the kitchen smelled of mint for days. Or maybe they had dried them for days.

In any case, it had been before—

Before.

She was quiet during the snack, despite the efforts of Amanda and Barbara to draw her out. They thought she was having a bad day over Michael. She still had those, but after five years, his loss had gone from a fierce open wound to a dull ache that hurt only when she pressed on it.

She left as soon as it was polite to do so, giving Corinne a reassuring smile from the door. Michael had been Corinne's second eldest son, the one who had decided against farming with his father, but who was willing to lend his hands to help his father and older brother Joshua. When Michael married Sarah, Corinne and Jacob had sold them a section of the farm and helped them build a house on it, with a machine shop behind, believing that Michael would be with them for years to come.

His death a scant three weeks after they'd discovered the cancer had put an end to that belief.

Their faith was as strong and unwavering as ever, though…an example Sarah would do well to follow. She crossed the creek on the log that had been worn flat and smooth by generations of feet, and climbed the hill between the two properties.

"Father *Gott*," she whispered as she walked the familiar gentle track, "help me to have faith in Your plan for me. Are You bringing me to the end of myself so that I must put my trust in You alone? If so, it's working. I don't see a way to keep a roof over my boys' heads as things are, so I pray that You will show the way to me. I ask this in Jesus's name."

It was plain to her that Ruth's odd request had less to do with the will of *Gott* than it did with the way Ruth managed her time and her family. Sarah was glad that so many people were able to find help at Ruth's hands, but the fact that she was a busy woman didn't necessarily mean that God intended for Sarah to take up that work as well. The thought of being a healer had never entered Sarah's head—and surely that was part of hearing the still, small voice of God?

At the top of the hill, she could look straight down into her garden, which was muddy and unkempt at this time of year. But from this vantage point, she could see the rows that had been and would probably be again . . . neat rows of corn, beans, peas, tomatoes, and onions. Practical rows that would feed her and the boys for months.

Why did people plant seeds in rows?

The wind pushed at the back of her coat, as though she were blocking its smooth passage down the slope of the hill. The lifeless grass bent under it, but she did not. Instead, she braced her feet and considered the expanse of the garden.

When plants grew in the wild, they grew in patches, didn't they? They seeded the ground and died, becoming fertilizer for the next generation, the clump extending farther with every passing year. But it seemed to be a purely human impulse to put things in rows: vegetables, fruit trees . . . the desks of the little scholars in the one-room schoolhouse...the buggies of the *Gmee* outside the homes where church was held every other Sunday.

*I should plant my garden like a quilt—in patches. It's probably the only way I'll make a good one.*

A giggle bubbled up in Sarah's throat. She could see it now—a nine-patch of garlic and dill. An Ohio Star of tomatoes and beans, with a border of cheery yellow marigolds to keep the slugs away. Or a Log Cabin of corn—no, wait, the corn would tower over everything and she wouldn't be able to see the humbler vegetables in the alternating pattern. The corn should go around the edges, and the silk from the ears would blow in the breeze like the lovely swirls of feathers that Corinne enjoyed stitching so much.

Oh, wouldn't her in-laws laugh over her patchwork garden! When her turn came to host church, everyone would have to walk across the lawn to look at it, and shake their heads at a woman who would never be able to use a hoe and harrow the way they were designed to be used.

*Plant more herbs. More than just the ones Mamm enjoyed. Plant the herbs that will keep the Gmee well.*

No, that was Ruth talking. Sarah would probably dream about her tonight, standing in the middle of the unplanted garden in her rubber boots, directing what went where.

"Sarah!"

Sarah jumped, then realized it had been a girl's voice, not Ruth's. A teenage girl in a lavender dress peeking out below a black winter coat like Sarah's own emerged from around the laurel hedge that protected the house and flowerbeds, and waved. "I didn't think anyone was home," Priscilla Mast called.

"I'm just coming from sisters' day at Corinne's." Sarah

left off daydreaming and scrambled down the path, hurrying through the trees and onto the lawn. "*Wie geht's*, Priscilla?"

"*Gut, denki.*" Priscilla's smile could brighten a cloudy day. "Are they all well at Yoders'?"

"*Ja*, very well. Ruth is there. I expect she'll stay the night and head back to Whinburg in the morning. It's too far for the horse this late in the day." Her farm was only about ten miles away, but even if she left now, Ruth wouldn't make it home before dark. "If you're looking for Simon, he isn't home from work yet."

Priscilla blushed scarlet, right up into the roots of the golden-blond hair partially hidden by her organdy *Kapp*, and behind her glasses, her lashes fell to hide eyes as blue as the bachelor buttons on the roadsides in summer. "I wasn't, actually. Mamm sent me over for some dill weed. She's making beet soup and we're completely out."

Sarah suppressed a smile and led Priscilla up the back steps and into the kitchen. Simon didn't talk much about girls, but she knew that he'd taken Priscilla home from the Sunday night singing once or twice. On the first occasion, before he had his own buggy, he'd had to drive the truck wagon in which they took the vegetables to market, but Priscilla hadn't been too proud to accept.

In her mind, that said good things about both of them. Simon had been grateful for the secondhand buggy. Before they'd got the second horse, if Sarah was using their mare, Dulcie, he'd simply walk, or hitch a ride with someone, with good humor and not a word of complaint.

"Just in here," she said. The pantry, being on the north side and on an outside wall, was cooler than the other rooms in the snug house Michael and his brothers had built, and Jacob had cut little screened doors in the back of one of the cupboards to allow air to circulate no matter the season. It was the perfect place to keep the herbs dry, and the coolness helped their savor last longer.

Sarah measured out half a cup of dill. "Will that be enough?"

"That should last us until next Christmas. I brought a couple of dollars. Is that all right?"

"More than all right. Here, let me throw in some caraway seeds, too." She wrapped the herbs in waxed paper and tied it all up with a bit of raffia. "I wish I had a better way to package things like this. I can't very well buy those nice labeled bottles of spices from the store and use them, but it sure is tempting."

"Mamm won't care how they arrive," Priscilla said with a smile. "It's how they go down that counts."

Sarah laughed and allowed as how that was true. "Give her my greetings."

"I will. And maybe you'd tell Simon I was by?"

For a moment, Sarah fought with the urge to hint to this pretty *Maedel* that Simon was in no position to be courting anyone. They were too young and he was too poor to be thinking of getting serious.

But that would be like standing in the creek and trying to stop it from rushing past her ankles, wouldn't it? She remembered how it had felt to be courted by Michael all too well.

"I'll tell him. 'Bye, Priscilla."

The girl ran off down the long gravel lane between the trees, her feet light with happiness that her message would be passed on, her skirts blowing against the backs of her legs with the fractious wind.

Sarah closed the door, her mouth softening with memory. Then she roused herself and reached for her kitchen apron. The boys would be home soon, hungry as hunters, and as luck would have it, Corinne had sent thick slices of leftover roast home with her for their supper.

She might know herself to be poor. But the boys themselves never knew anything but savory food seasoned with love and the very best her garden had to offer.

That in itself was something to thank the *gut Gott* for.

# CHAPTER 2

At the top of the Yoder driveway, next to the mailbox, Priscilla hesitated. She should go home and deliver the packet of dill that Mamm was waiting for. And she would. Just as soon as she walked to the corner and saw whether Simon was coming. It was only ten minutes away, and ten minutes could be explained by a whole lot of things.

Even if they couldn't, ten minutes with Simon were worth twenty minutes of lecture.

She stuffed the packet in her coat pocket and set off down the road. At the corner, she stood on tiptoe and craned her head to see into the big dip the road took down to Willow Creek. In the winter, the leafless trees allowed a great view of the road. It soared up the other side...and there was a black felt hat, just cresting the top.

Joy surged inside her as step by ambling step, Simon was revealed in all his glory.

Too late, she remembered that she should be trying to look as if she were waiting for someone else, or pulling up her socks in her gumboots, or anything but standing there like a grinning fool, waiting for him. Mamm said that when it came to boys, only a forward girl walked up to them and started a conversation, or did things like offer them rides when she had the buggy. "I don't want people to say you chased him until he caught you," she'd told Priscilla after Simon had brought her home from the singing.

Priscilla didn't care two hoots what people said. Nobody was chasing anybody here. There was nothing wrong with two friends walking home together, and besides, *forward* was such an old-fashioned word.

When he caught sight of her standing in the grass by the corner of the field Sarah rented to one of the Byler boys, he lifted a hand in greeting. He didn't change his pace, though, which was just so Simon. "Doesn't do to hurry, Priscilla," he'd told her once. "If whatever is waiting for you doesn't want to wait, then hurrying isn't going to make it wait."

"Yes, it will," she had argued. "If I'm waiting for you, and you hurry, then I know you're glad to see me."

"I'm always glad to see you," he'd said, and grinned, and she'd forgotten all about arguing.

He hadn't kissed her. Not yet. She wasn't sure she was ready for that anyhow. Simply being with him was enough for her—even the sight of him at church was a gift she held close to her heart, each glimpse a memory she took with her into the week, where sightings were few and far between unless she made them happen.

Which she was doing now.

"Hey, Priscilla," he called, finally close enough to speak without shouting.

"*Wie geht's*, Simon?"

"The wind blow you out this direction? Seems a cold afternoon to be standing waiting for a bus that doesn't stop here."

He had the most contagious grin under that mop of walnut-dark hair. A single long dimple creased his cheek, and his brown eyes crinkled at the corners because he figured he'd found her out.

It was only a matter of time before he looked around him and saw all the other girls who'd noticed his dimple, too—like Sallie Troyer, whose blond hair rippled to her waist when it was down, and who had flawless skin. Or Malinda Kanagy, who at eighteen was a year older than Simon, but who was the sister of Dan, one of his best friends. Priscilla was only a friend. How did a person go about changing that to *girl*friend?

"I thought you might like company on the walk home," she told him.

"I always like company. But your mother will be missing you. Don't you have to help with supper?"

She pulled out the packet of dill and waved it under his nose so he could smell it. "I am. She sent me over to get this from your Mamm."

He nodded, and changed his pace not one bit as she fell in beside him. Lucky thing she had a fairly long stride herself, or she'd be jogging home. Simon's amble looked leisurely, but it covered a lot of ground.

An orange-and-white box van towing a small silver car roared past them, and instinctively they veered over onto the grassy wayside to avoid splashes from the puddles in the road. Since they both had boots on, it didn't matter that they sank an inch deep in mud. Priscilla waved her hand in front of her face until the wind took the smell of diesel away.

"Wonder if someone's moving in close by?" she said.

"None of the places are for sale along here. It's probably *Englisch* folks going to Hershey or someplace, and taking a shortcut."

"There's the old Byler place," she reminded him.

"It's not for sale."

"It could be. Sadie Byler died at Christmas. It won't sit empty forever."

Both of them watched the van's brake lights come on at the stop sign where the road met the county highway. Then it turned right. The Byler place wasn't too far in that direction.

"It wouldn't be fair for an *Englisch* family to buy it," Priscilla said as if the van had stopped to argue with her. "Not with all the weddings we had this past winter and the young marrieds looking for places of their own."

"Why shouldn't an *Englisch* family move in? They could put on a new roof and rewire it for electricity. Put a big satellite dish out front. Give the place a whole new life."

She snorted at this poor attempt to rile her. "It would take a fortune to fix that place up."

"I'm glad we agree on something," he teased.

"Don't go getting big-headed about it," she warned, trying not to smile. "You still need to fit through the door."

And here they were at his driveway already. With a wave, as though she were nothing more than a neighbor in a passing buggy, he turned off and in a moment was lost to sight.

Priscilla sighed and walked on. Her boots seemed heavy with the mud they'd picked up, and the wind was colder than ever. She broke into a trot. It would help to warm her, and if Mamm saw her running home, it might go some way to making up those ten minutes.

She shucked her boots in the mudroom and fell into the kitchen, panting and holding out the packet of dill. "Here, Mamm. Sarah sent some caraway, too, because she said the money was too much."

"And who chased you home?" Mamm took the packet and

shook a little of the dill into the big pot of soup simmering on the gas stove.

"No one. It's cold out there and I was trying to warm up."

"I don't doubt it is. What took you so long?"

Drat. She should have run faster, and been in better shape so that she didn't sound like a winded horse, puffing and blowing. That was it. She was cutting out the rolls at dinner, starting tonight.

"Was I long?"

Her mother leveled a stare at her over the metal rims of her glasses. While some districts' *Ordnung* forbade gold rims—that smacked of wearing jewelry—theirs was pretty liberal. Mamm's looked like stainless steel, but even they weren't as steely as that gaze.

"It doesn't take nearly half an hour to run to the next place and get some herbs."

"Sarah wasn't home. I had to wait until she got back from sisters' day." Which was the truth, and it felt good to be able to say it.

"Ah." Clearly Mamm hadn't thought of this, and Priscilla would have heaved a sigh of relief if her sides weren't heaving already. "All right. Take off your coat and find your own sisters. It's time to set the table, and we need some biscuits to go with this soup."

She found fourteen-year-old Katie and twelve-year-old Saranne in their bedroom, agonizing over the torture that was long division. It came as no surprise when Saranne jumped up at the first suggestion of dinner.

"I'll make the biscuits," she said, and vanished, leaving her pencils and erasers on the floor, pieces of scratch paper drifting off the bed to land on them like big flat snowflakes.

"Poor thing." Katie gathered up the mess and tapped it

into a neat pile on top of Saranne's arithmetic book on the desk. "She just doesn't understand it, and I must not be very good at explaining, because I can't make her see how easy it is."

"It's easy for you." Priscilla leaned on the door frame and watched her tidy up the room. Tidiness seemed to follow in Katie's wake. She couldn't pass through a room without arranging newspapers or picking up kindling or putting away the six-year-old twins' toys. Half the time Priscilla wondered if she even knew she was doing it. Her sister had secret ambitions to be Teacher Katie someday, and Pris hoped that God would make it happen. She was perfect for the job. "You're the one who can double and triple a recipe in her head, and then divide it into six. And in the summer when you have the fruit stand, the receipts all come out even. They never do when I'm out there."

"That's why Dat gave the job to me." Katie smiled at her so she wouldn't think she was being proud. "I like numbers. I like knowing the answer."

"I wish I did," came out of Priscilla's mouth before she realized she was even going to say it.

She pushed off the door frame and went into her own room. Because she was the eldest, she had it to herself, and because she was by herself, it was the smallest room in the house, tucked over the porch like an afterthought. It was hardly bigger than the gable that held the window, but that didn't bother her one bit. It had a comfy single bed, a chest of drawers, a quilt she'd made herself, and a door that closed when she needed it to. It contained the things she valued most—privacy and a place to dream.

In a few weeks, the cherry tree that grew next to the back porch would blossom and leaf out, blocking her view of the fields. But for now, she could see quite a distance from her window. She moved the single curtain aside—two curtains was vanity, as was any other color but blue—and gazed in the direction of the old Byler place.

Had that moving van really been headed there? Could an *Englisch* family really be moving into the middle of their tightly knit Amish community?

There was nothing wrong with that, of course. In the summer, working at their roadside stand, she'd found the *Englisch* folks to be as neighborly as anyone for the most part, except for a tendency to stare and ask odd questions like did she ever miss television and having a cell phone.

But whoever was moving in there, they would bring change with them. Spring itself brought change—which was probably the reason why February and March were her least favorite months. Priscilla didn't have a lot in common with her sister Katie, but she did like things to be orderly. She liked to be able to tell what was coming.

Unfortunately, with spring and moving vans and boys, it seemed you very rarely could.

# CHAPTER 3

Henry Byler shut off the box van's engine and slid out of the driver's seat with a grunt, landing on stiff legs with both feet in the gravel. He slammed the door and stood there, hands on hips, while the engine ticked and the cold March wind pushed impatiently at his shirt, which was damp with a thousand miles of nearly nonstop driving.

The old place hadn't changed much.

His aunt Sadie had had debilitating arthritis, so her Amish neighbors kept the lawn mowed and the porches repaired. They got together for a work frolic to clean things up when it was her turn for church, so every couple of years it got a paint job, and a thorough scrubbing more often than that. But a lot could happen in between.

Like November storms. And termites. And eventually, death and probate and the letter that had surprised him one afternoon in his apartment in Denver, informing him that she had passed and left this old place to him.

Not to one of her four daughters, with their husbands and children. Not to one of her three brothers still living, nor their sons, the Byler boys, his cousins who leased the fields and kept them productively planted in soybeans and corn. All of them prosperous stewards of their land and full silos and fat cows.

Nope. To him, the runaway from the religion he'd been brought up in and had left more than two decades ago.

He reached into the cab of the van and found his jacket under the mess of hamburger wrappers and maps and motel invoices on the passenger seat. He shrugged it on, walked over to the flowerpot at the bottom of the stairs, and found the keys right where the letter from his uncle had said they would be.

The keys to the kingdom.

A kingdom he'd sworn he would never set foot in again.

He should know better than to swear—vows were for people who had the knack of keeping them.

The long lane curved over a shallow hill, just enough to shield the yard from view of the road. Old maples dotted the yard, one leaning over the house in a protective way that would have been poetic if a big, heavy branch hadn't been taking aim right at the gables on the second floor. That would have to be lopped off soon, before the sap got running.

The lock resisted him for about two seconds before releasing with a snap, and he stepped into the front room.

It still smelled the same—of furniture polish and cinnamon and the tart greenness she had once told him was the lemon balm she kept in sachets in the drawers.

*Please let the drawers have been emptied by my cousins' wives.* He didn't think he could handle going through an old lady's things. Not because of male diffidence, but because outside of Mamm, she was the only one of his relatives he had loved—and been loved by in return.

Unbidden, pressure rose in his chest and resolved itself into a lump in his throat. He swallowed, hard. "Thanks a lot, Aendi Sadie," he said aloud to the empty room. "I know you did this on purpose to get me out here, you rascal."

Her engagement clock on the mantel with its three golden

balls in the base had wound down, stubbornly pointing to twenty past two. He had been fascinated by those balls as a small boy, watching them swing around each other and trying to figure out what their action had to do with the movement of the hands on its face. He'd looked it up on the Internet once, having never had his curiosity satisfied by either Aendi Sadie or Onkel Jeremiah.

A lot of things had not been satisfied by an Amish up-bringing.

An equal number had not been satisfied by an *Englisch* adulthood, either.

He was a man caught between two worlds, like a guy with a foot in two canoes, both moving apart and a huge splash inevitable. When it came, it had been ugly and it had hurt.

Maybe that was why he was here, on this run-down farm in a community he hardly knew, with who knew what future ahead of him.

*Get a grip. You're forty-two, reasonably healthy, with a few talents that you think are useful even if nobody else does. Get it in gear and find yourself a place to sleep and something to eat.*

At this rate, he'd read himself a lecture as good as any Aendi Sadie ever had.

He climbed the stairs to the big bedroom that looked south over the tangle of the garden, a couple of sheds, and the fields, still in their winter sleep. The plot plan his uncle had enclosed indicated that these fields shared a fence with those of Jacob and Corinne Yoder, somewhere over there where a line of trees told him there was a creek.

He vaguely remembered playing in such a creek with the Yoder boys, who were a little younger. It was strange to think the Yoders were still there. Just like this house was still here, smelling the same, looking the same.

Only he was different.

Out of habit, he brushed the wall next to the door with the flat of his hand and, when he found nothing, looked at it.

Right. Amish house. No light switch.

Before somewhere to sleep and after something to eat, he would have to find a lantern or a candle. In Denver, winter days were lengthening and drying out, but here in Lancaster County it would be dark before he was unpacked, and he didn't much relish the thought of going to bed at six o'clock just because he couldn't see.

Someone had stripped the bed down to the mattress, which boded well for the drawers. Sure enough, when he pulled out the top one, it was empty, the neat lining of what looked like Christmas wrapping paper smelling faintly of lemon balm.

Had the cousins' wives been expecting that one of their number might move in here?

Or were they simply getting everything ready for auction and the property for sale?

He should do just that. Sell it all, then move on to a different state. Maybe California—though any money the farm brought probably wouldn't last long there. He could find an artists' colony in New Mexico, or join a commune in Oregon—did they have those there still?—or any number of things that didn't include returning to an Amish farm and trying to forge a life among a people he had abandoned.

*You didn't abandon them. You chose not to join church. Two different things.*

Not to Mamm, whose letters were invariably cheerful and always ended with her hopes that he would return to the life that belonged to him, not the one he had chosen for himself. "Our own will is no course to steer by," she had written in seventy-five different ways over the years. "It's God's will that matters, and His love that draws us back and gives us the strength to do it."

Well, he wasn't sure what had drawn him to Willow Creek, other than a crotchety old lady who had, for reasons he could not understand, left a farm to him instead of someone who deserved it or at least knew what to do with it.

He was doing it again. Feeling sorry for himself. He had no patience with self-indulgence in other people, so what was with the pity party? What he needed was some protein in his belly and some light on the subject. And then he'd better find his sleeping bag in the depths of the box van, because the cheery designs of the quilts in his memory had clearly been carted off to other people's houses along with the contents of Aendi Sadie's dresser drawers.

At least they'd left a lamp, he soon discovered. And the kitchen cupboards actually contained dishes—plain white Corelle ware that was indestructible, having outlived Sadie and was quite likely to outlive him, too. Matches stood in a holder on the wall next to the woodstove. It took him a few minutes to remember that you had to turn down the wick in the lamp once you'd lit it, or it would drool black smoke all over the glass chimney, canceling out its ability to produce light.

One lamp made him feel like a camper with a tiny fire in a big woods.

Two lamps were better.

Three really lit the place up, enough for him to see that while the propane fridge had been cleaned out and turned off, the cupboards contained flour and sugar and—eureka! Two Mason jars of what looked like chicken soup. The pilot light in the gas stove was still on, and there were copper-bottomed pots in one of the cupboards under the counter. So, with some cold pizza from yesterday and the hot soup, he was feeling almost cheerful by the time he'd finished and washed the dishes.

He'd had to heat the water in the soup pot. While the pilot in the stove was still on, it looked like someone had shut off the one under the propane water heater that supplied the faucets. He'd have to figure out who to call to get the propane topped up and the pilot lit.

And then he remembered.

No phone.

He took out his cell phone, which displayed one bar.

No power to charge it up.

Henry sighed.

He would have to plug it into the box van, which he should have done while he was driving. He'd completely forgotten what it was like to live without electricity, his body retaining worldly habits with much more persistence than it had those of his plain Amish upbringing. For nineteen years he'd never needed electricity, and here he was, twenty-three years after that, feeling as though he'd been tossed back into the previous century—a century that was hard and unyielding and could grind a man to dust as soon as look at him, if he didn't develop some survival skills fast.

His skills were rusty, but he could buff them up. He would get that propane and charge his phone and take up the reins of his life. And while he was at it, he'd call an electrician and see how much it would cost to have this house totally rewired and a phone put in, to say nothing of Wi-Fi. If a man was going to run a business from his home, he would need those tools, at a minimum.

The thump of booted feet on the planks of the porch was the last thing he expected to hear, and he half rose from his chair. Then common sense kicked in. This was not Denver, where a thump on the door could mean anything from a salesman to a home invasion. This was Lancaster County, where there were neighbors who believed in that old-fashioned thing called neighborliness.

And curiosity.

He opened the door, still undecided whether or not the occasion merited a smile. But it didn't matter—the grin on the face of the Amish kid on the porch was big enough for both of them.

"Evening," the kid said, and in rapid English went on, "We saw the lights across the field and Mamm told me not to come and impose on you so soon, but I just wondered...are you the new owner? Do you need a hand? I'm strong, and if you were looking for someone to help you move in and fix things up, I come pretty cheap."

Henry held up both hands under this torrent of unexpected information. "Whoa, slow down," he said in the same tongue. He still dreamed in *Deitsch* once in a while, but he hadn't spoken it since he'd jumped down from the bus in Missouri and thanked the driver in English. And he hadn't missed the fact that the kid had just assumed he was *Englisch*. It was a pretty good assumption, considering the van outside. "Who are you again? And what makes you think I need help?"

The kid gave him a look that said the answer to the second questions was so obvious it didn't even need expression. "I'm Caleb Yoder. I'm fourteen. We live over there." He waved in a general southwesterly direction that left Henry no more enlightened than before.

"We?" Was this a relative? He tried to remember if any of his cousins had produced a Caleb. It was likely; the pool of names the Amish drew on wasn't very deep.

"Mamm and Simon and me."

"Are you a Byler?"

"Nope. Yoder, I said. I'm Jacob and Corinne Yoder's grandson. Do you know them? Their second son, Michael, was my Dat."

"Michael." And now a memory came back to him, of a kid daring him to swing out over Willow Creek on an ancient rope swing, which had snapped under his weight and dumped him on his behind in three feet of water. In December. That's right—it had been Christmas, a green one, and the creek hadn't yet frozen over. He remembered the bare boughs of the maples and oaks as they'd wheeled overhead, seconds before the icy water closed over his face.

"I knew your dad when we were boys." And suddenly the kid's use of the past tense sank in. "Wait—did you say *was?*"

"He's dead now."

A pang struck him, though he hadn't known Michael all that well—hadn't thought of him in decades. Henry's parents had brought him out here to visit a few times, that was all, and the Yoder kids were the closest boys his age that his cousins played with.

Michael had been a couple of years younger than he. And now, already gone. Wow.

"I'm sorry to hear that," he said at last. "Was he ill?"

"*Ja*, the cancer. I meant it about helping you out," the kid went on, clearly a person who was either very private or who lived in the present. "I'm a hard worker. You can ask Mamm."

He had no intention of getting involved with the folks in the community, including asking some random Amish woman for a character reference for her son.

"I'm sure she would tell me you are. Mothers are like that."

He eyed the kid curiously. He was as gangly as a half-grown sapling, with that weedy look that probably meant a huge appetite. Dark eyes contrasted with blond hair—a combination you didn't see often in a Swiss-German culture. But Henry couldn't fault his attitude—the kid had jump.

"You still in vocational school?" Once they'd graduated from eighth grade, Amish scholars' formal schooling was over, but the state still required that they be in school until they were fifteen. So boys did a year in some kind of pre-apprenticeship, and girls stayed home, cooking and gardening and writing in their work journals and marking time until they were officially released to their lives of doing much the same.

"How do you know about that?" Caleb's lively gaze took in his *Englisch* shirt and jeans, his haircut, his clean-shaven face. Then it jumped to the three lanterns and back to him. "Do you know the Amish?"

Once the relatives knew he was here, his entire life—or as much of it as they knew—would be an open book for the entire community to read. He knew that. Had even been prepared for it. But knowing that and answering a curious boy's questions were two different things.

"You could say that."

"Did you used to be Amish?"

"Caleb, you ever heard of invasion of privacy?"

"No," the kid said.

He sighed. No surprise. "Yes, I used to be Amish. Holmes County. The Bylers here are my relations. I'm Sadie Byler's nephew, and she left me this house."

His eyes widened. "You're the one under *die Meinding*?"

Huh? For a second, he wondered if he was. But then common sense came back. "No. I never joined church. Why, did someone say I was?"

The kid frowned, clearly rearranging the rumors in his head. "It must've been someone else, then. There's only ever been one person put under *die Meinding* in this district since Bishop Troyer was chosen, like, before I was born. I thought you might be him." His face brightened. "I'm glad you aren't. I wouldn't have been able to take money from you, then."

"Who says I'm giving you money?"

"You will, once you've hired me and I've shown you what I can do."

"Caleb, I only got here an hour ago. I won't be making decisions like that for a while."

"Oh, I know. I just thought I'd better get my licks in before you hired somebody else." He glanced around the kitchen. "Because you're going to have to get help, you know. Unless you're a carpenter by trade?"

Henry shook his head. "Not even close."

This cheered him up even more. "*Gut*, then. Well, like I said, we just live over there, where the creek takes a bend toward town. When you're ready, you just let me know and I'll be here, guaranteed."

With that, he grinned again and loped down the steps, leaving Henry standing in the kitchen feeling a little bemused. He closed the kitchen door and went to lock it. Then his hand fell away.

*Dorothy, you're not in Denver anymore. Here in Lancaster County, in picturesque Willow Creek, on County Road 51, there is no need for locks and keys and the mistrust that produces the need for them.*

He'd opened his door tonight to find a friend. Or at least a potential employee.

That was good enough to be getting on with.

# CHAPTER 4

The most optimistic plant in the world had to be the crocus. Pushing its way through cold dirt, it sought the warmth of the sun—and more often than not found the crusty embrace of old snow instead. This year, though, the snow had all come early, and while it had been a rainy week, at least the crocuses hadn't had to push their tender petals against old patches of ice.

They always got their way, didn't they? Ice or not.

Sarah wondered if this wasn't how God's love worked. Human nature could be crusty and cold, resisting every overture of warmth from the outside. But the Spirit, soft and delicate though it was, pushed from the inside against earthy human stubbornness and against all odds, won through to bloom in all its beauty.

And wasn't it the crocuses you saw and delighted in, not the earth they grew out of?

Outside the buggy shop, Sarah waited for Simon to break free of Oran Yost's iron obedience to the clock, secretly applauding the crocuses blooming next to his fence for their temerity in sprouting there. The delicate work of the Spirit must be going on deep in that man's heart. Maybe someday it would bloom on the surface, too.

Simon had forgotten to take his lunch this morning, and rather than have him go hungry all day, or worse, walk into Willow Creek to spend his hard-earned money at the pizza place, she had brought it with her on her way in to the post office.

Oran housed his business in a big Quonset shed behind his place, and behind that, a row of buggies waited either for repair or pickup. As Sarah made her way toward the building, the rasp and scrape of sandpaper stopped when the hands of the clock hit twelve, and an exclamation of either anger or pain escaped through the big rolling doors of the shop.

"Boy, how many times have I told you to pick up your tools when you're done!"

"I'm not done," came Simon's voice over those of Oran's two full-time men and Simon's buddy Joe Byler, the other apprentice, who were straggling out the door for their break. "I'm going to finish these edges after lunch."

"You'll pick up your tools when you leave, whether you're done or not, so people don't trip over them and hurt themselves."

It was all Sarah could do not to dash in there and give Oran Yost a piece of her mind for talking to her son like that. But she could not. It was not her place to upbraid a man in his own shop, in front of the other men—especially not a man in a position of authority over Simon. It would shame Simon and show her to be an interfering busybody who didn't know how to submit—which was not the case.

Really. It wasn't.

So she studied the crocuses with the utmost self-control until Simon came out drying his hands on the front of his jacket. "Mamm? What are you doing here?"

She turned with a smile, and held up his lunchbox. "You forgot this."

"I figured that out around ten, when my stomach finished working over the bacon and biscuits from this morning." He took it with a smile, and she would have got a hug if they'd been at home, but they were out in public and young men did not hug their mothers where others could see them. "*Denki*, Mamm. Join me?"

"*Neh*, I had mine before I came." She loosened the strings of her black away bonnet, with its rigid U-shape and black ribbon bow at the nape, but didn't take it off. "I have to go to the post office to mail these letters to your aunts in Mifflin County, and then—"

"Simon, what are you doing?" Oran stopped in the doorway. "Michael's Sarah. Hallo."

"Hallo, Oran," she said politely, then looked at him more closely. He was limping, favoring a foot that obviously pained him a great deal. "Are you injured?"

"*Neh.*"

Men. They could be bleeding to death and they would still insist they were fine. "But you're limping."

"I'm perfectly well. I'd be better if your boy there wouldn't leave his tools lying around for the rest of us to trip over. If a customer comes in and hurts himself, there'll be a world of trouble."

Tripping over tools wouldn't make a man limp like that.

"It's the gout," Simon whispered out of the side of his mouth between bites of his ham, cheese, and pickle sandwich, and then gazed out across Oran's fields as if they held something much more fascinating than silage.

Aha. Gout could turn a loving, cheerful man into a shouting wreck. No wonder Oran was in such a temper this morning. Every time his big toe rubbed the inside of his boot, the pain would be excruciating. Michael's father had suffered terribly with it—until Ruth Lehman had come visiting her brother with the cure.

"If you're not injured, only one thing would make a man hurt that badly," she told Oran in a conversational tone, as if she were not putting her nose into his business at all. "The gout is an awful affliction, isn't it?"

He shot her a burning look from under his shaggy brows. He was not an old man—maybe sixty, maybe less—but pain had made him move like one. He clamped his mouth shut tighter than a rat trap.

She and Oran Yost were not given to exchanging much more than pleasantries in the yard after church. He wasn't what you would call outgoing to begin with. His wife, Adah, was laying up treasure in Heaven in heaps and handfuls, in Sarah's opinion, having to put up with a husband who rarely passed a positive opinion about anything, and who walked around with his shoulders and elbows hunched in, as if protecting himself from the interest and conversation of his neighbors.

But if he had the gout, only a cruel woman would withhold information that might help him. And Adah might get a kind word into the bargain.

"My father-in-law, Jacob Yoder, had the worst time with the gout," she said as cheerfully as if he hadn't turned his back on both her and Simon, and was limping slowly, painfully back into the shop. "He couldn't have so much as a cotton sheet on his feet when he slept at night—one night, he even fell out of bed because Corinne touched his foot by accident and he shot straight sideways. But curing it was the strangest thing."

Oran had stopped now, and was fiddling with the straps on the gray-sided buggy sitting next in line for repairs. "Medication ain't so strange," he muttered just loudly enough for her to hear. "It's putting that burden on the church for no reason I can't abide. Stuff's expensive."

"No, it isn't," she chirped. "You can find it at the supermarket. Sometimes you can get it on sale for a dollar fifty-nine."

He huffed as if she were babbling nonsense, and turned to make his way through the big sliding door.

"Black cherry juice did the trick, didn't it, Simon?" She raised her voice just enough to carry through the door. "A couple of glasses a day, and Jacob was right as rain in a week. It dissolves what they call uric acid, you see, that forms crystals in the toes. Jacob was cured—and he didn't mind Corinne nudging him in bed after that."

"Mamm," Simon groaned as the boys over by the buggy laughed. "Too much information."

With a smile, she untied Dulcie's reins, climbed into her own buggy, and dropped her voice. "He's as stubborn as a dandelion root, but if he doesn't ask Adah to get him some cherry juice, I'll buy it for him myself."

"Don't mind him. Mostly he's pretty fair. And he's probably right—I shouldn't have left my tools where people walk."

"A good example doesn't need to yell."

"Mamm, what happens between me and my boss isn't your business."

She touched his cheek. "I know. But you are my business—and if I can help a man who's obviously in pain, hopefully he'll forgive me for interfering."

Then she clicked her tongue to the horse, the buggy jerked, and gravel crunched under her wheels as she headed into town. She was content to have planted the seed. If Oran wanted a harvest, he would have to do the rest of the work himself.

After her errands were done, Sarah couldn't resist walking past the window of the fabric shop, where it was clear that Amanda had been at work. The spring fabrics were out, blooming in the window as beautifully as the crocuses and plum blossoms. And like a bee, Sarah was completely drawn in by the display.

Sarah's other sister-in-law, Miriam, wife of Michael's older brother Joshua, had been running the fabric shop for as long as Sarah had lived in Willow Creek, which was fifteen years. Michael's youngest sister, Amanda, who was twenty-four, had been working for Miriam a couple of days a week for a few years now, stocking the shelves and bolts in the beginning, and then moving up to cut fabric and help with the ordering.

Amanda bagged the purchase of a teenage girl, who smiled and bade Sarah a soft greeting as she and her friends left the shop. Then Amanda came out from behind the cash register and gave her a hug.

"I just knew that yellow would pull you in. As soon as I unpacked it, I said, Sarah will love this. She'll never buy it in a million years, but she'll love it just the same."

"Am I so predictable?" The sun came out from behind a cloud and illuminated the yellow cotton hung cleverly from the corner of the window. Beside it, Amanda had draped a soft peach, and next to that, a beautiful raspberry cotton. "I bet that red is going like hot cakes."

"Two of those girls bought the peach, and the last one got

the yellow. By the time we have Heritage Days in June, the *Youngie* will be out in all the colors of the rainbow."

"I'm so glad our district tolerates all the colors God made...well, except those neon ones. I think Bishop Troyer will draw the line there."

"I love color." Amanda fingered a length of cotton scattered with butterflies and what looked like gold leaf—the kind of thing that brought the *Englisch* quilting ladies in by the busload. "I'd never make a living in Whinburg, for instance, where the brightest a woman's dress can be is... burgundy."

"Oh, now, don't say that. One or two have worn pale blue."

Amanda just rolled her eyes, and Sarah grinned. While many things remained the same in the *Ordnung* from district to district, the finer details were often left to tradition and acceptance. Even here in Willow Creek, the oldest ladies wore black and dark green and purple. But as the generations got younger, the colors got brighter, until you got to the teenagers, who could buy that lovely golden yellow and get away with it.

But something about that soft raspberry called to her.

"I see what you're looking at." Amanda got a bolt from the rack and shook out a length. "This would be pretty on you. You're not as pale as some. It just brings out the color in your cheeks."

"Never mind the compliments, you. Flattery will get you nowhere." She checked the end of the bolt. Nine dollars a yard? "Besides, I can't afford it until after next Saturday...or it goes on sale."

Amanda laid it on the cutting table and measured out a dress length.

"What are you doing?"

"Tell you what." The cutting shears hung suspended over the pool of fabric. "How about I cut it now and put it in the back? It's going to go quickly, Sarah. This way, you can pick it up when you have the money."

How kind she was—and how crazy! "I can't let you do that. It isn't honest to cut something that isn't paid for."

"Call it the layaway plan." Miriam came out of the back, her hands full of fat quarters from the bolt ends that she'd been tying up with ribbon. She arranged them in a basket next to the cash register, where they would tempt the impulse buyer who hadn't succumbed to the fabric on the bolts.

Before Sarah could say another word, the scissors sang and a dress length fell to the table.

"*Denki*, Miriam," Sarah said. "That's very kind of you."

"I know you're good for it," Miriam said comfortably, settling herself on a stool with a sigh to rest her feet. "I hear Sadie Byler's house has a tenant."

"Yes, so Caleb tells me. The man had barely shut off the engine in his moving van when my boy was over there looking for work. If I'd known he was going, I'd have at least sent a plate of cookies with him to soften the imposition."

"Caleb is a good boy," Amanda said loyally. She adored her nephew, and it was no secret that Caleb thought his young Aendi was pretty special, too. "He knows an opportunity when it goes speeding past his driveway. Who's this man who bought the place?"

"Sadie left it to her nephew," Miriam said before Sarah could. "He's *Englisch* now, though he was brought up Amish. I don't know what possessed her. That farm would fetch a good price, and there are any number of Amish men around Willow Creek who would jump at it."

"Including the Byler boys," Sarah said thoughtfully. "I hope they don't have a bad spirit over it."

"Human nature being what it is, I expect it was a tough pill to swallow," Miriam said.

"Maybe this Henry will come back to church, if he grew up Amish," Amanda said, always the optimist. "Does he have a family?"

"There wasn't any evidence of one, according to Caleb," Sarah told her. "Maybe he's going to get things fixed up and then send for them."

Amanda's spine wilted a little at this possibility, and Sarah wished she'd kept her mouth shut. But what difference would it make to Amanda? Henry Byler was not Amish, and therefore a single woman couldn't cast her eyes in his direction. Much as Sarah wanted Amanda to find the man God had chosen for her—which didn't seem to be happening in Willow Creek—there was no point in getting her hopes up.

An *Englisch* man could be a productive member of the community, the way the folks who ran the restaurants were, or the men who drove the milk trucks that took the Amish dairymen's milk to the processing plant. But he could not enter into true fellowship, the kind that fed the soul and helped it grow, with a member of the Amish church. Could not develop the kind of relationship that might lead to something deeper.

Which was why Sarah gently led the conversation away from men and back to fabric and color and what she planned to take to the market on Saturday.

Topics that were safe, and held no danger to a woman's heart or home.

# CHAPTER 5

On Friday evenings, Sarah and the boys walked across the cornfield to the Jacob Yoder farm for family supper. She was pinning a fresh *Kapp* to her hair—one straight pin on top, and one on each side—when Simon leaned on the frame of her open bedroom door.

"Are you ready to go?" she asked him, tying the ribbons of the *Kapp* in a neat bow on her chest.

"I'm going to pass this time."

Her fingers got all tangled in the strings, and she looked down to see what the problem was. "Oh? Not feeling good?"

"I'm fine. There are always so many people there, they'll never notice."

Simon was the kind of boy whose absence was always noticed. But she didn't say so. "You have other plans?"

He shrugged himself off the jamb. "A few of the boys are driving over to Strasburg for a hockey game. I thought I'd go."

Sarah grasped at her common sense, which was being flooded by the maternal urge to hold him close. "You're seventeen—I suppose it's time for you to get out and see a little of the world."

"Strasburg isn't exactly the world, Mamm," he said with a

laugh. "It's ten miles away. What's up? I've been out with my buddies before."

"I know." Now she did succumb to the urge to hug him. "I'm being silly, thinking of you growing up. You go and have fun. Just be home at a reasonable hour. Does Oran need you tomorrow?"

*"Neh."*

"That's *gut*, because I do." She smiled brightly. "If I want to put my peas in, it's time to turn the garden over."

He smiled back at her—every spring they watched her with one eye on the calendar, anxious to get her hands into the soil. "I'll go over to *Daadi's* early and get the tiller."

A little while later, she and Caleb walked over the hummocky fields. The sun had sunk below the trees in the wild lot behind Sadie Byler's farm, and a chilly breeze fingered the nape of her neck and tried to get through her black woolen stockings.

There should be three of them. And in less time than she wanted, there would only be one. Caleb would be going out with his friends, too, and seeing girls, and getting married...

And then what?

Sarah practically bolted up the steps and into Corinne's kitchen, which was warm and welcoming and full of sisters-in-law and children. It took all the bustle of finishing the meal and getting it on the table, and then the clatter of cleaning up afterward before she felt settled in her spirit again.

"I need to face it, I know I do," she confessed to Corinne later in one of the bedrooms, where the partially finished quilt was rolled on its frame. "Of course young men grow up and get married and leave home. And I want them to—I want them to find the girl God has chosen for them and to make homes of their own. But..."

"But that leaves you in that house all alone," Corinne said gently. "Unless Simon wants to open a business of some kind in the barn and build a little *Daadi Haus* onto the house for you."

Sarah frowned at the place in the border star where the drops of her blood had been dabbed out and someone else had taken up the work, finishing it with much more skill than she possessed. Probably Amanda.

"I'm not a Grossmammi. Not for a while yet."

"I never said you were. But it's a possibility."

"Corinne, a young woman isn't going to want to start housekeeping in a house already run by her mother-in-law."

"With the shortage of land and more men doing lunch-pail jobs and opening small businesses, lots of young women are learning to adapt."

"Maybe so, but it's foolish to imagine such things and get all worked up about them when they may never happen."

"Are you getting worked up?"

Sarah sighed. "I was worked up when I got here, I'm afraid."

"What you need is faith, *Liewi*. God's plan is always right. Instead of getting worked up about what could be, why don't you ask Him what He has planned for you?"

Sarah had to smile. Her mother-in-law always referred to the God of Heaven as if He were in the next room—as if you could lean on the door like Simon had earlier, and ask Him what His plans were for the day.

"*Ja*, I know you're right."

"That would be the wise thing to do." Corinne touched a completed star gently. "After all, He might have something good in His plan for you yet."

"Corinne..." She could not mean what Sarah thought she meant.

Corinne cleared her throat, as if it had swelled with the same emotion welling up in Sarah's heart. "You may not be a widow forever."

"That is one thing I am not worked up about. And you're the last person I would expect to say such a thing."

"I've learned to be open to God's will," her mother-in-law said simply. "Whatever that might be. There was no one happier than I when you and Michael were married. And there will be no one happier than I if God brings you a second chance."

*I don't want a second chance. I was Michael's wife, and after you've had the best, you're spoiled for the rest.*

*Ach, neh.* That kind of attitude did not show *Gelassenheit*, the quality of yielding and submission that was becoming in a daughter of God.

"Truly?" she said softly. "You would really be happy if I married again?"

"If you were happy, then I would be, too."

"I don't think that kind of happiness comes twice in one lifetime."

"Don't be so sure. Lots of women marry again. Lots of men do, too."

"But do they marry for love, as young people do when they're starting out and forming a family? Or do they marry because she needs a house to keep and he has one, or he needs a mother for his children and she would be a good one?"

"People marry for all kinds of reasons. As long as the reason is grounded in God's will, a couple can make it work."

"That's true, but being a man's choice because he needs a mother is different from being chosen because you're first among women."

"Is that how you felt about Michael?" Corinne asked quietly. "He needed a mother for Simon."

The memory of those heady days of courtship made Sarah smile. Her family had rented two vans and come down to Lancaster County for a wedding—her father, her two older married sisters and their young families, and her youngest brother and sister. There must have been romance in the air, because before they'd left the bride's farm, Michael had introduced himself...her cousins had invited her to stay over Christmas...and by the time the ice had begun to melt, they were engaged. "He did, but you see, he was first among men for me. And there was no doubt in my mind that he was marrying me for myself, not for my maternal qualities. I didn't have many of those in the early days."

"Another man might see those qualities, too."

Sarah shot her a glance. "If I didn't know better, I'd think you were softening me up for a little matchmaking."

Corinne patted the unfinished quilt and walked to the door. "I wouldn't dream of it. But the *gut Gott* might."

She hoped Corinne meant it. Because if her mother-in-law got it in her head to smooth the way for a second marriage, Sarah's life would get far too complicated.

Sarah followed her out and made her way into the front room, where she settled on the couch to watch Caleb and his young cousins in their game of Scrabble. Jacob looked up from the paper. He wasn't a man who sat still very much, but he enjoyed a few quiet moments while his family entertained themselves all around him.

"Oran Yost spoke to me at church on Sunday," he said, folding the paper to the next section and laying it on his knee. "He said he'd been having a little trouble with the gout."

"From what I saw, it was more than a little. I saw him last

week and told him the same as what Ruth told you—black cherry juice."

"He took your advice. Sounds like it worked."

"Did he?" Perhaps she shouldn't have sounded so surprised. Her father-in-law's lips twitched.

"When a man is in that kind of pain, he'll do just about anything to find relief. Even take advice from young women with no business in his yard." Now his smile broke out in earnest.

Sarah laughed. "I had business there. I was taking Simon his lunch. Well, I'm glad he's feeling better. I don't know how he could walk—it looked to be a pretty bad case."

"So in small ways, you're happy to pass on what my sister teaches you."

Sarah turned her full attention to him. "Yes," she said slowly, wondering what he was getting at.

"But not in the larger ways?"

"Jacob, *was sagst du?*"

He shrugged and picked up the paper. "Ruth says you have the knack. You plant herbs that could be used for helping and curing, but you only sell them in the market. You're the first to offer help on the side of the road, but the thought of people coming to you of a purpose frightens you. Why is that?"

Sarah wished she could think of a reason to go into the kitchen, but Jacob's calm gaze held her. "I—I have enough to do," she said lamely. "Making a home for the boys, feeding and sewing and cleaning for them, selling in the market..."

"If it is God's will that you learn these other things, then He will give you the strength to do them."

"And how do I know it is God's will, and not Ruth's?"

He gazed at her, and she realized a second too late that that had not been a very wise thing to say to a man about his sister.

"If it is God's will, you will not be able to resist it," he said quietly. "Though my sister comes a close second when she gets the bit in her teeth."

Sarah relaxed. "What do you think I should do?"

He shook out the paper and his gaze followed a column for a moment. "It is not up to me. It is between you and God."

"But if Ruth has spoken to you about it, you must have an opinion. What did you tell her?"

"Are you looking to me to make up your mind for you?"

"You know your opinion counts for something with me."

"She asked me to help her convince you. But that is not my place, and I told her so. All I will say is that your own actions seem to lead you in Ruth's direction."

She was going to have to rein in her actions, then. It was no sin to be unwilling to do what someone else wanted.

*Unless you believed in* Uffgeva, *and wanted to live out that belief.*

That was submission to God. Not to man. Besides, imagine all the things she would have to learn if she were to agree. Her days were full enough already. She had not been exaggerating—keeping house for the boys and washing and sewing and trying to earn a living, not to mention helping where there was need in the church, kept her busy from dawn until after sunset. Where would she find the time to drive over to Whinburg every week and be schooled in the ways of teas and tinctures? Maybe there would be classes to take, and books to pore over, and if there were, that would mean her evenings, too.

Oh, no. She had a place to fill that she could not leave just because she "had the knack."

Whatever that meant.

# CHAPTER 6

In Priscilla's opinion, hockey was the last thing a person should think about once the crocuses came up. Who wanted to sit at a cold rink surrounded by ice, with the clash of skates and sticks ringing in your ears, when flowers were blooming and you could actually imagine the smell of grass and blossoms, even if you couldn't see them yet?

But that was before she'd found out about the tournament the boys were playing at the homemade rink in Reuben Esh's field outside Strasburg. Before all the girls in her buddy bunch had decided to go and cheer on the Woodpeckers' team.

Simon belonged to the Woodpeckers, the local gang of *Youngie* in Willow Creek. The young folks didn't run in gangs the way she understood that inner-city kids did, on the news you sometimes saw on the TVs in the electronics store in town. No, these were groups of friends around the same age who called themselves by all kinds of names—the Pine Cones, the Canaries, the Avalanche. Some gangs were a little fast, and some were downright rowdy—enough that parents worried that their sons or daughters might get into trouble with the police. But the Woodpeckers were pretty moderate—more interested in having a good time than in acting up and bringing the wrong kind of attention to themselves.

Priscilla's older brother Christopher was a Woodpecker, too, so of course she would go with him in the buggy to the game. And the only reason he agreed to that was because he was taking Malinda Kanagy and Malinda's younger sister Rosanne, the latter of whom just happened to be Priscilla's sidekick.

All in all, she couldn't have planned it better if she'd tried.

Being best friends, she and Rosanne chattered all the way to the rink, heroically resisting the urge to tease Christopher and Malinda for the awkward little bits of conversation they managed to get going between them.

"Those two were lucky we were here," Rosanne confided to her as Christopher found a place along the fence to tie up his horse and they made their way toward the rink, hands full of snack coolers and hot thermos bottles. The rink was outdoors, of course, but Reuben and the players had made a makeshift set of stands from used lumber. A row of lamps hung between poles behind the nets so the players could see after sunset. "It would have been the quietest buggy ride in the history of man if we hadn't been there to keep the conversation going."

"I know." Priscilla found them a seat two rows up. "I don't know how my brother plans to get himself a girlfriend if he can't put two words together—how on earth did he manage to ask Malinda out tonight?"

"Come to. Hockey game. With me." Rosanne lowered her voice into the male register and dissolved into giggles.

They waved over the other girls in their bunch, all of whom had worn rust-red dresses like theirs—the Woodpecker color. There was quite a lot of rust-red in the stands, despite the fact that most of it was covered by winter coats. The boys wore knit caps in that color, and shirts of the same. In contrast to the red was the peculiar shade of turquoise that their opponents, the Badgers, claimed as their own—and since the Badgers were local, there was a lot more of it.

"Never mind," Priscilla said to the girls around her. "We'll make up in skill what we don't have in numbers."

And then the teams skated out onto the ice. Priscilla drew in a breath at the sight of the familiar figure with the mop of dark hair under his helmet.

Rosanne glanced at her, then out at the players, who didn't wear padding except for shin guards. Only the goalies had homemade blocker pads, heavily festooned with silver duct tape, and heavy masks and gloves.

"I didn't know Simon Yoder was playing tonight."

"I didn't, either." At Rosanne's snort of disbelief, Priscilla added, "I didn't. He usually goes to Corinne and Jacob's for a big family supper on Fridays."

Rosanne nudged her as the puck dropped and the Badger center popped it over to his left wing. "Maybe he heard you were coming."

"I wish. He's so nice. And yet he never…"

"But he's taken you home from singing twice since last summer."

The Woodpecker defenseman stole the puck and passed it to Simon, who whirled and raced up the ice, the blades of his skates singing in a way they never got a chance to on the bumpy ponds and stock tanks the boys practiced on at home. There was something to be said for a made-on-purpose level rink, with boards along the sides and everything.

"*Ja.* He was being nice. We live on the same road, after all."

"There's more to it than that," Rosanne said loyally. "Look! He scored!"

They jumped to their feet, cheering, as Simon skated back to center with a grin so wide they could see it all the way up in the stands. But as it turned out, that was the only puck the Woodpeckers got past the Badger goalie on their way to a 4–1 defeat. Still, it didn't seem to bother them any as they streamed through the field afterward and gathered in a knot out by the buggies, congratulating each other on a game well played.

Priscilla and Rosanne stood on the edge of the crowd of boys, watching as Christopher slapped them on the back and rough-housed a little, ruffling hair and shaking hands. Malinda joined them after a few minutes, looking as cool and neat as if she were about to go in to church on a Sunday morning.

"Boys will be boys," she said, snugging her fashionable store-bought scarf about her throat and buttoning her coat over it so that it draped in a flattering way. "Come on. Let's go find our buggy before it gets too much later."

"I just—I wanted to—" Priscilla stopped in embarrassment, and Malinda gazed at her, waiting for her to finish her sentence.

"She wants to congratulate Simon Yoder on his goal," Rosanne said for her, and Priscilla could have pushed her into a mud puddle.

"No," she said defensively. "I wanted to tell Chris we're ready to go."

Rosanne made bug eyes at her while Malinda tried to locate Simon in the pack of boys. "Are you sweet on Simon? I know he took you home a time or two."

Did everybody have to bring that up? Especially when things had gone no further, no matter what she did to move them along? "*Neh*, I just wanted to be friendly. It was the only goal we scored, after all."

"Well, here's your chance." Malinda nodded toward

Simon, who had emerged from the pack with Christopher and was headed their way.

Priscilla took several deep breaths to calm her bumping heart, with the result that by the time the boys joined them, she was feeling a little light-headed.

"Hey, everyone," Simon said. "Glad you could come." His gaze landed on Priscilla, and she wondered if he'd meant *you* in general, or *you* as in herself specifically.

"Well done on your goal, Simon," she said. "If we only got one, I'm glad it was you."

He shrugged. "It was a surprise to me, especially since I wasn't supposed to play. Josh King couldn't make it, and I was the only guy who had a helmet. So they put me in."

"Maybe they'll put you in more often now."

He shook his head. "*Neh*, that's it for this year. The ice is getting too soft. Soon as the ground dries up a little more, we'll be planting and there won't be time to practice."

"Who did you come with, Simon?" Rosanne asked. "Do you have a ride home?"

Priscilla could have died. Either Rosanne planned to ride home with someone else, leaving Priscilla looking like she was trying to engineer a double date with her brother and Malinda, or Rosanne expected Simon to wedge himself onto the rear bench in the buggy, between the two girls. Not that that would have been so bad. But how obvious could you get?

Priscilla's cheeks began to burn.

"*Ja*, I came with your brother Dan and Joe Byler," he told Rosanne. "We're going to get a coffee. Do you want to come?"

Priscilla did the math in a flash. Three girls plus four boys equaled a fine time. And if they got their coffees pretty quick, they could even get home by midnight.

She and Rosanne grabbed Christopher by either arm. "Sure, we're going to come. Right, Chris?"

"It's up to Malinda," he said like a gentleman.

Malinda could read a desperate plea in a younger girl's eyes as well as anyone. "I could use a coffee," she said easily. "The longer we stand out here, the colder I'm getting."

At the coffee shop, they crowded into a corner booth shaped like a big wedge of pie, and Dan and the Byler twin—Priscilla could never tell them apart, but if Simon said it was Joe, then she believed him—dragged chairs over for themselves. To Priscilla's great disappointment, Simon didn't slide into the booth next to her. Instead, he waited until everyone was in and then sat on the end, next to Dan's chair.

An opportunity lost.

She ordered a cappuccino because she liked the picture of the foam with the cinnamon sprinkles on top. It took several tries before she discovered that every time she took a sip, she had to wipe the huge mustache off her upper lip with a napkin—and when Simon gently tapped his nose, she realized with horror that she'd got foam on her nose, too.

She blushed to the roots of her hair, and now everyone could see it.

Why did she have to be such a goofball? Simon was never going to date someone who behaved like a three-year-old.

"So, Joe, tell them about the guy who moved into your Aendi's house," Simon urged him, which turned the attention away from her, thank goodness.

"He's not just a guy, he's related, isn't he?" Christopher asked.

Joe's Adam's apple bobbed as he gulped coffee. "He's Aendi Sadie's nephew. Her brother Henry moved his family out to Holmes County and died out there. So did the wife.

Henry—the nephew is named that, too—never joined church and lived all over the place, according to Mamm. He's some kind of artist."

"What kind of artist?" Malinda asked.

Joe shrugged and sucked back another big gulp of coffee. Maybe he had a midnight curfew, too. "Shame about the farm going to him. If she'd left it to Dat, Jake and me could have planted it."

"Maybe you can deal with this Henry," Simon pointed out. "The leases will have to be done over."

"*Ja*, but my uncles have them," Joe said glumly. "They ain't going to just hand them over to a pair of *Youngie* like us. I'm going to be working for them, same as I did last year."

"You never know," Priscilla said. "Caleb talked to him and there's a lot of work to be done. You might be able to get a carpentry crew together and help out with the house and buildings."

"Yeah?" Joe brightened, and actually looked at her as though he hadn't noticed her sitting there before. Which was silly, because they'd known each other all their lives. "Caleb say what kind of artist he was?"

She shook her head. "He goes over every couple of days to see if the man needs him yet, but the answer's always no. He unloaded his moving van straight into the barn, which I thought was strange."

"House has all its furniture," Christopher put in. "Makes sense to fix it up and then move your own stuff in."

"Or maybe he doesn't plan to stay," Simon mused. "If he hasn't unpacked, maybe he's just going to sell up after all. I hope he does. Auctions are always interesting."

"Whatever he's got, it's all in the barn now." Priscilla

glanced at the clock over the cash register. It would take them a couple of hours to get home. "Chris, we need to get going."

"You're not going to make it by midnight, *Schweschder*," he said, as immovable as a stone as he tipped his coffee cup up over his nose. "Besides, I need to take Malinda home first."

Oh, *wunderbaar*. And he'd leave the buggy in the lane so she and Rosanne could sit there in the dark while he walked Malinda to the door hoping for a kiss on the step.

"I can take Malinda and Rosanne home," their brother Dan said innocently. "I'm going to the same place, after all, and Joe can ride with you."

"But—" Chris couldn't very well tell the girl's brother he was angling for a kiss now, could he?

Priscilla kept her face straight. "Then Simon could come with us, too, and not have to walk two miles home in the middle of the night."

Simon shrugged. "It doesn't matter to me. I've got plenty to keep my mind busy while my feet travel."

"Dan, I'll come with you." Malinda's voice was calm as Chris's face fell. "Simon, you go with them and save yourself the walk. Then we all might get home at a reasonable hour. I have to be up at five to go with Mamm to the market anyway."

Priscilla felt sorry for her brother, having his plans all squashed like that. But she couldn't help the delight that began to fizz through her veins. She pinched Rosanne's knee under the table, ever so softly, and Rosanne pinched back.

It was settled. Joe would ride up front, and Priscilla would go on the rear bench with Simon.

Where it was dark. And you could hold a perfectly dignified conversation with the people up front, and all the while be—she practically hugged herself—doing something else.

Like holding hands.

# CHAPTER 7

Henry leaned on the big barn door and surveyed the huge, echoing interior for about the twentieth time that week.

It hadn't changed—still smelled of earth and ancient hay and cows.

Nor would it until he made up his mind as to what he was going to do. Had he really given up his Denver apartment, loaded up his things, and come blasting across the country for...what? Nostalgia? The prospect of a home that had been welcoming and warm in memory, but in cold reality was...Amish?

It had taken two nights of freezing his hands and feet to get the woodstove to work properly, and even then, all he had been able to burn were scraps he'd located in the barn. He'd stocked up on food and could cook easily enough, but he'd gone the first three days without a hot shower until the propane truck had come, filled the tank, and got the pilot lit.

It was lucky he'd had no guests except for the ever-present Caleb, whom he was going to have to hire just to keep the kid from pestering him to death. Caleb had not appeared to notice that for three days, he'd smelled.

Which was a miracle, because he sure noticed everything else.

As if he'd summoned him into being, Caleb popped out from around the corner of the barn, which Henry had observed was the terminus of a path that had now been worn across the field, wavering over a hill, and winding down to where the creek took a turn toward town, as promised.

"Ready to unpack those boxes?" he called cheerfully.

"No. Not yet."

"*Warum nichts?* Er, why not?"

With a kind of tingle in his mind, Henry realized he had not needed the translation. He had not even heard the English in his head—had simply understood the *Deitsch*. That was a bad sign.

"Because I haven't made up my mind about whether I'm staying or not."

Caleb circled the stack of boxes and crates that held Henry's ability to make a living. Or they would, if he could get his backside off the fence and decide whether he was staying or going. "Joe Byler apprentices at the buggy shop with my brother Simon, and he says his Dat and uncles are going to come talk with you about the leases."

In the paperwork he remembered some mention of leases. Somewhere down about number ninety-six on his list of things he needed to think about.

"They'd be your uncles, too, wouldn't they?" Caleb persisted.

"My cousins. My father, Henry, and Joe's grandpa Silas were brothers. My family tree could use a little clarification, what with all the boys out here."

"It'll be in Sadie's Bible," he said. "She was probably like my *Mammi*, Jacob's Corinne. She keeps track of everyone— and with the Yoders, that's something. *Mammi* had to paste an extra sheet in for us." Something else caught the boy's eye, and like a magpie, he swooped in to investigate. "High Temperature Firing Clay," he read. "What's that?"

"Just what it says. It's a block of clay."

He straightened, giving Henry The Look. That Amish look that said, *You spent good money on something that most people can grow or make?* "There's plenty of clay around here. What would you buy it for?"

"The clay around here probably has a lot of impurities in it. That stuff has been processed specifically for what I do."

"Are you a potter? Do you make stuff with clay? Joe says you're an artist. Is that true?"

"Caleb, did anyone ever tell you that you ask too many questions?"

"Mamm does, all the time. And then she makes me look up the answers in the dictionary. But I don't need a dictionary here. What's in that big crate? Do you have a whatchacallit—a potter's wheel, like in the Bible?"

"Yes," he said, trying to stem the tide. "Not exactly like in the Bible, but... don't you have things to do at home?"

"No. Mamm's at the market and Simon went out with the twins. Say, why don't you take me to the market? If you're a potter, I bet you could sell the stuff you make there. I can introduce you to people."

"No, thanks," came bursting out before he could even think, the way a foot kicks out when the doctor taps a knee with his little mallet.

"Why not? If you're not going to unpack today, either, and if you're not going to start work on the house, you might as well."

"And will I be expected to pay you for your services as my personal guide of the market?"

Caleb grinned. "No, but I wouldn't stop you if you wanted to."

The thought of a crowded market was abhorrent to him. Too many eyes with too many questions in them. Too many strangers who thought they had a stake in his business. Or maybe that was just his family, whom he'd made a point of still not seeing, and it was now the end of March.

*You are a great big chicken. What do you think they're going to do? Judge you? Convert you? Make you go to baptism classes?* He was not a child, and here he was, behaving like someone younger and more stubborn than Caleb.

"Who do you know at the market?" he asked.

The boy, still investigating, spoke up from behind the crate containing the kiln, which was higher than his head. "Everybody. Mamm sells herbs and things to the tourists, but now isn't a very good time of year for it. She'll probably have lots of time to talk."

"Who else is 'everybody'?"

"The twins' Mamm, Paul's Barbara. That would be, um..." He paused for a moment, and came into view around the other side. "Your uncle Silas's son."

Maybe he'd better look into signing up on one of those genealogy websites, so he could plug people into their branch of the family tree and keep them straight.

"He's one of the ones who wants to see about the leases."

"Ah. Right. Who else?"

"Oh, a bunch of people. The bishop's wife, Evie Troyer, sells quilts at the first stall you see when you go in. Lots of the women make quilts to sell there."

"And the bishop?"

"Our bishop is pretty young—he was called when he was barely thirty. He does conversions—you know, making electric washing machines run on propane and stuff. Has a big shop on his place, but he lives real close to town. He won't be at the market, though."

"Not a farmer?"

"No. His brothers are, but they live a ways out."

"So how does your Mamm keep two teenage boys fed and clothed selling dried herbs every Saturday?" Even he could see there must be something more to the story.

"That's why I want to work for you," Caleb said in a tone that hinted this was the hundredth time he'd had to explain it. Which it was not. Maybe it was the hundredth time the boy had thought it. "Simon gives her nearly everything he makes, and I would, too, if I could only get work. I have to put it in my journal, see, and—"

"All right, all right." Henry held up both hands and Caleb closed his mouth with a click. "Let's go to the market, then, and you can be my personal guide. I'll feed you lunch and give you five bucks for your trouble, all right?"

The grin that broke out on the kid's face could have lit up the barn. In fact, Henry wasn't sure if maybe it didn't. "*Denki*, Henry! You won't be sorry. I'll find you all kinds of customers for your pots, don't worry!"

He'd need to find customers eventually. Maybe getting off the farm wasn't such a bad idea. A change of scenery might give him more information to base a decision on.

And he could use a meal that didn't involve his own cooking.

The Willow Creek Amish Market was housed in a big shed with a tin roof and removable sides. Around it had grown a cluster of *Englisch* businesses catering to tourists, like the Dutch Rest Café and the Amish Attic Gift Shop, which Henry doubted actually contained anything from an Amish attic.

He didn't know why things like that still bothered him, after all this time. A person had a right to make a living, and if they wanted to sell quasi-Amish gifts practically outside the doors of a market where people could buy real ones, he supposed that was one of the benefits of a free economy.

Caleb looked back at him impatiently, and he lengthened his stride to catch up.

"We'll go see Mamm first, so she knows I'm here with you," the boy said.

Henry finally thought to ask, "It'll be okay with her that I drove you here?"

But Caleb was already out of earshot, and if Henry didn't hurry, he'd lose him in the busy aisles. Booths were set up flea market style, but looked fairly permanent, as if families had been doing business this way for years. Tight, durable Amish carpentry was evident in the false fronts and porch-style showrooms in some of the booths, where small furniture was on display. There in a corner booth close to the entrance was a woman who must be the bishop's wife, a very pretty woman in her forties who was almost invisible behind counters heaped high with quilts, table runners, place mats, and pot holders.

Not for the first time, he wondered what had happened to Aendi Sadie's quilts. He could sure use a few, since the wood scraps weren't going to last forever and spring was taking its time arriving.

Caleb hailed him and he turned down a row devoted to the products of the garden, which consisted of a lot of fruit and pickles in glistening Mason jars, and a few bunches of very early rhubarb. Toward the end, the boy stood in front of a simple booth containing a table in front and some standalone bookshelves in the back, covered in dried bouquets of herbs and flowers, along with some dolls and decorations made of twisted and braided wheat.

"Henry, this is my mother, Sarah Yoder," Caleb said.

Henry looked into the startled gray gaze of a woman in her early thirties. Dark blond hair was tucked modestly under her *Kapp*, and if he'd been expecting a matronly Amish *Fraa*, he didn't find her. Wide cheekbones and a small but determined chin gave her face a heart shape, and a mouth that should have lent itself to humor was at the moment open in surprise.

"Caleb, what on earth are you doing here?" She spoke in English for Henry's benefit, but he could practically hear the lecture in *Deitsch* trembling in the air.

He did his best to head it off at the pass. After all, he had been complicit in the plan. It wasn't fair that poor Caleb should take all the heat.

He held out a hand, and after a second's hesitation, she took it and gave it a single shake. "Good morning, Sarah. Don't be too hard on Caleb—your boy has a good heart and a good mind for business. I'm Henry Byler, Sadie Byler's nephew."

It was clear she'd already figured out who he was, having taken him in from haircut to hiking boots. "Good morning." Her gaze moved to her son, who was busy moving the herb bouquets into a line instead of the casual bunches in which she'd arranged them. "Did you come in the car?"

"Yes. I hope it's all right that I gave him a ride."

In Denver, a mother faced with her son accepting a ride from a male stranger would have gone into hysterics and then called 911. But Sarah Yoder merely frowned. "I hope he was no trouble."

"No, not at all. We're on a fact-finding mission. He wants to introduce me to some of the people here."

"He's a potter, Mamm," Caleb put in. "I told him this was the place to sell his pots."

"And what are you doing telling an *Englisch* man to do anything?" she said in rapid *Deitsch*. "Remember your place, Caleb."

Again Henry felt that tingle of recognition. He got about half the words as she said them, and then his brain caught up and translated the rest.

"He's not all *Englisch*, Mamm," Caleb told her earnestly. "He was born Amish. His *Dat* was the brother that went out to Holmes County."

"I haven't seen much of my relatives yet," he said smoothly in English, as if they'd been including him in the conversation, "but Caleb said he'd take me over today to meet my cousin Paul's wife. He says she has a booth here."

Her skin reddened and it took him a minute to identify the odd feeling in his chest as compunction. Sure, maybe they shouldn't have conversed in *Deitsch* in front of him. But it had been rude for him to interrupt a mother's remonstrations with her son and reveal he'd understood it, but wasn't willing to share that language with them.

He wasn't Amish. He was *Englisch* now. But he shouldn't have done it, and apologizing would only make things more awkward.

"You'd best go do your business, then," she said to him. "But when you are finished, you can leave Caleb here. He'll go home with me."

"Mamm..." Caleb began, and stopped when she raised an

eyebrow at him. He gulped. "Come on, Henry. I'll show you around."

He ambled off down the next aisle at about half speed. Clearly he intended to make his time with Henry stretch out as long as possible.

"I hope I didn't get you in trouble," Henry said, catching up in a few steps. "Maybe we should have waited until next week, and asked your Mamm first."

"It's okay," he said glumly. "She's just worried that I'm bugging you. But I'm not, right? We're doing business and you need me."

"Right. For today, I guess I do."

Caleb brightened, clearly the kind of person who made lemonade when his Mamm handed him lemons. "Look, there's Barbara Byler, with the place mats and things. She's my *Aendi*, too. My Dat's sister."

So his cousin Paul had married the girl next door, Michael's sister, the comfortable-looking *Fraa* he had expected Sarah Yoder to be.

Again, he held out his hand, and Barbara took it. "So you're the long-lost cousin," she said. She had a grip like iron, and he resisted the urge to shake out his fingers once she'd released them. "We thought you might come over long before this."

"I would have," he fibbed, "but it's been decades since I was here last. Things have changed and there's a lot to do at the house."

"You could have asked for help," she said. "But then, the road goes both directions, so we should have made the first move. Hallo, Caleb. *Wie geht's?*"

"*Gut*," he said. "I'm showing Henry around the market. He's a potter, and there might be some people here who need pots."

"Oh?" Barbara gazed at him with interest. "A potter? I heard you were an artist."

"I can make pretty artistic pots," he offered, smiling. "But they probably wouldn't sell as well as practical ones. Jugs and platters and cups, for instance."

"I don't need any of that." She indicated the stacks of cheery place mats and pot holders, pieced and quilted in intricate patterns. "But others might."

Small talk was not this lady's strength, evidently. It wasn't his, either, so they had that in common. "How is Paul? Sorry I couldn't come to your wedding. You probably have teenagers by now."

"We do," she said. "Three girls and three boys. The elder two are twins. They'll be eighteen in August. The girls are fourteen, twelve, and ten, and my baby is two already."

"I told you about Joe and Jake," Caleb elaborated. "Joe works with my brother, Simon, at the buggy shop, remember?"

"Ah, the many pieces are falling into place," Henry told him.

"You should come for supper," Barbara said. "Are you all alone over there? You could probably use a good meal."

That was true. But before he could reply, she went on, "Is your family coming soon? It's been a couple of weeks, hasn't it?"

"No family," he said slowly. "Just me."

"No family!" she repeated, as if he'd said no lungs, or no heart, and planned to walk around that way until he keeled over. "But I thought—we heard you'd—"

"I was engaged some years ago, but it didn't work out." He clamped his lips shut on a subject that was so private that the very words hurt in his mouth.

She gazed at him, those round blue eyes taking in every line of his face, every wrinkle in his *Englisch* clothes, every frayed thread on the hems of his jeans. He braced himself for another graceless comment, for expectations, for words like stones, no matter how casually tossed.

"You'd be very welcome for supper. Why don't we say tomorrow?" Her gaze returned to his face. "Please come—it's our off Sunday so we'll be home. We would like to get to know you."

Graceless she might be. Blunt and sweating and not quite comfortable with the tight waistband of her green dress and black cape and apron. But her voice was gentle, the voice of a deeply compassionate woman, and Henry found his throat closing up.

Without another word, he nodded abruptly and plunged down the nearest aisle, heading for the light of day at the end of it.

# CHAPTER 8

During the off season from November to April, the market was only open Saturday mornings, but even then, between 7 A.M. and noon Sarah could usually sell all the herb bundles she'd made up, to say nothing of packages of *Schnitz*—sliced dried apples—with pretty handmade recipe cards so that the rare winter tourist could make a pie at home and take the taste of Amish country with her. Picking apples in Corinne and Jacob's orchard in the fall was hard work, as was drying all the apple slices in the dehydrators set up in the big south-facing room upstairs, but it was worth it to have something to sell on the wet Saturdays of spring. After that, neat loaves of seed bread filled out the table and usually sold pretty well.

At noon, traffic dropped off and she packed away the remaining bouquets and packets of *Schnitz*, as well as the wheat dollies that Simon made during long winter evenings. Michael had taught him how when he was a boy, and Jacob, who had taught Michael, had spent many a snowy night after Michael's death showing Simon fancy twists and how to give the impression of life even when all he had to work with were broken stems.

Sharing the wheat dollies with his grandfather—sharpening

the skill his own Dat had passed on to him—had helped during those hard months. Love and sorrow were twisted into their little bodies with their wild hair and stiff limbs, but the knots and kinks of grief got worked out as well. By the time the year had wheeled past that first spring and into the summer, the sharp edges of missing him had softened, and the memories of laughter had been easier to take out and appreciate. Soon those memories were the ones that came out most often.

Sarah carried the big cardboard box out to the buggy behind the market. Where was Caleb? If he didn't catch Dulcie and have her between the rails by the time Sarah cashed out and settled up with the management—who got twenty percent of everything the stall keepers made—there would be *Druwwel* on the way home.

He said they'd been heading over to Barbara Byler's stall. Maybe they were still there.

She turned down the textiles aisle, where others were packing up as well. Barbara was bent over a cardboard box with about half her place mats and pot holders put away when Sarah leaned over the counter.

"Hi, Barbara. Have you seen my Caleb in the last few minutes?"

Barbara straightened with a smile. "Not in the last few, *neh*. He and Henry Byler came by about an hour ago, but..." Her face clouded. "I asked Henry over for supper tomorrow and he lit out of here in a big hurry. I hope it wasn't the wrong thing to say."

"How could asking a cousin to supper be the wrong thing to say?" And if he'd left, where was Caleb? "Is he going to come?"

"I think so. He nodded. But he looked upset." Barbara

lifted a pile of pot holders while Sarah took the other pile and helped her stack them in the next box. "I think it was my asking about his family. I didn't mean to upset him. I meant to offer kindness."

Sarah had to smile at that. Anyone who knew Barbara knew that kindness was her first reaction to just about anything except the cat licking the butter and the chickens breaking into her tomato starts. "Kindness takes some by surprise, I hear."

"If you're not used to it, I suppose it might. It's good that he's moved here. A man should know his family."

"But his parents? Brothers and sisters? Where are they?"

"In Holmes County—the siblings, at least. His parents are gone now. His mother never saw him join church, and I know it grieved her right up until the last."

Sarah handed her a stack of table runners made of strips of fabric woven in a three-way lattice pattern. There was a lot of math in those runners—it made Sarah's head hurt to look at them—but Barbara put them together in the evenings while she was supervising her brood as if it were as easy as making applesauce.

"Well, maybe that's why God has brought him back," Sarah said. "To show him that his place is here, with his family and his church."

"He has no family of his own." Barbara folded the flaps of the box together and raised her gaze to Sarah's.

Sarah felt a clutch at her heart. "None? But I thought they were coming later."

"So did I. I mean, I assumed. We would assume, wouldn't we, that a man in the prime of his life would have a wife and several *Kinner* by now. But he says not."

"The poor man," Sarah breathed. How dreadful it would

be, to be all alone in the world. She tried to picture herself in such a position—no boys, no in-laws, no sisters and brothers whose wives wrote a circle letter to keep her up to date on all the family news in Mifflin County.

No church. No God in his life, directing his steps, being there to count on and ask advice of.

If she thought her life was troublesome as it was, maybe she ought to look at it again—from Henry's point of view.

Compared to him, she had everything. Love. Family. Home.

Faith.

"It's right that you asked him," she told Barbara with sudden fierce certainty. "Even if he's never willing to let the Lord work in his heart, at least he will have you and Paul and his family here. And who knows? Maybe if he learns to love his natural family, the love of his spiritual family will draw him in as well."

"I hope you're right," Barbara said. She hefted the boxes onto the counter. "Now, I wonder where those boys of mine have got to?"

"Maybe they're with mine. I told Caleb he was coming home with me—he'd better not have disobeyed me just to get a ride in a car. I'll take a quick look around for all three, if you like."

It didn't take long to cover the aisles of the market. She found the twins in the buggy of one of the older boys, admiring the battery pack that powered the stereo he had tucked under the bench seat. He was just so proud of it that she didn't have the heart to tell him that boys had been doing that kind of thing when she was running around—and probably for years before that.

Which was something that an old person would think.

Go on, Sarah, she chided herself. Next thing you knew, she'd be saying, *When I was a girl*, and then she'd have hit middle age for sure.

Well, she wasn't there yet. She didn't have time to get old.

She sent the twins off to their mother and asked around, but no one had seen Caleb. If that didn't beat all. What kind of car did Henry drive? She gazed out at the parking lot with her hands on her hips, noting that yes, Dulcie was still foot-loose and fancy free in the meadow.

She caught her and hitched her up, and by the time she drove around to the front of the market, the edge of her annoyance was beginning to melt into concern. Had something happened to her boy? Or had Caleb merely gone home with Henry in his car? If he had, the consequences would fit the crime—not turning over the garden, because Simon was to have done it while she was here. No, it would have to be something he hated. Something like—like cleaning the chicken coop. That was it. She'd have him wash down the walls with soap and water. It would take him the rest of the day, and—

Her wide gaze skidded to a stop on the Dutch Rest Café, where her missing son sat with Henry at a table right there in the front window, both of them waving their soup spoons in the air as they discussed something wildly entertaining.

With a long breath of relief, Sarah tied up the horse at the rail in front of the place and went in. "Caleb!"

He looked over at her, grinning. "Hi, Mamm. Henry is taking me to lunch to say thank you for showing him around."

"After I told you to come back to help me put the boxes in the buggy?"

The smile faded a couple of notches as he realized he was

in the wrong. She hated being the cause of the dimming of that smile, but she hardened her heart. Obedience was vital—when a child learned to be obedient to his parents, he learned to be obedient to his God, too.

Henry put out a placating hand. "Don't be too hard on him, Sarah. I told him I'd take him to lunch. It only seemed fair, after he gave up his morning for me."

"I wish you had told me. I've been worried, not knowing what had happened to him. Caleb, I'm going now. *Kumme mit.*"

"But—"

"The rest of our meals haven't arrived yet," Henry Byler said. "Here, why don't you slide in next to him and join us?"

Caleb wasted no time in moving over onto the other chair so that she could sit. "*Ja*, Mamm. Come and have lunch—I'm getting a hamburger. Do you want one, too?"

"No, I want you to come home with me, and—no, Henry, I'm not going to—well, honestly—"

And somehow, despite all her good intentions, she found herself sitting in an *Englisch* restaurant opposite an *Englisch* man with her disobedient son beside her, feeling *verhuddelt* and…and hungry.

"We can have everything on here at home," she muttered behind the menu he handed her.

"But home is two miles away," Henry pointed out with a smile, "and I don't know about you, but markets make me hungry. Would you like me to order you some soup, too?"

"Just a small cup." She didn't think she had enough in her pocket to buy a sandwich, and she wasn't about to touch the cash she'd made this morning.

"It's on me," Henry said quietly. "Have a bowl if you want, and a sandwich to go with it."

"I can't let you pay for my meal."

"Why not? Caleb put in a morning for me, and I owe you for allowing him to do it."

"You do not." He was so *Englisch*, worried about who owed what when sometimes generosity was simply that. Though, to be sure, the generosity seemed to be all on Caleb's and Henry's side at the moment. "I'm not even sure what I'm doing in a restaurant with a man I didn't know yesterday."

Caleb slurped up the last of the soup. "I've known him for a couple of weeks." He laid down his spoon.

"There's a character reference for you," Henry said. The waitress came back to take the bowls and he ordered a bowl of broccoli cheese soup and a club sandwich for her.

She was committed now, so she might as well enjoy it. "Thank you. It was kind of you to invite me, though it strikes me as being more like the wages of sin." She gave Caleb the kind of look that held an entire lecture, and then saw her sister-in-law Miriam, Michael's older brother Joshua's wife, over his shoulder, stopping outside next to her buggy.

She obviously recognized it, and put a parcel on the front seat that had to be the rose-colored fabric she'd cut for Sarah last week. She looked around, then—

Oh, my.

Sarah resisted the urge to giggle at Miriam's expression when she took in the tableau in the big front window. Sarah gave a wave and got up, her hand going to the billfold in her pocket. But before she could go out to pay her for the material, Miriam collected herself, waved back, and hurried off down the sidewalk.

She'd have to go by the shop on the way home, and explain. Sarah subsided into her chair. "You couldn't have got a table farther inside?" she asked, spooning up soup as though it were going to escape if she didn't. "I think we just shocked Aendi Miriam."

"We sat here so you could see us," Caleb told her. "Or so we could see you when you came out, and invite you. Why is Aendi Miriam shocked?"

She would not look at Henry Byler, who did not have to explain himself to anyone. She would need to see Miriam before the Yoder family got together—which would probably be tomorrow, since it wasn't a church Sunday.

"She doesn't like to eat in restaurants," Sarah said. "She believes it's a waste to spend money on something you do at home three times a day."

The rest of their meals arrived and Henry would have picked up his burger and bit into it, but she bowed her head and spoke to Caleb. "Whether we're home or not, God still deserves our gratitude."

Caleb bowed his head while they said a silent grace. And to Sarah's surprise, Henry waited quietly until they'd opened their eyes before he picked up his burger and took a big bite.

She would have loved to know if he'd said grace himself, once he'd seen them do so. But that was not the kind of thing you asked a stranger.

"How are you settling in?" she said instead. "Caleb tells me you have nothing for him yet, but I don't want you to feel pressured to start something just because he wants work."

"I'm as settled as I can be without being settled in my mind, if that makes any sense."

She found the nerve to raise her gaze and study him for a moment before she dropped it to her sandwich. But in that moment she saw a number of things.

A narrow scholar's face. Blue eyes. Tired lids with long lashes. Long fingers that held the burger, but that somehow managed to convey strength—no doubt from working clay.

"I could help you unpack the clay," Caleb said around a mouthful of grilled meat and bacon and lettuce. "Then at least you could start making pots and selling them."

"We don't have any potters in these parts that I know of," Sarah said. "What kind of pots?"

Henry shrugged, and swallowed before he spoke. "Not just pots. Abstract sculptures. Garden gnomes." Then he cleared his throat. "Anything people need. I was telling Barbara Byler at her counter that I can make plates, cups, pitchers, bowls... I made a complete matching set in blue and gray and white once, for a wedding gift. Four of everything, plus serving pieces and a pitcher. It was challenging to get everything uniform and matching, yet give each piece a little something unique."

"That's a very Amish way of looking at it," Sarah said into her sandwich, then finished it off.

He paused, as if listening to what she'd just said. "What, everybody looking the same, but different underneath?"

Sarah knew how to leave a seed in the ground and not disturb it. She said nothing more, merely wiped her fingers on the paper napkin. Then she asked, "I have a little problem— I wonder if you would be the person to help me with it?"

"Of course," he said instantly, almost as if he were relieved at the swerve in the conversation. "What can I do? Something with the horse outside? I'm a little rusty, but if you need something driven to your house—"

"No, no, it's to do with pots."

"Oh." He sat back. "What would that be?"

"In the summer I make bouquets like the ones I had today, but along with that I have bags of herbs—you know, rosemary and thyme and such, for cooking. I just wondered if it would be possible to put the herbs in a container of some kind. The zip-top bags get punctured on the way home...but a pot, now, that would be more stable. Of course, how you would keep the lid on is another question."

He nodded, gazing into the middle distance over her shoulder as if he were building something in his head. "Not a lid. A cork. Cut to fit the mouth of the clay jar exactly. In fact, I could design a different kind of jar, just for you, to make your herbs unique. Then, after the herbs are used up, people could put things in them."

"Pretty jars, as well as useful." Sarah nodded. She didn't have a lot of use for pretty by itself, unless you were talking about the flowers God made. But add practical to pretty, and she was sold. Maybe other women would be, too.

"I can carve the corks," Caleb said. "We could make them out of other stuff. I bet restaurants have lots of corks left over from bottles."

"No leftover corks, I'm afraid." Sarah smiled at him, because part of his idea had merit. "The health inspector probably wouldn't like that. But if we ordered corks and they didn't come in exactly the right size, you could carve them." She craned her neck to look across the table. "What are you doing?"

Henry had extracted a pen from his pocket and was drawing on the scallop-edged paper place mat. With just a few strokes, a row of pots materialized on a board, as if they were all on display.

Caleb leaned over, his eyes practically bugging out. "You really are an artist. How do you do that?"

"Years of practice, and several years of an art degree that I could have used to start the stove with a few nights ago." A few more strokes of the pen. "Do you like any of these?"

Goodness. "You invent half a dozen pots in less than a minute, and expect me to choose?" Sarah said, half laughing.

"No." With a smile like a ghost of hers, he sat back. "It's been a long time, and I guess I got carried away. I only meant that if there was a shape you liked, I'd have somewhere to start."

"Well…" Sarah brought her hands up on the table and shaped them around an invisible object. "They would need to be easy to carry in your hand. Big enough to hold, say, a cup of the dried herb, but not so big they would get in the way in the kitchen."

"Big enough to go in a row on the windowsill," Caleb said.

She raised her eyebrows at her smart son. "Exactly."

"Tall and thin, or squat and round?" Henry's pen hovered over the row. "I vote for round. We don't want people knocking them over every time they reach for something."

"You're right." She pointed to one of his drawings. "I like this. It's round, but not really."

"That's what they call a ginger jar, slightly fatter on the shoulders and narrower toward the base. How do people get their herbs out of it?"

Her hands moved slightly as she mimed a woman measuring out some rosemary for a roast chicken. "I would put a measuring spoon in it, or fingers to pinch up a bit. The round shape wouldn't allow for easy pouring, would it?"

"Not unless you wanted them to look like teapots or small pitchers."

She shook her head.

"So, an opening on the top big enough for a tablespoon or fingertips, a ginger jar shape…" His busy pen made a pot materialize in a different corner of the place mat. "And a cork for the opening to keep the herbs fresh."

And there it was. Her mouth opened and she shook her head in amazement.

But the pen did not stop. In a moment, a branch of rosemary wound itself around the base of the pot, complete with tiny flowers.

"So you can tell what's in it," he said. "I can paint them with one of the glazes, or score them into the clay with a stylus."

She had no idea what a stylus was, but the simple fact that such a good solution existed was enough for her. "You should choose what is easiest for you."

"That would probably be painting. Guess I'd better brush up on my nature studies—you know, drawings from nature. If you find me in your garden some morning, sitting on a rock with my sketchbook, don't be surprised. I'm just working on filling your order." Her eyes widened, and he said hastily, "That's a joke. Sorry. Don't take me literally."

"No, no." It had been an amusing picture, but the timing was wrong. "We're months away from you having anything to sketch, unless you count the herbs I have growing in the kitchen window. But I just remembered that my son Simon is turning over the garden today, and maybe my order from the seed catalog has come. Caleb, have you finished?"

"Can I have dessert?"

"You may have it at home. We have *Schnitz* pie from last night, and there should be some gingerbread and cream cheese whoopie pies left, if Simon hasn't eaten them all." Henry looked up with the most pathetic expression she had ever seen. Not even Michael's old pointer had looked at table scraps with that much longing. Without missing a beat, she said, "You can take some of them over to Henry this evening as a thank-you for lunch."

"You are a saint," Henry said in a tone people usually reserved for prayer.

She blushed, hot and prickling, and embarrassment coupled with the silliness of that blush made her feel awkward, lunch or no lunch. "Nonsense." She put on her coat and stood. "None of us are saints—all men have sinned and come short of the glory of God. Caleb, *kumme mit.*"

Her boy must have sensed that she couldn't be persuaded to stay any longer, for he rose meekly, thanked Henry for lunch, and followed her out to the buggy. When she took the reins, he backed the horse and then jumped in beside her. Caleb was not easily subdued, and any other day she might have marveled at it. Today she was just glad for the clop of the hooves, the rattle of the wheels, and a little time to think before she faced her sister-in-law.

Or not think, as the case may be.

About Henry Byler. And his little pots.

And what on earth she'd just gotten herself into.

# CHAPTER 9

"So, what did you think of him?" Caleb finally spoke when they were halfway home from the fabric store, jolting Sarah out of thoughts that were as scrambled as a dropped egg.

"Henry Byler?" She thought plenty. She just couldn't say much of it to a little pitcher with such big ears. "He seemed nice."

"I think he's lonely."

"I'm sure he is, with no family of his own, and not many friends...and cut off from God."

"I'm his friend. And it doesn't matter that he's not in church, because neither am I."

A chill darted through Sarah's stomach and her fingers tightened on Dulcie's reins. The horse tossed her head and Sarah made an effort to relax. "That's because you're too young to make such a decision yet. He's a man grown who chose to take his own way."

"I know. I just think we have something in common."

Sarah did not like this line of thinking at all. "You do. You both need to give your lives to God. And there's nothing to prevent your encouraging him to do that."

"So you don't mind if I go over there?"

She wanted to laugh at how neatly he'd outmaneuvered her, but if she did, he would think she wasn't serious about this.

"It was *gut* that I met him, and he does seem nice, but Caleb, you must remember that our decisions prove what is in our hearts. Friendship and companionship are one thing, but you mustn't think that you can have real fellowship with him, or let yourself get too close."

"I won't. I just want to help out."

For the second time in an hour, she saw the moment to step away. This time, though, it was harder to hold her tongue. Harder to give herself peace by lecturing him on the dangers of becoming too friendly with the world.

And mostly, it was hard because she needed to hear that very lecture.

How had she allowed herself to be drawn into what was practically a partnership with a worldly man, a man who had turned his back on God? A partnership that had literally created something from nothing, right there on the place mat. She had fallen into that moment headfirst, been seduced by the magic of creating something that had not been there before... and had seen a tiny germ of possibility blossom and grow into something that was almost real.

*Almost* being the important word.

Because that feeling—that excitement she had shared with him in the moment of creation—it was not real. She had been carried away by his clever pen and the art that had been put at her disposal like a gift, asking for nothing but that she allow it to be.

She had allowed it, and now it would bear fruit, and what kind of harvest would it bring?

Miriam had made good use of the few minutes they had together. She was not a judgmental woman, but she had a wise soul, and while sometimes Sarah chafed against her advice, she usually found it was right in the end. So if she had any sense, she would send over a note tonight with the whoopie pies, saying that she had thought some more about it, and decided that little muslin bags like sachets would be a more practical way to sell the dried herbs, not pots. She would say thank you for his time and for the sandwich, and that would be that.

There would be no more reason to see Henry Byler than in the normal course of a day, passing on the road, or bumping into him at the post office or the dry goods store. Caleb would soon tire of asking for work that wouldn't come, and maybe Henry would eventually move on, leaving the farm to people who would know how to be good stewards of it.

Feeling a little more settled in her spirit, Sarah let Dulcie make the turn into their lane. The horse knew well enough what direction it should take to get back to its comfortable barn; it needed no help from her to make the right choice.

"Look, Caleb." She pointed, the reins loose in her fingers. "Simon's finished turning over the garden." Her elder son waved from the far side of the rectangular plot, dark with fresh, damp earth, all the old plants and the tillage radishes turned under to make fertilizer for the new. The soil was cross-hatched in the way she liked it, for he'd tilled longways and then across, breaking up the clods and bringing up earth from deep beneath to feed the new roots.

Ferd, their workhorse to which the tiller was hitched, cropped grass against the fence behind him while Simon used the shovel to give the sides of the plot a nice crisp edge. "Not so fast," she said as Caleb made as if to jump out and join him. "I want you to let the hens out and clean the coop."

"But Mamm," he protested, "Simon needs help."

"Simon is nearly finished, and the coop needs you."

"I can do it tomorrow—the sun is almost down."

"Caleb Yoder, it is only one thirty in the afternoon. You disobeyed me earlier, and this is the price you must pay. I want the bedding from the coop in a pile there"—she pointed—"so I can spread it once we've planted, and the walls must be scrubbed down before you put out new bedding."

He knew better than to argue any more, because she could think of an endless series of jobs that would keep him working late into the evening, and then he wouldn't be able to go over to Henry's at all. So he unhitched Dulcie and let her out into the field, and then got his rake, his shovel, the wheelbarrow, and his reluctant self over to the henhouse.

By the time she had unloaded the buggy and put everything away, Simon had finished. He leaned into the kitchen, standing in his muddy boots on the porch outside, and she gave him a big slice of schnitz pie and a glass of milk. "Ferd and I will take the tiller back to Daadi. After I put him up, I promised Chris and some of the guys I'd meet them in town."

"Not too late," she reminded him as he gulped down the snack. "It's Saturday night, and we need to prepare ourselves for the Lord's Day."

Even though it was an off Sunday, they still spent the morning together, singing a hymn or two, and reading from the Bible and the *Martyrs' Mirror*, enjoying the quiet and each other's company.

"I won't be late."

From over the hill, his cheery whistle floated back to her as she helped herself to some cake and walked over to the garden.

This was the part she liked—deciding what would go

where, and how much. But this time it would be different. She wished she could climb up into one of the maples and gaze down through the delicate haze of budding branches at the rectangle of rumpled earth, visualizing the garden the way some women could look at fabric and visualize a quilt.

Or a man could visualize a ginger jar.

*Neh, don't think about that.*

She walked the perimeter and thought about patterns. How did Corinne design her quilts? Sarah wished she'd thought to ask. Some women grew up with a needle in their hands, and could sketch a pattern as easily as—

—a branch of rosemary—

*Stop that!*

This was a garden, so it had to have some kind of order. She'd changed into rubber boots, which made wide, flat tracks as she quartered the rectangle. Four quarters. A path dividing them by which she could weed each quarter. Hm. These were awfully big. Better bisect the quarters, forming eight diamonds. That was more like it. What about diamonds on their sides on one quarter, like a pinwheel? She could alternate chard with beets for texture and color.

Her boots pressed the pattern into the soil.

An Ohio Star went in the quarter closest to the house. Tomatoes in the points and bush beans in the middle.

Borders of orange calendula here, here, and here to keep the slugs away.

A spiral of potatoes in this quarter, with lots of garlic in the curving spaces between. She would probably regret not being able to hoe a straight line, but my goodness, she'd been hoeing straight lines all her life. Maybe it was time for a little creativity—a little fun.

Final quarter. Squash hills and pea vines, alternating in a simple Nine Patch, but when each plant blossomed, it would be breathtaking. With satisfaction in every thud of her rubber boots in the soil, Sarah drew the garden with her footprints.

And when the thought flitted through her mind that Henry might be the only person in the settlement who would appreciate her craziness, she chased it away. Some thoughts were like starlings in the tomatoes. You could never let them actually settle down to roost, or they'd never leave.

Sarah stood at one end of the garden and gazed at her handiwork. Or footwork, she supposed, though it didn't look like anything useful at all from this angle. In fact, it looked as though the entire congregation had tromped through the dirt, leaving a host of footprints.

Never mind. She knew what they all meant.

A breeze wafted past her, pressing her skirts against the fronts of her legs. She lifted her face, welcoming the air movement. It was warmer today than it had been yesterday, but you never knew in March—it could snow tomorrow. But if the weather held, she could do more than tramp around in the dirt. She could plant.

*What about the herbs?*

This was a vegetable garden, meant to feed her family and keep them through the winter. She had enough herbs growing in the kitchen and close to the house to make her little bouquets and packets for the tourists.

*You should plant more. You should talk with Ruth and find out what she uses most in her practice. Think of the health of the Gmee.*

Wouldn't Caleb laugh if he came out with his wheelbarrow of bedding and found her arguing with herself in the middle of an empty field? The point was, just because everyone thought she should do a thing, didn't make it the right thing to do. The Lord made decisions like that.

*Have you been praying that He would show you His decision?*

Of course she had. Well, some. All right, then, she had prayed about it once and asked the *gut Gott* for some guidance. But had He sent it to her?

*Neh.*

Or had He?

Her father-in-law had spoken to her about it. And Ruth, of course. And Barbara.

Was she waiting for a voice from on high, or was she simply not paying attention when it spoke from homelier sources, like her friends and her family?

Sarah sank into the boys' old swing that still hung from a thick branch in one of the maples. She pushed herself back and forth, gazing out at the garden.

This could not be what God wanted for her. To sacrifice her strength and time for others instead of her family and the ones closest to her? To involve herself more deeply in the lives of the people in the district?

Though, to be honest, Ruth's time was taken up so much because she was the only one with her skills in quite a number of miles. If there were two of them, there would only be half the work, wouldn't there? It wasn't like she would be taking on Ruth's entire job.

Still, even half that job was more than most women had to cope with.

In her mind's eye, she saw Simon and Caleb, so strong, and getting taller and manlier by the day. They would be grown sooner than she wanted to think about it. They would find the girls God wanted for them, and maybe they wouldn't settle in Willow Creek. Maybe they'd want to create homes of their own, and leave her here on these five acres. Maybe if that happened, she'd be glad of good, useful work to do. Work that might pay the bills.

Was that why God had sent Ruth, with her angular figure and no-nonsense manner, to shock Sarah out of her comfortable but somewhat isolated path and put her on a different one? One where He could use her for His own purposes?

If she looked at it a certain way, she had all the signs she needed that this was His plan for her. The swing came to a stop. The breeze touched her cheek as gently as a mother's fingers and passed on.

*Please, Lord, help me know what to do. Help me to know Your will. And Lord, along with knowing it, help me to be willing to do it. Because I'm not. I don't like change, and You know I've been through enough of it. If I say yes to Ruth and agree to this work, will You hold me up and enable me to do it? Will You help me heal the ones who come to me for help? Will You give me the right plants in the right season—and the right words in their season, too?*

Sarah's lips trembled with the desperation of her prayer.

*What should I do, Lord? What is Your will for me?*

"Mamm!"

Sarah looked around blindly, half wondering if the Lord would speak in such a panicked tone.

"Mamm!"

Her head cleared and she saw Caleb running toward her, his hands held out in front of him as if he'd been burned.

With a clutch at her heart, she leaped out of the swing and ran across the lawn to him. "*Was ischt*, Caleb? What's wrong?" She grabbed his hands and turned them palms up.

They were covered in white welts from fingertip to wrist. She let out a breath of relief. No blood. Welts.

Stinging nettle. From the clump behind the henhouse.

He was trying hard not to cry, but the pain was about to get the better of him. "It hurts, Mamm. It feels like my hands are on fire."

"They would, if you stuck them in a clump of stinging nettles. What were you doing back there?" She pulled him with her toward the house.

"That big rooster was chasing me and then he got between my feet and I fell over him, right into that big patch of weeds!"

"They're not weeds." She ran cold water over his hands at the outside tap. "Those are nettles. I let them grow back there because the young greens are good in soup. I thought you knew not to go near them."

"They look like weeds to me." He snuffled, but held the tears back manfully, though she knew he had to be in a lot of pain. "I don't know the difference."

She knew the difference because her mother had cared enough to take her out behind the barn and show her that sometimes weeds—chickweed, miner's lettuce, nettles—were good to eat when you didn't have much else.

She knew the difference, and her sons did not.

Sarah's hands stilled on those of her boy. She had spent the afternoon preparing the soil for what she had planned for it.

What if God had spent years of her life preparing her for what He planned? What if it wasn't simply a matter of a "knack," or of planting things because their scent brought back memory for her? What if God had separated her out for this work years ago, at her mother's knee, and had been softly working the soil until her boys were grown and she was ready to turn her hands to something outside her own home and kitchen?

Outside her own self?

Because the simple truth was, she was standing here at the sink without a single idea of how to lessen her boy's pain. She couldn't remember her mother ever treating her for nettle stings. All Sarah could do now was run cold water over them, maybe try a little burn and wound salve, and wait until the pain subsided, which could be hours.

*Ruth would know. If you let her teach you, you would know, too. And your heart's delight, your Caleb, would not be standing here waiting for you to do something useful, with tears in his eyes.*

Shaken, humbled, she went with Caleb out to the coop and helped him wash the last unfinished wall. Luckily, he'd already taken out the soiled bedding, because there was no way he could hold a shovel or a rake until the welts subsided. Then together, they put down a thick bed of straw for the delighted hens, who would spend until sunset entertaining themselves by picking the seeds out of it.

And as she worked—as Caleb's unquenchable spirits came back to life again—she felt herself teetering on the edge of a decision. Caleb picked up the brushes gingerly to put them back in the shed, and looked at her cautiously. "I'm sorry you had to help me, Mamm. I didn't mean to trip over that rooster."

She smiled at him. "Don't be sorry. I was waiting on the Lord."

"Did He tell you something?"

"He's been telling me something for quite a while. But I didn't want to listen."

His eyebrows rose. "You?"

"Where do you think your stubbornness comes from?" she

asked with a smile, and carried the bucket around the coop to toss the dirty water on the nettles.

The breeze rustled through the orchard, shaking the branches where buds had begun to appear.

*My grace is sufficient for thee: for My strength is made perfect in weakness.*

# CHAPTER 10

Saturday nights were pretty quiet at the Mast farm. Priscilla usually read one of her library books, or worked on a puzzle with her sisters. But lately, she'd been restless, wanting more than the way things had always been and what she'd always done. Her blood seemed to be moving faster, and she was on the alert, waiting for something interesting and exciting to happen.

The fact that *interesting* and *exciting* were not words you'd use to describe the lives of the *Youngie* in Willow Creek didn't mean she wouldn't be ready for them.

"Come on, Katie," she urged her sister. "Let's go for a walk up the road."

"And see what?" Katie put down her own book—something that had to do with sea life. "The same mailboxes and trees that have been there since we were born?"

"She's hoping Simon will drive by and give her a ride into town for an ice cream." Saranne giggled. "Then she can say she went on a date with him."

Priscilla didn't even dignify this with a reply. "Never mind," she said, and pulled a jacket off a hook in the mudroom before she let herself out the kitchen door.

She wished she'd never said a single word about Simon

Yoder to her sisters. Because if he liked her, their teasing and ribbing would have been embarrassing, but it would have had a glow behind it. But since he clearly thought of her as nothing more than a friend, every word out of Saranne's mouth was like a needle slipping through skin unprotected by a thimble.

Ten miles home after the hockey game the other night and he hadn't even tried to hold her hand. Ten miles, and the most she'd had to hang her hopes on had been the occasional bump of his shoulder against hers when the buggy had dropped off the asphalt onto the gravel, or they'd gone around a turn just a little too fast because they'd been in a hurry to get home.

Well, she was simply not going to think about him anymore. She'd made it clear in every way short of actually saying so that she would welcome the idea of being his girlfriend, and he hadn't responded. Even when God gave them the perfect opportunity to begin something—an opportunity so perfect and so obvious that no one could have missed it—he'd, well, missed it.

Priscilla shrugged into the jacket and gauged how much time she had before full dark fell as she walked up their lane to the road. The horizon still glowed, so she had maybe half an hour to walk off some of her energy and try to wash the image of Simon Yoder out of her imagination. She wasn't sure how she was going to forget someone she saw a couple of times a week, not to mention all day Sunday, but it was a start.

Spring was on its way, but as twilight came on, she could smell it more than see it. The grass, greening and growing after the rain. Freshly turned earth. She and Mamm had already seeded the garden, the neat rows guided by yellow string on stakes at each end, and they'd made string tents for the peas to climb when they got big enough.

Seeds and string and flowers all had their purpose.

What was hers?

If God hadn't revealed her to Simon as His choice for a girlfriend and maybe someday a wife, then what did it mean that He had revealed Simon to her? Was it really a revelation, or just wishful thinking?

A lump formed in her throat as for the first time she wondered if maybe there was a little more to the will of God than she thought. How did two people know they were meant for each other? And how was she to find out?

Her sister Katie knew even less about the subject than Priscilla did, since she didn't have eyes for anyone. Would Malinda maybe?

No, she couldn't ask Malinda. That calm, assessing gaze would see too much.

The clop of hooves moving at a spanking pace sounded behind her as a buggy crested the hill, and she stepped over into the muddy grass so the driver could pass her. But instead of doing so, the buggy slowed, the horse snorting and jingling its harness as it shook its head.

"Going somewhere, Pris?" a boy's voice said.

She turned to see Joe Byler in a brand-new courting buggy, so shiny that the light over the phone shanty a few feet away glinted off its panels. "Where did you get this?" she breathed.

"It's mine." He tried hard not to seem proud, but the grin betrayed him. "I just finished polishing it at the shop. Hop in, and I'll take you for a spin."

The first passenger in his brand-new buggy! "Sure!" She ran around the back of it and climbed up, feeling the springs bounce, and settled onto the smooth leather seat. "Oh, this is nice."

He clicked his tongue to his mare and she took off, pressing Priscilla against the comfortable cushioning along the back rest, which had been upholstered in royal blue. She smelled new leather and fresh paint, and under it all, the sour tang of fiberglass that would fade in a few days of use.

"How long did it take you to build it, Joe?"

"A few weeks. I kept it in the back, you know, because Oran, he don't like us working on our own projects where folks can see them."

"I'd think he'd want the shop to look busy."

"Well, sure, but not too busy. He don't want customers thinking he don't have time for them, and have them go on down the road to another shop."

"I suppose."

"So . . . you're not over at the Kanagys'?"

One, he could see she wasn't. And two, what was happening over there?

"Simon said he was going to head over when his chores were done. They invited me, too, but I wanted to put the finishing touches on this baby." He held the reins like a king would hold a scepter—king of his own rolling castle.

"No," she said, as if she knew what he was talking about. "I had things to do, too."

It was one thing to see Simon by accident all the time. It would be crazy to go to things deliberately, hoping she would see him, like she'd been doing for months now. She was not crazy.

Not anymore.

"Where are we going?" she asked as he crossed the county

highway and stayed on Willow Creek Road, which would eventually take them into town.

"Just taking her for a test drive," he said. "It's getting dark—time for the lights." He flipped a switch, and practically under her elbow the headlight on her side came on, illuminating the road. Every buggy had headlights, and taillights, too, but Joe looked so delighted that you'd think he was the first ever to install them. "Want to listen to music?"

He fiddled with the storage compartment under the seat where the battery for the lights was, and in a moment a CD slid into its place and a song by a bluegrass band filled the air. Against the last of the light in the sky, she could see his horse's ears swivel back.

"I don't think your mare likes music."

"She don't have any taste." His foot tapped in time to a fiddle and a banjo, and she recognized Alison Krauss's voice when she began to sing. "Do you like this?"

"Sure, but it's kind of hard to hear over the wheels and hooves and cars going by."

"I can turn it up—or I have some rock and roll if you'd like that better."

"Joe, just turn it off, all right? It's nice, but I don't need it to enjoy your buggy." Besides which, if he put rock and roll on, the entire settlement could hear them and know exactly where they were.

To her surprise, he did, and the quiet of the evening flowed back in.

"Say, Pris, did anyone ever tell you that you look nice in that color?"

For a second she couldn't remember what she had on. She looked down at her sage-green dress, which was mostly hidden under her black jacket, and what you could see was getting harder to make out as the light faded. "This? It's for-ever old . . . it's just a house dress."

"Maybe. But you look nice."

Goodness. Priscilla sat back, feeling a little startled. Joe Byler was the kind of boy Mamm referred to as the "salt of the earth." The kind of boy who was always under the farm ma-chinery fixing it, or standing in a field with his arm slung over a horse's back as he shot the breeze with the other boys, or energetically hip-checking another player on the frozen ponds of winter. She wouldn't have believed him capable of such a flight of fancy as a compliment. To a girl. Unprompted.

"*Denki*," she managed to push out past her surprise.

"Got any plans with anyone after singing next time? It won't be this Sunday because church is at our place, but the one after?"

What on earth . . . Was he asking her out? Joe *Byler*?

"No . . ."

"Maybe you'd like to go home with me. I promise I won't give any other girls a ride before then." He laughed, as though there was sure to be a teeming horde of females scrambling for the honor over the next couple of weeks.

*Neh* trembled on the tip of her tongue and she clamped her lips shut on it.

That wasn't like Joe. He'd be pretty sure there would be *no* females scrambling for the honor, more like. Joe Byler wasn't the first guy you thought of when you thought about a date, but why shouldn't he be? And why shouldn't the girl that Simon Yoder had overlooked go home in his brand-new courting buggy? Why shouldn't she enjoy someone else's company if Simon didn't want to enjoy hers?

"You can give a ride to whomever you want, whenever you want," she said as Joe pulled into someone's lane and turned the buggy around. "But thank you. That would be nice."

"Great." He flapped the reins and the horse picked up its pace as it headed back the way it had come. "Want to swing by Dan's before I take you home?"

"No, I told my folks I was taking a walk." She shrugged. "They're pretty strict about Saturday nights."

He nodded. "It only took once of staying out all night and then having to sit up on them hard benches next to my pa without daring to fall asleep, and I was pretty much cured of Saturday night get-togethers."

"Why did you stay out all night?"

"Went to a band hop over east of Whinburg. A bunch of kids from every district around were gathered in someone's pasture. They towed in a flatbed and put the band up on it, and kids who had cars parked them in a circle with their lights on so people could see to dance. A bunch of people brought beer and some of the girls brought food. I should've had less of the first and more of the second."

"Why, what happened?"

"Aw, I passed out face down in a big honking cow pie and them rascals I was with just let me lie there, sleeping like a baby."

"Ewww!" Priscilla covered her mouth with one hand, torn between laughter, distaste, and sympathy. "So you went to church smelling like a . . . rose, did you?"

"Lucky for me it was summer. There I was at four in the morning in somebody's pond, swimming laps like I was training for a race. When I got home, I scrubbed down with hand cleaner and hosed myself off again, and was the last man into church before they closed the doors."

"The boys always go in last."

"But I was the last of the last."

"You know what they say." Her smile warmed her tone. "The last shall be first. No matter what they smell like."

He chuckled, and they passed the phone shanty once more. "You can let me off here, Joe. That's our lane up there, past the second mailbox." But he didn't stop until they were across from the Mast lane, so that she wouldn't have to walk at all.

He waited until she'd crossed the road, and then he turned the buggy in the mouth of their drive.

"See you next Sunday, if not before," she said. And as he waved and clicked his tongue to his horse, she wondered if he might take that as an invitation.

And what she would do if he did.

# CHAPTER 11

Since it was an off Sunday, Sarah and the boys were invited along with her in-laws to Elsie King's to share a simple lunch of *Bohnesupp*, a meal Caleb loved. Elsie made it and kept it hot in the big boiler in her water heater, which always struck Sarah as being very smart, since it didn't waste propane and Heaven knew the boiler was enormous. A couple of hours of visiting passed quickly, and she and Caleb were just crossing the road on her way to the field on the other side where Elsie kept the horses, when a buggy stopped on the side of the road and a tall, stooped figure climbed out of it.

"Sarah Yoder." Oran Yost greeted her solemnly, holding the horse's reins. She sent Caleb off to hitch up their buggy, then changed direction and approached him.

"Hallo, Oran. *Wie geht's?*"

"I'm well."

He was walking without pain, that was true, but he still carried his body as though his stomach hurt—sort of curved in on itself. She'd seen enough of Michael's back troubles when he'd been alive to recognize that a posture like that probably wasn't doing his spine any favors, either.

"And Adah?"

He hesitated, glancing back at the shadowy figure sitting in the buggy. "I have a little concern for Adah. Since your cure did so much good for me, I wonder if you might know of something that would help her."

"Oran," she said gently, "you would do better to write to Ruth Lehman. The only reason I knew about the black cherry juice for gout was because she told Jacob about it."

"*Ja*, so you said. But it was not Ruth who spoke up when she did not have to, to try to help someone who was not looking for help."

"She would have if she'd been there in your yard at the time."

"But she was not, and you reached out your hand."

"I reached out my nose to put it in your business, you mean."

What might have been a smile twitched briefly on his lips. Or maybe he just had an itch. "May she come and speak with you?"

"Oran, I really don't think—"

"*Bidde,*" he said, and the simple fact that Oran Yost had said *please*, had asked anyone outside of almighty God for help, so astonished her that all she could do was nod helplessly.

He glanced across to the buggy again and this time Adah Yost climbed down and picked her way across the road like a sparrow, looking up and to the side every few seconds as though she expected a hawk to land on her and carry her away.

Sarah walked with her to the fringes of Elsie's enormous garden, which had been turned over earlier than Sarah's, and was already coming up. Sarah lifted her face to the second really warm day of the whole month. Adah looked instead at the dark, crumbly earth as if that were the reason she had come.

Sarah took the bull by its figurative horns. "Oran says you're not well, Adah."

The other woman was in her early sixties, as round and solid as her husband was tall and stooped. Her *Kapp* strings were tied neatly on her chest, her apron was pinned so that the *Leppli* was exactly in the center of its opening in the back, and the straight pins marched down the center of her black cape with barely a dimple. But for all this, she looked wind-blown and harassed and thrown together. Maybe it was the gray hair escaping from under its white organdy covering. Or maybe it was in her face—that same sparrow expression, longing to take flight and escape before something else sur-prised her.

Sarah had noticed that to people who anticipated happy things, happy things generally came. After all, if the *gut Gott* held even a sparrow in the hollow of His hand, should not a child of His hope to find good things there? But some braced themselves for the unexpected and counted on the worst…which tended to arrive right on schedule, confirming their sad belief.

Adah risked a glance away from the garden. "It's not me. It's Oran."

Oran said she was unwell. She said he was. Or did she mean that Oran was the cause of her complaint? Sarah wished Ruth were here. She would know what to do.

"Maybe it is me, a little," Adah said. "Oh, I don't know. I just know that something is not right, and Oran seems to think you can help."

"I think he's optimistic."

Adah shot her a longer glance. "Oran?"

She knew her husband well. "Tell me."

"A—a spirit has been in our house since the girls left to

get married." At Sarah's widening eyes, she clarified, "I don't know how to describe it. It's like a gray cloud weighing on me, so heavy that I don't even want to get up in the morning, and I used to be the one singing in the kitchen, teaching the girls the words to the songs in my little book."

Sarah hardly knew what to say. Why had she ever believed that Oran wasn't kind to his wife? A woman bearing that burden wouldn't be singing in the kitchen. Maybe Sarah ought to be begging their forgiveness for thinking such things.

"And you said it's Oran..."

Adah took a step away, as if to check that nothing was coming, though there was nothing to see but the road, the buggy, and on the far side of it a couple of horses, nodding over the fence. "Maybe I spoke hastily. It's probably me, with my silly fancies, making his stomach gripe and spasm. There's nothing wrong with me but a rash on my legs, and all that needs is calamine lotion."

A gray cloud that made you want to pull the covers over your head didn't sound like a silly fancy to Sarah. It also sounded like something way out of her depth. "Adah, I told Oran that I don't feel able to help you. I have no knowledge except what my mother taught me, and that was more along the lines of insect bites and burns."

"Oran thinks very highly of you." Sarah was surprised into silence. She went on, "You may well look like that. He doesn't warm to people easily, you know, so when he told me to come speak to you, I was surprised, too."

"But—"

"The thing is, it is not so much what a person has to offer as how they offer what they have. The way you offered him help made him trust you a little, Sarah. And believe me when I say I have not seen that kind of confidence in his fellow man in a long time. Trust in the Lord, yes. But in others? It is difficult for my husband, more than for other people."

Finally, compassion for this woman who had stepped out of her husband's shadow and her own shell to ask for help won out. "I will write to Ruth and find out if there is a tonic she would recommend for a woman in your situation." When Adah looked alarmed, she rushed on, "I won't use any names, just give the details as you've told them to me. I'm not a healer, despite what Oran thinks, but I can write a letter for you."

Another woman might have thanked her and said she'd write the letter herself, but Adah did not. Instead, her pale blue eyes flooded with tears. "*Denki*," she whispered, and fumbled in her sleeve. She pulled a well-used tissue out from under her leather watchband and blew her nose on it. "I would not want anyone to know—Oran would not—"

Ah. Sarah suddenly understood. A man who could not trust, who held himself so closed up that even his body echoed it, would not write to anyone for a cure. He would trust in God to send it somehow...maybe even in the guise of a chattering woman who tossed information over her shoulder like it was an apple core, and then found to her surprise that the seeds had sprouted into vigorous life where she didn't expect them.

## Chapter 12

On Sunday night, Henry approached the Byler house with something akin to trepidation. Not fear, exactly...more of a healthy urge to turn and run. He gripped the bouquet of carnations so hard they would probably get shiny bruise marks on their skinny stems. In Denver, he'd bring his hostess a bottle of wine as thanks for her efforts to prepare dinner. In Willow Creek, none of the stores even carried alcohol—you'd have to drive to Lancaster to find it, and if it was Sunday, the stores would be closed anyhow. Not a lot of demand for a fine Merlot in an Amish district.

He went around to the kitchen door, as family would, instead of giving the impression that he expected to be greeted at the front door like a guest or someone important. Funny how his mother's teaching surfaced after decades of disuse, cropping up the way stones did every time you plowed a field—even if it had been under the plow for generations.

The door swung open and there was Barbara, smiling. Her eyes widened at the carnations.

"For you," he said. "For being so kind. I hope you like them."

"I don't need a present for inviting a cousin to supper," she said, burying her nose in the pink and white blooms. "Oh, these smell *gut*. Come in."

She found a Mason jar to put the flowers in, and set it in the middle of the table. His cousin Paul extended a hand and Henry shook it, aware the whole time of his cousin's unsubtle head-to-foot examination.

"So, Henry. After all these years, we see you again."

"Things have changed around here in some ways, and not at all in others," he said, striving for an easy, cordial tone. "The old house still smells the same, looks the same. And yet here you are with a wife and children."

He was introduced to them as they took their places at the table—the eldest, Jake, next to his father, then an empty chair, then three girls like stair steps of fourteen, twelve, and ten, and the toddler next to his mother.

"Our Joe is still at the buggy shop, working on a project," Paul said. "He is Jake's twin. I suppose you heard that they're working one of your fields for their uncle?"

"I did, and more power to them."

The girls folded their hands in their laps and bowed their heads without being told, all except for the toddler, who had to be reminded by Barbara. A silent grace followed, which made the clatter of plates and bowls afterward seem loud by comparison. Henry couldn't remember having a meal like this since...well, the last time he'd been here thirty years ago. How had Barbara, who to his knowledge had spent the day at the market, been able to rustle up a meal like this? Had her eldest daughter taken the job in hand and produced cabbage salad with apples, biscuits, a pork roast with potatoes cooked in the roaster with it, corn, asparagus, bread, jam...

The table might not be groaning, but he certainly would be. Cold pizza and hard-boiled eggs were no substitute for an

Amish woman's cooking, and his regard for Barbara and/or her daughters went up another notch.

The girls ate silently, their eyes flashing to look him over behind their glasses of milk, and dropping again when he smiled. Their father put away most of his first helping before he cleared his throat and took up the conversational thread once more.

"How are you making out over there? It was a surprise to us all when Sadie left you the place."

Henry wiped his mouth with a paper napkin similar to the ones in the restaurant yesterday afternoon. "It was a surprise to me, too."

"Maybe God has plans for you," Barbara added.

He hoped not. "I meant to ask you, Barbara—Aendi Sadie had a number of quilts, didn't she? I seem to remember them on all the beds, and even draped over the couch. The nights are chilly and I wondered if you knew where they'd got to."

"Oh, I have them," she said comfortably. "Would you like them back?"

Henry said, "I could sure use one or two, if you haven't put them to use already."

"I didn't know how long the house would be empty, so I took the linens and bedding so the moths wouldn't get into them. I took a couple of the thicker ones for the girls' beds, but you should take the others home with you."

That solved that mystery. "I'll do that, thanks. As for the fields, Paul...thank you for being such a good steward of them."

His cousin shifted in his chair. "I need no thanks for doing what is right." He went on, "But we would like to know what your plans are. The seed should have gone in a week ago or more, but the boys have been holding off. It shouldn't wait much longer or the oats and corn won't be ready when all the men go out to harvest."

"My plans." Henry shoveled in the last of his potatoes and one of the girls handed him the bowl for a refill. He hesitated, but the thought of the gravy did him in. He might not get a chance at gravy like this again. As he ladled it over the spuds, he said, "I've been on the fence about staying."

"The boys were saying so."

Henry glanced at Jake, to whom he couldn't remember ever speaking. "Oh?"

The boy, who though seventeen was clearly not finished growing into his shoulders and feet, looked uncomfortable. "We were talking with Caleb and Simon, and Caleb says you've got a big pile of pottery stuff out in the barn, but none of it's unpacked."

"That's right," Henry said, straight-faced, as if he'd just remembered something. "I never got him to sign that nondisclosure agreement."

Six blank faces gazed back at him. There would have been seven, but the toddler was busy grabbing for his mother's slice of bread and jam.

"Caleb's right. They're not unpacked."

Paul scraped his plate clean with his fork and sat back. "If God has brought you here, then it was for a reason."

"God, or Aendi Sadie?" He meant it as a joke, and was glad to see that his cousin still had his sense of humor.

"Maybe both. But if you are going to move on, then you should do so, and give others a chance to look after that land."

"Paul..." Barbara murmured.

Henry began to feel a little like a balky mule with someone tugging on his halter. But on the other hand, he had not forgotten what it was like to be a farmer. "Do you want me to sell the place to you?"

"If that is what you feel led to do."

"That's the whole problem. That letter from Uncle Gideon was the last time I felt led to do anything, and now that I'm here, I'm wondering what I'm doing."

Where had *that* come from?

Paul's blue eyes were as guileless as the spring sky—and maybe just as likely to blow up a storm at a moment's notice. His cousin said, "If you want some direction, maybe you should pray about it."

Here it was. He just knew that religion would come into it somewhere, even in a conversation about farming. "I'm not a praying man, Paul. Not like you."

"That wasn't how you were raised."

"No. But it's how I choose to be."

"And you wonder why you feel so directionless. Why your life doesn't have a purpose."

Now, that was getting a little too personal, and in front of these girls, too. "Careful, cousin," Henry said softly. "You're sounding a little holier than thou."

To his utter surprise, Paul flushed at the rebuke—or maybe it was the tone. When he spoke, Henry realized he had underestimated the other man. "Forgive me. I didn't mean to offend you. I only meant that when God guides our steps, He leads us into green pastures."

His humility made Henry redden in his turn, and wish he'd held his tongue. And that he had the strength of character to apologize just as readily.

Instead, he said, "God—or Aendi Sadie—has led me into green pastures, or at least, orderly fields and healthy lawns. Which, like I said, is thanks to you and your boys and the uncles." That was as close to an apology as he could come. He went on, "Barbara probably told you I was at the market yesterday. I might have a commission to make some storage jars, which means I'll be unpacking all that stuff in the barn. If that goes well, and I get more work, I could stay."

"*If* and *might* are not enough to hold up the planting," Paul told him. "I guess what we want to know is whether you'll renew the leases so we can get to work."

"Paul, I'm not a farmer now, and have no plans for those fields out there. If you and the uncles want to keep doing what you're doing with them, it's fine by me."

*And if I decide to leave, at least I won't have that worry holding me back.*

"*Gut*, I'm glad to hear it. Jake, you'll go over and tell your uncles first thing in the morning, and then I want you and Joe out there with the plow."

"Soybeans this year for our section," Jake said. "Me and Joe already decided."

There was no standing around waffling in this house. Henry was glad someone could make a decision. Or maybe the decision had been made for him when he'd begun drawing designs for Sarah Yoder.

As if she'd read his mind, and forgiven what she found there, Barbara said, "What are these storage pots you're going to make? We've never had a potter in these parts. How are you going to find customers if people have never needed pots before?"

"Well, the thing is, first you create the desire, and then you fulfill it. That's called marketing."

She gazed at him with humor in her eyes, and a dimple winked next to her mouth. Pulling the toddler into her lap as the girls began to clear the dishes, she said, "That sounds like an appeal to human nature."

"In a way, it is. A lot of times people don't know what they want until you show it to them."

"Like Eve and the apple?" one of the girls ventured as she took his plate. It was the first thing any of them had said all evening.

"I hope my pots don't lead anyone into sin and bring about the downfall of humanity." He smiled, and her wary expression flickered into a smile, too. "But maybe there are uses in the kitchen for stoneware or porcelain that the women have been working around, just because they don't know there's a solution."

"Like what?" Barbara asked. "I know my kitchen pretty well, and it's been working fine all this time without what you said. Stoneware and porcelain."

"I don't doubt it has. But do you have a teapot?"

"We're coffee drinkers."

"What do you put the milk in?"

"A pitcher."

"Plastic or metal?"

"Plastic."

"If it were stoneware, it would stay colder once you'd put it on the table."

"And I want it to be colder?"

"Maybe not for coffee, but in the summer, when you're eating outside and it's ninety degrees and you don't want the milk to sour, you might."

"Ah." Barbara sat back, looking thoughtful. "Sadie always liked a cup of tea when I went over there. She liked the peppermint blend that Ruth Lehman used to bring."

"It tastes better when you brew it in a pot than when you

simply pour hot water into a mug. I can make teapots in all shapes and sizes."

"What about a sauerkraut crock?"

He remembered his mother's kitchen, and the kafuffle every fall when the cabbage was harvested, shredded, and put up in brine in big stoneware crocks the size of a five-gallon bucket, to steep for however many weeks or months it took.

"Those, too. I might have to hunt up someone to make the metal parts—you know, that hold the lids down."

"I broke the lid on one of mine and never had the heart to throw away the bottom."

"I could make you a new lid."

Paul said, "Jake could make the metal parts, I bet."

"Jake can make anything," said the middle girl, whose name Henry had already forgotten. She was clearly her brother's favorite, if the grin was any indication.

"Maybe a potter would be a good thing in the neighborhood," Barbara conceded. "Alma, take Amos in for his bath while I cut the pie."

Alma, that was the middle girl's name.

"Mamm, you won't start without me?"

"No, we'll let our dinners settle until you're back. So," she said to Henry, "do these storage pots have anything to do with Sarah Yoder?"

Henry got a distinct sense of whiplash. It took him a second to get his head on straight. "We talked a little about it. You must have been talking to that woman who saw us at the restaurant."

Did her gaze have something more than polite conversational interest in it? "That was Miriam Yoder who saw you, and so did anyone else coming out of the market and walking by. You be careful, Henry Byler."

He raised his brows. "Me? What did I do?"

"Around these parts, if a man takes a widow woman to lunch, it makes a pretty strong statement. You've only just arrived in town. You don't want to make people think she's fast."

It had been a long time since something had made his jaw sag in astonishment. "Fast?"

"There aren't many Amish women in Willow Creek who would go to lunch with an *Englisch* man. They might be friendly, might accept a lift in a car or offer his family some help if they needed it, but lunch? In public?" She shook her head.

Henry couldn't wrap his mind around what she was getting at. He looked to Paul for support. "I didn't mean—I just—"

"Miriam Yoder is her sister-in-law, so she would know better, but others might not. Sarah Yoder is a *gut Fraa*, Henry," his cousin said. "It looks bad."

"It was just a thank-you to her kid for showing me around the market. She didn't even come until later, and we talked her into having a sandwich."

"Still. It gives the appearance of evil."

"Having lunch with me is evil?"

"Not if it were me, or Barbara, or my brother or one of our aunts. Your family. But to invite a woman to lunch who is not family, who does not share your beliefs, who can never return your...interest...you are putting her in an awkward position."

Interest? There was no interest on his side. As for Sarah, no wonder she'd been so agitated when she'd realized her sister-in-law had seen them.

"I'm sorry. I didn't realize. It was a business lunch, nothing more."

"You do not have to apologize to us," Barbara said. "But you might think of apologizing to her. And then not doing it again."

Oh, he'd already made that decision before he'd even arrived home. The last thing he needed in his rootless life was a blond Amish woman with big gray eyes, whose entire face lit up with delight at something as simple as a sketch. And the second to last thing he needed was the urge to draw another one, and another, just to see that look again.

To know he had put it there by giving her a simple gift.

"I can safely promise you that I will never do it again," he told his cousin's wife, devoutly believing that he meant it.

# CHAPTER 13

Dear Sarah,

I received your letter in this morning's mail. I have seen posture such as you describe before. If this man's stomach is "griping and spasming" as his wife told you, his body would try to protect itself, even if he doesn't know he's doing it. Part of what we do is observe what the body is telling us even when the mouth doesn't speak the words.

You did not ask me for a mixture for him, but if he is willing to take it, you might offer him this tea I've put in the brown bag. It is chamomile to soothe a troubled mind and stomach, fennel, mugwort, dried gentian, and a very small measure of rue. He should put one or two teaspoons in a cup and pour hot (not boiling) water over it. Let it steep for a quarter of an hour and drink the tea. He'll want to take a cup three times a day.

If a woman is unhappy but can't tell the cause, I often give her my Sunshine Tea. You probably have everything you need to make it in your own garden, except borage flowers and rose petals, which I enclose in the zippy bag.

2 parts chamomile
1 part borage flowers
1 part lemon balm
a palm full each of lavender flowers and rosepetals

Mix up enough to make an ounce, then boil a quart of water and pour it over the mixture. Let it steep for half an hour or an hour, whichever feels better to you. Strain out the bits and have her drink a cup of it three times a day. Give her the recipe and she can make it up herself. If she doesn't start feeling sunnier after two weeks, let me know and we'll try something else.

Ruth

P.S. Next time your boy falls in the stinging nettle, tell him to crush up some dock leaves and rub them on his hands. God arranged it so that dock and nettle often grow together for this very reason.

P.P.S. If you want to drive over sometime this week, I can give you slips of some of my plants. And you might want to start a recipe book.

Sarah folded up Ruth's letter and laid it on top of the bags of flowers, which had smelled lovely when she'd opened up the package. The screen door banged and Caleb came in. "What's that, Mamm?" He hovered over the two bags of flowers as if they might be an afternoon snack.

"It's a package of herbs from Ruth Lehman. She's giving me some advice for someone."

He took an orange from the bowl, peeled it, and wolfed it down. "Who?"

"Never mind. People's troubles are their own."

He swallowed with a gulp. "Are you going to be a *Dokter-fraa* like Ruth?"

"Maybe. I haven't decided," came out of her mouth before she could even blink.

"Why not?"

That was so like Caleb. "Because for one thing, my dear son who must always know the reason for everything, I don't have time to drive all over the district giving herbs to people."

"You wouldn't. They come to you."

"*Die Kranken* can't hitch up the buggy. What if they're too sick to get out of bed?"

"Their husbands could, or their *Kinner*. Would they pay you?"

"Do you think it's right to pay someone for their help? Would I ask you to pay me when I scrunch up dock leaves to put on the stinging nettle welts, which is what Ruth tells us we should have done?"

With a grin, he said, "I'd have paid a dollar to know that. Those things hurt. Henry is going to pay me to take flyers around town about his pottery business."

"That's different. That's a task. When someone comes to you for help with their health, it doesn't seem right to charge them for it. It is merely what a friend would do to help another."

"Ruth cured Aendi Miriam's headaches and charged her twenty dollars. That's a lot for a headache."

"How do you know that?" Her sister-in-law had suffered

from terrible migraines, until Ruth had left one of her little
packets of powdered herbs. Miriam had told them at their
Friday night dinner that it was a miracle she could get some
relief—but she didn't recall any of the *Kinner* being around
to hear it.

"Zeke told me. He said it was the best twenty dollars his
Mamm ever spent, if she could come out of the bedroom and
be Mamm again." Caleb took another orange and Sarah made
a mental note to visit Miriam before too long. One of her
*Englisch* cousins had sent a big box of oranges from California, and Miriam had been trying to give them all away before
they spoiled, since one family couldn't eat their way through
such a big box in time.

"Mamm, why don't you do it? If people pay you, then you
wouldn't be so worried about money all the time."

For the second time in five minutes, she stared at him,
shocked.

"I know you say that worrying about stuff just shows that
you don't have enough faith, but I know how it is with us.
I've been trying to do things for Henry so he'll pay me and I
can give you the money."

Never mind that he was fourteen and practically a young
man—Sarah folded him in a hug, grateful that God had given
her such a thoughtful, pure-hearted son. He hugged her back,
then wriggled free. "And if you do have to drive out to help
somebody, me and Simon can just eat leftovers or make macaroni or something."

"And are you going to do the laundry on Mondays and the
sewing on Tuesdays and the baking on Thursdays and Saturdays, too?"

"I can bake," he said gamely. "I make biscuits sometimes."

She laughed and ruffled his hair. "I'm just trying to help

you see that being a *Dokterfraa* isn't just about money coming in. It's about helping people, and sometimes that involves going to them. It means spending time with Ruth to learn. Maybe it might even mean reading books and taking classes."

"Well, if Simon moves out to Colorado, you won't have him to cook for or clean up after, and you'll have more time to do all that."

A prickly chill trickled down Sarah's face, her chest, her arms, and into her stomach, as though someone had just up-ended a bucket of cold water over her head. "What?"

Caleb clapped a hand over his mouth. "*Ach, neh!*" he said, his voice muffled behind it. "I wasn't supposed to blab!"

"What did you say about Simon?"

But he only shook his head, his hand still pressed against his mouth.

"Caleb Yoder, you stop being so foolish this minute, and tell me what you meant."

The hand lowered, and Caleb hung his head. "I told him I wouldn't say a word. I promised."

"Obedience to your mother is more important than obedience to your brother. Simon is thinking of moving to *Colorado*?"

Caleb squeezed his eyes shut, and nodded.

"Why?"

"Mamm..." he moaned.

"Tell me," she demanded, sounding so stern while underneath, her stomach rolled with nausea and her knees shook.

"That's all I know. He wants to go. Him and Joe Byler, they were talking about it out in the barn and they didn't know I was there, and then when I sneezed, they caught me and made me promise not to tell. But I didn't hear very much, honest, Mamm."

The fact that her elder son wanted to go so far away for unimaginable reasons was enough for anyone to hear. She would give anything to have the last two minutes back— to rewind the clock to the moment before those words had struck her like a blow.

"I'll ask him at supper, then," she said.

"Don't do that—he'll know it was me," Caleb wailed.

"I'll tell him it slipped out accidentally. That's the truth. And then we'll see what he says." She took a deep breath and struggled to control the ache in her throat. "Have you finished washing the buggy?"

"*Ja*," he said miserably.

"*Gut.* That's all I had for you, then." *Dear one, please go before I cry in front of you.*

He perked up infinitesimally. "Can I go to Henry's? And take those whoopie pies you promised him *days* ago?"

"I made some more this morning. Take him half a dozen."

He whooped and raced around the kitchen like a whirlwind, dashing out the door with the frosting-filled cookies on a plate and no plastic wrap or bag or towel or anything.

The screen door had barely banged shut behind him when she dashed down the hall to her room, fell on the bed, and wept…for something that hadn't even happened yet. Oh, she was so foolish. This wasn't about Simon being old enough to think about where God wanted him to live. It wasn't even about him traveling so far.

It was about her own fear of being alone, which probably made her the most selfish woman in the entire family.

*You stop blubbering and get up right now. March out to that kitchen and do something useful, and get ahold of yourself enough to speak reasonably and calmly to your son when he comes back.*

This was probably why Simon had not talked it over with

her. Because—manlike—he was afraid she would make a scene just like this.

Well, it was all wept out of her now. She'd had her wallow and now it was over. But there was a second reason he'd kept silent, if she knew her boy—because he feared she would say he could not go.

He knew her, too.

She got up, splashed cold water on her face, and repinned her covering. Then she obeyed her own lecture by marching out to the kitchen to make dinner. She kept one eye on her potatoes, and the other on the window over the sink, which had a view across the Byler fields to a rise in the road.

The sun was just sinking behind the laurel hedge and her *Schnitz-und-Gnepp* casserole was filling the kitchen with the savory aroma of apples and ham and dumplings when her boy crested the rise. In a moment she could hear the rattle of the wheels on the gravel lane and the clop of Dulcie's hooves slowing to a stop. At the same time, Caleb's voice hailed his brother from the back forty.

With increasing resolve, she scraped carrots and sliced them up in diagonals the way Caleb liked, to be served with melted butter and a sprinkle of dill. The boys came in after they'd put the horse away, and she indicated a bowl on the counter.

"All right, young baker, would you mix up some biscuits?"

He took a couple of seconds longer to hop to it than usual, and she could see him wondering if she'd jump on Simon with a dozen questions about Colorado, with the consequence that Simon would jump on him about telling her.

So she simply smiled at them both, and when the biscuits were ready and they'd said grace, she kept the conversation light and as far away from the subject of Colorado as the house they were sitting in.

Unfortunately, there was more than one subject she'd prefer didn't come up, and that wasn't so easy.

"Henry says thank you for the whoopie pies," Caleb told her. "He ate three right off the bat."

"Someone won't be sleeping well tonight. And how many did you eat?"

"Only one," he said defensively. "He said he was going to have the last two for breakfast."

"That's a terrible breakfast. You should take him some eggs next time. The chickens are laying better now that the days are longer."

"He wants to know when you'd like to come over and see some sample storage jars."

She felt a hitch in her spirit, as though someone had taken up the reins and given them a good yank. "I've…well, I've been having second thoughts about the jars. I think maybe it would be better if the herbs were in little fabric bags, like sachets, almost. Then I could get more in a box and sell more at the market."

Caleb reached for another biscuit and buttered it. "But Mamm, he already unpacked his stuff. He was getting ready to—what did he call it?—*wedge* some clay when I left. That means to whack it until you get all the air out."

"I would hope he would unpack anyway, if he plans to stay. I'm sure he'll find other people who need pottery."

"He'll need more than one customer, *ja?*" Simon put in. "Besides, this family could afford to spend a little less time around him. He's *Englisch*, not Amish. We can be friendly, but he never joined church, and we don't want to forget that."

Caleb swallowed his biscuit. They were a little bit dry and

crumbly, but Sarah thought they still tasted pretty good. She took another herself and spread a generous dollop of butter on it. He said, "It's not that he never joined church. He just hasn't joined church *yet*." Simon looked a little surprised at being corrected by the boy who usually hung on his every word. "He had supper at Joe and Jake's last night, and they treated him like family. *They're* not keeping up the walls of separation."

"That's because he *is* family." Simon picked at the *Schnitz* layer in the casserole pan and slid out a nice slice of apple. "We're just the people on the other side of the cornfield. The *Amish* people." His emphasis mimicked that of his brother.

"We could be his friends. He needs them, Simon. And besides, you haven't joined church, either."

"Caleb!" Sarah remonstrated softly. "Simon is on the opposite side of that choice from Henry Byler."

"So am I, then." Caleb straightened a little, as if he were bracing himself. "Will you join church in this district, Simon, or the one in Colorado?"

Simon froze, and it seemed as if even the clock stopped ticking. His gaze locked on his little brother in accusation and betrayal.

"Mamm knows," Caleb said casually, and sound flooded in—the clock, the clink of Caleb's fork as he ate the last carrot, the creak of Simon's chair as he sat back.

He looked half ready to leave the room, and Sarah got up to get the coffeepot and pour him a cup.

"*Sich getempert,*" she said when she came back, one hand on his shoulder as she poured, and passed him the little pitcher of cream. "He let it slip this afternoon. So you and Joe have been making plans, then?"

Her calm question seemed to startle him, as though he'd

been expecting a storm, and he relaxed a little in relief. "Not—not plans exactly. Just talking about it."

"Tell me." She cleared the table and began to dish up the rhubarb pie left over from yesterday. She would have to pick some more—the boys loved the first rhubarb of the season, and theirs came up before anyone else's, tucked near the lemon balm in the south-facing corner of the house.

Sadie had had a huge plant on the edge of her garden. Did Henry even know what to do with it? Would it bolt and go to seed because no one was there to harvest it?

Simon accepted his pie and poured some of the cream for the coffee over it, still watching her. What a good thing Caleb had let the secret out and she'd had time to get past the tears and into the calm of a decision.

"There isn't much to tell," Simon finally said. "His uncle Elias—not Henry's father, but the other uncle who was out there in Ohio—wrote to say he and his family had joined the new settlement in Monte Vista last year, and did any of the boys want to come to help out for the summer."

Sarah had no idea where that was, but an Amish settlement sounded promising for them, at least. "Are there many families there?"

"Not yet, only a couple, including Joe's uncle. I've been an apprentice for two years, so we were thinking I could help with the buggies, and Joe can farm, so if we went, we'd have something to bring to them. There are also a couple of dude ranches near there, so if all else failed, we could maybe get jobs with the horses."

*If all else failed.* "What do they farm in Colorado?"

"Beef and wheat," Caleb put in. "I looked it up in one of my old geography books."

"It's not the same soil as here," Simon told them, "but I'm sure Joe can grow whatever the soil will let him."

"And where is everybody living?" Sarah said carefully. She would not say, "Where would you be living?" because that would sound too much like she thought he would actually go. It was a fine conversational line to walk—getting as much information as she could while making it sound like the subject wouldn't affect anyone in this room.

"Joe's going to write to his uncle and ask if we can stay with them." Simon finished off his pie and peered at Sarah's piece, which she hadn't touched yet. "Are you going to eat your pie, Mamm?"

She pushed it across the table to him. "So Joe's uncle has a house built, then?"

"*Ja*, they were glad to have him. He built their house, and now he can't keep up with the demand for carpentry. That's another job Joe and I could do, if he needed people on his crew."

"And what about Paul and Barbara? Don't they need Joe, too?"

"*Neh* ... Paul and Barbara ... well, they ..."

"They don't know yet," Caleb said around a mouthful of rhubarb. "I'm glad I'm not the one to tell Paul Byler he's losing a hand in his fields."

Fortunately, no one was going to be in that position.

"Mamm," Simon said eagerly, leaning toward her in his chair, "maybe you could talk with Paul's Barbara about it. If you're okay with it, then she would see it's a good thing and she could talk Paul around."

Sarah put up her hands to stop this idea before it bolted. "Oh, no you don't. One, a man doesn't ask his mother to do his work for him. And two, the only thing I would say to

Paul and Barbara would be that they should give Joe a little more work to do, because he obviously has too much time on his hands if he can stand around talking and dreaming with you."

Simon's mouth fell open in a protest.

"Simon, see sense," she said gently, firmly. "You can't go to Colorado. You have responsibilities here. You have two more years as an apprentice before anyone will hire you, and we need the money Oran Yost pays."

"I know a lot about buggy making!"

"I imagine you do—but Oran knows more, and he has committed to teaching you and Joe. And speaking of commitments, would you back out of yours so easily?"

"People come and go all the time." He put down his fork. "And maybe there's a buggy maker in Colorado I could hire on with."

"If I were that man, I'd think twice about someone who abandoned his apprenticeship."

His brows had lowered in a mule-like expression she didn't see very often, but it reminded her so much of his father that it was eerie. "I'm no quitter, Mamm."

"Then work out your four years. When you're twenty, you'll of course do what you believe God is leading you to do. But when you're seventeen, you're still under my roof and that time is not yet."

He pushed back his chair. "Joe says two of his cousins are going, and one of them is barely nineteen."

"But are they apprentices?"

Instead of answering, he mumbled something about cutting more kindling for the stove, and pushed out the kitchen door.

With a sigh, she pulled the half-eaten piece of pie toward her and dug her fork into it. Then she glanced up at Caleb.

"He really wants to go," he said in a wondering tone. "Do you think he was mad?"

"Not getting our own way often makes us mad," she said, and her dinner rolled uneasily in her stomach. She hated having to crush her boy's dreams. The taste of it was sour in her mouth, and suddenly the pie was the last thing she wanted to finish.

But at the same time, what kind of mother would she be if she let him go off with skills that were only half-baked and an innocence of mind that would only be bruised by the journey?

She had done the right thing—and it had had to be done. But that didn't stop the cry in her heart later, when he didn't come in and she realized that if he was angry, he was going to let the sun go down upon it. She stood by her darkened window slowly braiding her hair and gazing out over the fields and farther, up into the stars.

The world was enormous and unfathomable and her son was only seventeen.

Truly, being a mother took more faith than she ever would have dreamed.

# CHAPTER 14

"You sure spend a lot of time walking these days." Katie leaned on the door frame and watched Priscilla lace up her running shoes on the back step. "Still hoping to meet Simon on one of them?"

"For your information, walking is good for you. I need to wear off that second helping of dessert."

"Oh." Katie looked wise, that *I know what you're up to* look.

Priscilla rolled her eyes. "I am not interested in Simon Yoder anymore, and Joe Byler is taking me home from singing on Sunday, so never mind looking like you know everything."

"I know more than I did a minute ago." She pushed off the wood frame and stepped back into the kitchen. "Have a nice walk—and say hi to Joe for us."

Priscilla made a rude noise with her lips, which only made Katie laugh behind the door. Well, when it was her turn to go boy crazy, Priscilla would make sure she got every bit of teasing she deserved. Besides, it was all completely unjustified... she really was just going for a walk.

She walked across the lawn and climbed the fence into Dat's front field, which he was leaving fallow for hay this year.

Already the new grass was as high as her knees from all the rain they'd had, and soon there would be meadowsweet and daisies and shoots of Queen Anne's lace, Priscilla's favorite wildflower. They weren't up now, of course, but when they were, she'd pick a big bunch of them for the blue pitcher on the dining table.

She looked at her watch. She could walk exactly one mile in twenty minutes, which would take her halfway to the town of Willow Creek in one direction, or past the Yoder farms and down to the dip where the creek the town was named for ran.

She picked the creek. It was pretty down there, even if she had a little climb out of it. It would be good for her.

So of course, now that she had decided Simon was a lost cause, what should she see but that familiar lanky body, standing on the bank of the creek under the covered bridge and skipping rocks. But his aim was off today—they just plunged into the water instead of skipping.

"Hi, Simon," she called, leaning on the wood rail.

He looked up, but instead of smiling like a friend would do, he just sighed and picked up another flat stone.

*Chunk.*

"You need to change your angle if you want it to skip," she said helpfully. "Of course, if all you want is to drown them, then keep doing what you're doing."

"Come on down, Pris."

It was clear something was wrong. The good thing was, now that she wasn't interested in him as a boyfriend, she could talk to him like a friend.

She swung her legs over the railing and dropped onto the path that wound down the bank and under the bridge, where the water had washed away all the soil, leaving a flat apron of shale that made a good place to spread your towel in the summer. Hunched into his jacket and wearing his rust-red Woodpeckers knitted cap, Simon was standing a little way upstream, where the bank was grassy and the sumac and willows pressed close to the path the kids had worn along it.

"What's the matter, Simon?"

*Chunk.* "Nothing."

Boys. Honestly. "Have you seen Joe's new buggy?"

"I've been helping him work on it."

"I think it's beautiful. He showed me last Saturday and took me for a ride."

*Shame on you, Priscilla Mast.*

"Yeah?" For the first time, his tone held something other than that sad note. "He came over to take you out?"

Well, this was interesting. Why should he care? "No," she had to admit. "I was out for a walk and he was taking a test drive. I think it's the first time I've ever been the first ride in someone's buggy."

"Someone's *courting* buggy. Careful, Pris, you'll be giving him ideas."

"Nothing wrong with that," she said with airy unconcern. "What *is* wrong is whatever is bugging you. Want to talk about it?"

He seemed to realize he'd picked up another rock. He took aim and skipped it twice across the big pool where they swam in the summer.

"Aw, there's no point in talking. Mamm doesn't want me to do something I wanted to do, that's all."

"What was it?"

"Nothing."

Good grief. Here they were back at square one.

Someone hailed them from the far side of the bridge, and she looked up to see Joe Byler, as if they'd spoken him into existence. His boots thudded hollowly from their vantage point under the bridge as he jogged across, and then he slid down the bank to join them.

"Hey, Pris. So what's new?" he asked Simon.

"My little *Plappermaul* of a brother spilled the beans to Mamm before I had time to prepare her, and now she's set against it."

"Aw, no." Joe let out a long breath and kicked at a clump of grass so hard a big muddy chunk of it sheared off and flew into the creek.

"Set against what?" Pricilla asked as if she had every right to be in this conversation. Which she had been, up until now.

"Something me and Joe were thinking about. But I guess that's all it's going to be. Thinking."

"What did she say?" Joe wanted to know.

"Oh, she said I'd be a quitter if I left Oran before the two years is up. She didn't even consider that there's probably a buggy maker out there, and I could finish the apprenticeship with him." Now it was Simon's turn to abuse the grass.

Priscilla flipped through what she knew of Joe's family and tried to reckon up the number of uncles he had and where they lived.

"Are you two planning to move out to Ohio?" she asked. That was where the other uncles lived, wasn't it?

"Never mind, Pris," Simon said, straightening up and clearly trying to lighten his tone. "We probably shouldn't be talking about this in front of you."

"What, is it some kind of big secret? You two make it sound like you're going to rob a bank, not go for a visit."

"We're not going for a visit," Joe said, then glanced at Simon. "Well, in a way we are, but if all goes well, it might turn into something permanent. My uncle moved to Colorado to a new settlement, and he wrote asking if we wanted to come out there and work."

For a second, it felt as though the creek had detached the bit of bank she was standing on, and was whirling her off downstream while she tried to keep her balance.

"Oh," she said, while her mind flew back to what he'd said about Sarah, forbidding him to go. "I see."

"I'm glad you do, because Mamm sure doesn't," Simon said. "I'm seventeen and I'd sure like to see something of the country. I've never been farther west than Smicksburg."

Priscilla hadn't even been that far. She had gone to Florida once, though, when *Grossmammi* Martha had turned ninety-nine and they'd had a big family reunion there in Pinecraft. But Florida wasn't way far away like Colorado. Days and days of travel away.

"Did you tell your *Dat?*" Simon said to Joe.

"*Ja.*"

"Same thing?"

He nodded. "He wouldn't even talk about it—which isn't like him. He talks plain, but at least he'll hash things through with me usually. Mamm was out in the barn with him when I left."

"Pris is right." Off to the side and watching them like a spectator at a volleyball match, Priscilla perked up at this unexpected compliment from Simon. "It's not like we're going to rob a bank. I don't understand why this is such a big deal."

"*Dat* needs me and Jake on the farm. It'll be a hardship with one less pair of hands, and Alma and the girls can help, but they can't drive the team or do the heavy work."

"So what should we do? We already wrote your uncle saying we wanted to come."

Joe drew his chin in, like a bull that's been tapped on the nose. "I don't know what else to do. You know how he is. Once he says no, it's no until kingdom come."

"Well, we have to think of a way around it. For both of us. Unless you just want to take off one day, and see what happens."

Joe rubbed his nose and watched Simon from under his shaggy mop of hair. "Go anyway? Disobey my old man?"

"It was just a thought." Simon's neck reddened.

"Ha ha. Not funny."

Were all boys like this? All in or all out, with no compromise? Maybe now was the time to stop pretending she was just part of the scenery.

"Do you have to move out there for good and leave everything behind?" she asked, and they jumped, as if they'd really forgotten she was there. "What's wrong with just taking a two-week holiday? People do that in the summer."

Joe looked puzzled. "But we don't want a vacation. This could be our lives we're talking about."

"It could be what your parents are talking about, too. Don't try and stuff the whole cow down their throats when maybe all you need is a bite of steak."

Now she'd lost them.

She sighed. "You have two things to worry about here. Your folks need you to keep things going, and they're worried about you going so far away. So why not solve both those things? Just go out there and have a look around. Lend a hand for a couple of weeks, meet the church there, see what's what. Then come home and tell your families all about it. They'll see there's nothing to worry about, and you'll know what you're getting into."

Brown eyes and green gazed at her. Well, she'd done her

best and it was a good idea, and if they couldn't see that, she would just have to leave it with them.

"I'm going home. Good luck with your plans."

She climbed the bank, and once she was up on the road again, she could hear their voices coming up out of the creek bed. She couldn't tell if they were arguing or not, but really, it didn't matter.

They weren't going to listen to a girl anyway.

# CHAPTER 15

Dulcie came to a halt in the Yost yard and Sarah climbed out of the buggy. The morning had dawned through a blanket of fog, but it was clearing up now. She tipped her head back to watch the new leaves combing the last trailing skeins of mist the way a woman might run her fingers through her hair. As it thinned and the sun warmed it, the mist seemed to glow.

The gently moving light touched elements of the Yost property—a barn that sparkled with a new coat of paint, a lawn that had been rolled flat and mowed with surgical precision, a fence beyond which no wildflowers dared bloom. The only part of the yard that seemed relaxed enough to express its nature was the rock garden pressed up against the house.

She picked up her handbag containing the envelope of herbs and crossed the yard, where she found Adah already waiting in the kitchen doorway. "*Guder mariye*, Sarah. If you're looking for Oran or Simon, you passed them—they're in the shop."

"I'm looking for you." The kitchen smelled of ginger and butter—Adah was baking, but the counters were spotless. She had already done the dishes, and a couple dozen cookies and two pans of gingerbread cooled on racks on the counter. "I have the herbs from Ruth Lehman here, but I have a feeling Oran will not be brewing his own tea, so I brought you the instructions."

"Oran?" Adah gazed at her curiously over her shoulder as she poured two cups of coffee from the pot on the stove, and put some of the cookies on a plate. "But I thought you had written to Ruth on my behalf."

"I did. The herbs she sent for you are right here. But I also mentioned Oran's stomach troubles, so she sent along something for him, too." She pulled out a piece of paper on which she'd written Ruth's instructions. "Here."

Adah scanned the brief lines and looked up. "Griping stomach? This is what you told her?"

"It's what you told me."

"Sarah, I can't give him this."

"Why not? Maybe it will help."

"I am not even going to tell him that you brought it. If he knew that I was speaking out of turn about something so personal, he would be very angry."

Sarah couldn't think of a single thing to say. "But—"

"Worse, now Ruth knows. It will only be a matter of time before she speaks to him about it and he finds out what I have done."

But he had been so concerned for her when they'd spoken last Sunday. "Adah, you spoke up out of your feelings for him. How could he be upset about that?"

Adah shook her head and took a sip of her coffee. "He would not see the concern. He would only see that his business has become common knowledge."

"Then I'll write to Ruth and tell her not to talk about it."

"That is not the point. The point is that I spoke up, and I shouldn't have."

"Well, what's done is done." There was nothing she could do about this now, especially when it made no sense to her. "You can offer him the tea and the possibility of help, or not. That's up to you. Now, here are the herbs Ruth sent for you—she calls it her Sunshine Tea." She had compiled the rest of the recipe from dried herbs and flowers she had on hand, and added the flowers that Ruth had sent. "Smell."

Obligingly, Adah dipped her nose in the zippy bag and breathed in. "*Wunnerschee.* But I can go out in the garden and smell the flowers."

"It's not the smell so much that will make the cure—though I suppose that's a benefit. I imagine Ruth has had to give people plenty of tonics that smell awful and taste worse. The benefit comes when you make a tea of it. See? Drink a cup three times a day. If Oran would drink his, you could do it together."

Adah said nothing, which made Sarah feel as though her words had fallen into a well and she was waiting to hear them hit the water.

The silence in the kitchen lengthened until Sarah felt compelled to say again, "I'll leave the rue mixture for him, and you can do with it as you like. I'll be on my way now."

Adah rose, took Sarah's mug and her own, and instead of putting them in the sink as Sarah might have while she saw her guest out, she ran water and soap in and washed them carefully. Then she dried them and put them away in the cupboard. The entire procedure took less than a minute, as though it had been practiced so many times that it had become habit.

"Thank you for the tea," Adah said at the door.

"Don't thank me, thank Ruth. I might have contributed

some of the herbs, but this is her recipe and her skill. I hope they work for you."

Adah nodded, and the polite blandness in her face compelled Sarah to add, "You will take the tea, won't you?"

"I don't see how a lot of flowers can help. I don't see that it's worth the trouble."

"It's only boiling a pot of water and pouring it in a container."

"I might not have time. Or I'd forget to drink the three cups."

Didn't she want to feel better—to have that gray cloud lift? How did Ruth handle people who didn't care enough about themselves to act on their own behalf? Then again, when people came to Ruth, they were doing it because they did want help. In Adah's case, help was being imposed on her by her husband. Therefore, it looked like her husband was going to have to watch over Adah.

Which meant Sarah was going to have to go and talk with Oran again—a prospect she didn't relish.

"Well, I hope you will," was all she said.

She should just go home. She flapped the reins over Dulcie's back, and when she got to the end of the lane and the parking area for the shop, she almost didn't pull on them to stop the horse. A sensible woman would just keep on going and leave them both in God's hands.

But Oran had said he had confidence in her. Surely Adah was mistaken. After all, if the black cherry juice had worked for one complaint, it was likely the rue tea would for another.

That decided her. She turned into the lot, climbed down, and tied Dulcie up at the rail.

When she went inside, she found all the men busy amid a maze of tools and benches and lengths of wood. Simon had on a mask and a heavy plastic apron and was sanding the edges of what looked like a squarish bathtub, but was actually a buggy body, the black part to which the gray top would be attached. He looked up and lifted his chin in greeting, but didn't stop. None of the men stopped work.

Oran was working, too, in a separate area, painting an undercarriage assembly. But just because his work needed to be separate so as not to get sawdust on the sparkling new chassis, that didn't mean his eagle eye wasn't moving from one apprentice to the other, then to the clock and back to his workers. He saw her, of course, as soon as she stepped into the shop, looking as out of place in her dark green dress and organdy covering as a butterfly.

"It is too early for your boy to stop for lunch," was his greeting.

"I wouldn't want him to stop," she said pleasantly. "Could I speak with you a moment?" Sarah glanced over her shoulder to see how close the others were, and Oran caught it.

"They will continue their work. And if you don't mind, I will continue mine." He dipped his brush in the black paint and got back to work.

Sarah lowered her voice. "The herbs came for Adah so I took them to her."

"*Ja*, I saw you go by. But you needn't have gone to the trouble of stopping to say so. I would have seen it when I walked down for lunch."

"I wanted to speak to you, though, because Adah doesn't seem...inclined to take them. She doesn't see the point, she says. So I want to ask your help in making sure she does."

Carefully, he laid the brush across the mouth of the paint can, then waved her out the door. When they were both standing out in the side yard with only the buggies to hear, she said, "If you want to see her get better, you might try to convince her that it's a good idea to follow Ruth's instructions." She wished she had brought her handbag or at least a shawl with her. It would have given her something to do with her hands. "Ruth also sent along a packet of rue and chamomile to make a tea for your stomach."

Oran frowned at the rear wheel on the nearest buggy. "I asked for nothing for myself."

"I know, but Adah mentioned it, so I asked Ruth if there was something that might help."

"I am not the one who needs help."

"Those were Adah's words, too, or close enough. The truth is, you asked me to help her, and she asked me to help you. You are both concerned for each other—and if each of you insists that the other drink the tea, then you'll both get well."

"Why did you go to Ruth Lehman?" And suddenly his full attention was on her.

"There must be a dozen men in the *Gmee* with stomach problems. It's nothing to be ashamed of."

Under the brim of his straw hat, a flush crept up his neck. "I am *not* ashamed."

What was going on here? "Oran, you are making a mountain out of a molehill. I brought a packet of rue to make a tea. That is all."

"So you said. I appreciate a hand held out to help. But I do not appreciate Ruth Lehman's hand in my business. It has been there before, and the results were not good."

"*Neh*, I didn't tell her it was you. But she's a healer—she probably knows enough about the *Gmee* to fill a book. Why should you or Adah be different from all her other patients?"

"We are not her patients. And I am thinking we should not

be yours, either. You will do better to mind your home and your own business."

Well, this just beat everything. "I don't understand. You asked me to help."

He raised his head to look over her shoulder as the door behind them opened. Simon stepped out, looking first into her face, and then that of his boss, before he closed the door behind him. "Oran, where are the—"

"Go back to work, Simon," she and Oran both said over each other. Her boy grinned—and stayed right where he was.

"What are you smiling at?" Oran said.

"You...you both said it together..." Then he seemed to sense the depth of the tension in the air. "Is everything all right?"

"It's fine," Sarah said. "I brought some tea for him and Adah, and Oran takes exception to it. I'll be going now."

She turned to circle around the shed so she wouldn't have to walk back through the shop, but behind her, Simon said to his boss, "Why should you take exception to something as harmless as that?"

"Those are your mother's words. And what do you know of harm, Simon Yoder?"

"I know words can harm. What have you been saying to her?"

This was becoming worse the longer she stood here. Sarah gripped her son's arm. "Go back to work, Simon. It's just a misunderstanding, is all."

"I want to know what kind of misunderstanding makes you all red in the face, Mamm."

"Nothing that needs to cause offense, and we're in danger of doing that."

"Only the proud take offense—and give it," Oran said

grimly. "I don't want this kind of interference in my home, nor this spirit in my shop. Sarah, take your boy with you."

A chill seeped into her cheeks. "I don't understand."

"Simon, pack up your things and drive your mother home. I won't be needing you anymore."

"Oran, no, please don't let this—"

"Come on, Mamm." Simon's work-roughened hand closed around her elbow, and he led her around to the buggy. She was still trying to figure out what had possessed Oran to behave this way while Simon stripped off his heavy apron and gathered up his few tools and possessions—including the lunch she'd made that morning that he wasn't allowed to eat before noon.

He untied Dulcie and gently pushed Sarah over to the passenger side.

"What just happened, Simon?" She felt a little dazed.

"It's all right, Mamm." He snapped the reins over the horse's back and turned her in the lot. Sarah got a glimpse of the other men with their heads down, sanding and painting as if their lives depended on it.

"It's not all right. Did Oran Yost just end your apprenticeship?"

"*Ja*, he did, and I can't say I'm sorry."

But she was. She had sinned, and now Simon was out of work. It was the beginning of the month and for the seventh month in a row she wouldn't have enough money, and...

Oh, what had she done?

Nothing Simon said could make Sarah feel better. It was a good thing he had taken the reins, because it was all she could do not to break down in front of him. If he knew how upset and *deschperaat* she was, it would only make him feel guilty and ashamed—as if the sin had been his, not hers.

"Simon, please forgive me," she finally managed when he turned into their drive and the relief of being off the public road calmed her a little. "I did not show Oran Yost the humility I should have, and because of it, you've lost your apprenticeship."

"Of course I forgive you."

But that did not make the situation any better.

He pulled up the horse in the yard, but it wasn't until Sarah had climbed out of the buggy that she realized he hadn't got down, too. "Aren't you going to put her away?"

"I'm going back into town. To look for work."

The tears welled in her eyes. "Maybe it could wait at least until you've eaten your lunch?"

"I want to do it now, Mamm. One of the guys was laughing this morning about seeing a Help Wanted card up at the Hex Barn. If I'm lucky, the job will still be open. I'll take the lunch with me."

"The Hex Barn?" No one in his right mind would want to work there. It was one of those fake Amish restaurant and souvenir shops in a strip mall out on the highway past Willow Creek—the kind that sold whoopie pies made by a bakery in New Jersey and passed them off as "homemade in an Amish kitchen." The kind that put Pennsylvania Dutch hex signs on coffee mugs and hot pads and sold them as being Amish. Since the Amish did not believe in embellishing their homes and barns in any way, this misled well-meaning tourists to the point that they got kind of upset when there were no hex signs to photograph on the barns of the *Gmee*.

Simon backed Dulcie around. "It's a job, Mamm. Sure, it's

a little goofy, but maybe they could use a real Amishman in there."

"But Simon—" And then she closed her mouth. They were in no position to be fussy about jobs at the moment—in fact, she should be asking Simon to check whether they needed a woman to unpack the whoopie pies and rewrap them in plastic to look like they'd just come out of her Amish kitchen.

Stubbornness had gotten her into this fix. Humility was the only thing likely to get her out.

Simon clattered off and she took his toolbox into the barn, setting it on the workbench where he would see it. Then she considered the shape of her day so far.

If she had been thinking of a career as a *Dokterfraa*, she'd better think again. Neither Adah nor Oran wanted her help, though it was clear that both of them needed something that perhaps only God could give them.

She needed a few moments alone with her heavenly Father. Pride seemed to be her failing today—that and fear. One told God she didn't need Him, and the other whispered that even if she did, she didn't think He could help.

The way the day was going, she should just walk over to Henry Byler's farm and tell him not to trouble himself with the ginger jars.

Distracted, she rambled across the lawn to the garden, which she'd only managed to get half planted. There was no excuse for leaving a job half done just because she had been feeling silly and rebellious when she'd begun it.

She needed a garden. Her family needed to be fed. Silly or not, that garden had to go in today and that was that.

She went and got the seed packets out of the shed, but left the flats of tomato starts that Simon had brought home with him from Corinne's on Saturday in the south bedroom under the sunny window. It could still snow, after all. And while she dug and seeded and covered, she prayed. The squash hills heard about Oran. The cornrows on the north side heard her sorrow over Adah. Lettuce, carrots, and onions witnessed a cry for forgiveness and her need of help—for faith, for trust, for the confidence she'd once had and didn't seem to any longer. And the star made of string for the runner beans...well, that heard only the sigh of the breeze in the maples on the lawn. A sigh like the ones her Daadi used to heave, seeing all the things that she had done wrong and thought and said...and loving her anyway. A sigh that she could only hear because she was finally quiet.

Despite her mistakes, the God of Heaven still loved His daughter.

And the garden was done.

She sat on an overturned bucket on the grass, feeling the damp ground cold under her sneakers. Despite the fractious wind that told her some heavy weather was on its way, she was hot and sweating and her headscarf had come loose somewhere over there, where she'd been struggling to get the chard and spinach into their spiral and finding out that circular patterns were a lot harder to manage than straight ones. It now hung around her neck and had probably managed to catch a handful of soil.

There was a purring sound behind her that was not the wind, and the gravel crunched in the lane. She swung around to look and, to her horror, saw Henry Byler climb out of his car.

He hadn't seen her yet.

She leaped to her feet and smoothed down her dress with one hand while she pulled her *Duchly* up with the other. She tried to tie the knot more tightly, because she certainly couldn't talk to an *Englisch* man bareheaded. Tiny hairs got caught in the knot and pulled, but she could put up with that for the five minutes she'd need to see what he wanted and wave farewell.

She stepped into view and got her first proper look at him...and concluded that, however bad her day had been, his had been even worse.

# Chapter 16

There was something in a garden that always made Henry feel calmer. He couldn't quite put his finger on why this should be, but as he leaned on the hood of his car and gazed at the neat flowerbeds next to the house, and then at the lawn that really was a lawn and not the howling wilderness that his was beginning to resemble, he felt the quiet and the—the obedience of it sink into his soul.

Maybe that's what it was. An Amish garden was full of vigorously growing things, but they had a purpose, and they responded to the hand of the gardener because it pruned and cultivated and *cared*. The hand might be ruthless, and sometimes harsh, but it acted in order to make the plants grow better. To do better what they were designed to do.

Look at the difference between Sadie's garden—his, he had to stop thinking of it as someone else's—and this one. If you let plants go wild, sure, you'd have a lush, verdant place. But the price you'd pay was the loss of the smaller plants and the dominance of the more vigorous ones. There was a big difference between enabling a plant to do what it was designed to do, and letting it have its own way. His yard was an object lesson in that.

His yard...and other things.

"Hallo."

Henry turned at the sound of her voice, and saw Sarah Yoder walking across the lawn toward him. Talk about someone perfectly attuned to her setting...she wore a dark green dress, a blue scarf, and a black kitchen apron, but it wasn't even the colors that made him think so, though they made her skin look translucent with its glow of exercise. She had that sense of belonging in her garden that he'd run into only once or twice in his life.

In Denver, the climate didn't lend itself to lushness and calm. The plants seemed to know they had only about three months to get the business of flowering and seeding completed, and so they grew thin and quick and went to seed and threw themselves on the ground gasping just as the snow fell and covered them up until next year.

Sarah's cheeks were flushed and she touched her covering nervously. "Is everything all right?"

Was she psychic? Or had he been talking out loud all this time? "Sure. Why wouldn't it be?"

"Oh, I don't know. You just looked..." She stopped. "Never mind. I was in the garden."

"So I see. What are you planting?"

Her lips turned up as if the joke was on her. "You might as well come and have your fun now. You can be the first."

Wondering what she meant, he followed her past the huge, whispering maples to a rectangle of garden that had to be half an acre. She stood to one side and waited.

He gazed at it. Squash hills, bean and pea teepees, furrows. What was there to laugh about?

It was only rows of—

Wait a minute.

No rows. Furrows where seeds were, but no rows. Instead,

there were squares and triangles and even a big spiral of something, but not one thing had been planted in the usual obedient Amish rows. A laugh erupted like a quail flushed out of its cover. "It's a quilt."

She nodded with a kind of resignation, flavored heavily with *what have I done?* "I think I went a little bit crazy. I'm never going to hear the end of it."

"We artists get that a lot. Is it finished?"

With a long breath, she leaned down and tweaked some tiny weed out of the soil. "I had toyed with the notion of planting herbs for cures, but after today I'm going to stick to vegetables like a sensible person. I'll just ask Simon to turn over another section and plant pumpkins or something practical that the tourists like."

Something like relief swept over him—or maybe it was simply the calm that came when you had a reason to give up.

"What happened today?" The moment the question slipped out, he knew he'd overstepped the boundaries of this woman's privacy. But what man looking at the reddened cheeks, the back that stayed straight through will alone, could help himself?

She heaved a sigh. "I tried to give someone a cure, and I not only caused offense, I also caused Simon to lose his job."

"Someone? Would that be Oran Yost?"

Her eyes widened with alarm. "Oh, please don't tell anyone. He's upset enough that I wrote to Ruth for a cure for him. How did you find out?"

"Caleb. He's told me all about Simon's work situation, so when you said Simon had lost his job, it was pretty easy to make the connection."

Her gaze turned to the squash hills and held. "My boy trusts too quickly and talks too much."

"Your boy has an innocent mind. Don't wish that away too soon."

To his surprise, she didn't tell him to mind his own business—or at least state what he'd come for. Instead, she said, "*Ja*, you might be right. I wouldn't want to think that trust could be a bad thing."

"It's safe with me anyway." For the first time, the corners of her lips flickered upward and he felt he'd accomplished one good thing today, at least. "You're probably wondering what I'm doing here."

"*Ja*, but I figured you would get to it in your own time. And when you're done, I have something to say to you."

Any reason to put this off was a good reason. "Go ahead. Ladies first."

Another microscopic weed met its doom. "I've been thinking—about the herb jars—that maybe it's not such a good idea."

Something in him sank, which was ridiculous, because wasn't that why he was here? "Oh?"

"I was thinking…that maybe it would be better if I packaged the herbs in little bags, like sachets. They would be easier to carry and not so heavy. And then you wouldn't need to go to all that work."

If this hadn't been so cosmically apropos, he would have laughed. "Great minds think alike, it seems. That's why I came over—to tell you that I wouldn't be able to make the jars, after all."

"Oh, why not?"

What could it possibly matter now? A little lost sleep, fifty-seven different conversations with himself as he tried to come up with a way to let her down gently, and she'd already decided she didn't want them anyway. "I just couldn't get inspired."

Now her gaze was curious. And something else. Something sad. "You need to be inspired to make pots?"

For some reason that hurt, though he doubted she meant it to, and would be sorry if she knew it had. "Were you inspired to make your garden?"

He'd succeeded in turning that gaze away and back to the furrows and whorls of her seeding patterns. "If you call crazy inspired, then yes, I suppose so."

"Artists have been called crazy before."

"I am not an artist."

"I beg to differ. But that's neither here nor there. The point is, to make something out of nothing, you need to have a vision for it, a kind of confidence in your own imagination. And I just...didn't."

He couldn't tell her the truth. Fear had suffocated his inspiration. Wasn't that the original meaning of the word *inspiration*? Breath of God or something? But that wasn't the kind of thing you said to your Amish neighbor on whom you were reneging. Even if she had reneged first.

"I guess I don't understand," she said. "You drew those pots very confidently."

"But drawing something and making it with your hands are two different things. I just got blocked, I guess. I couldn't get the idea from my head into my hands."

He'd sat there for most of yesterday, trying to work past the paralysis of fear—the thing that had ended his fledgling career in the first place. But instead of giving it a clean death years ago, he'd hung on to the remains—the wheel, the kiln, the boxes of clay, his recipe book for glazes—unable to give them away and unable to work.

Unable to blot out the criticism, the words overheard in the neighboring stall in the bathroom, the art bloggers who had been so honest that it had shattered his confidence in himself like a piece of not-quite-dry green ware.

"How did you manage before?" she asked, her voice gently damping the jagged sounds in his memory, the babel of criticism.

"Before what?"

"Before you came here. If you were a potter, you must have made pots for other people pretty well."

"It doesn't work like that. Well, maybe it does for some people, but not for me."

She straightened and laced her fingers together loosely in front of her, the way you'd give someone a boost. "You mean you don't just have a booth at the market, and sell them there?"

Now it was his turn to almost smile. "No, in Denver you'd try to get a place in a gallery, or be a member of a bigger art show at a festival of some kind. I got lucky. The sister of one of the guys I worked with at the design firm had a gallery, and she agreed to show some of my pieces."

"Ah," she said. "A show."

And in that word lay all the condemnation of the Amish for this world's pride—and the triumph of *Gelassenheit* over worldly ambition.

A show. Showiness. Showmanship. Show-off.

"It's not like that," he repeated, beaten before he could even start. "It's just pieces on display in a room, that's all."

"Did you sell many of them?"

*Byler's pieces teeter on the line between utility and ubiquity— you always have the feeling you've seen something like this before.*

"One or two. But it doesn't matter now. It was the only show I ever did."

"Only one show? Why only one?"

His lips twisted. "The critics weren't very kind." He quoted, *"'The eye sees where he's going, but the imagination never quite gets there.'"*

"I don't even know what that means."

"Sometimes I wonder if the critic did. But the point is, if the reviews are bad, people won't come in and look. And if they don't look, they don't buy. So it was back to designing marketing collateral for me."

Her hands clenched, as if they'd just realized they were empty, and she took a few steps toward his car. "One show. And you let other people's opinions stop you from doing something you loved?"

"Hey, now. That's hardly fair."

"But it's the truth, isn't it?"

She had no idea what he'd been through. How late he'd lain awake trying to think of ways to spare her feelings. "You're a fine one to talk, Sarah Yoder. Here you made one cure and gave up. Seems to me the pot is calling the kettle black."

She sucked in a breath through her nose. "At least I tried to help someone. I wasn't putting on a *show*." Her mouth trembled, and he knew that a dozen more *Deitsch* words were rushing to see which would be first to get past that iron control, that lifetime of training in *Uffgeva*, in the giving up of the self, in nonconfrontation.

The same lessons his Mamm had tried to teach him all those years ago—to no purpose.

With a sense of shock, he realized he was mimicking her body language—hands on hips, feet planted apart, mouth zipped shut so nothing would get out, and a glare that could singe the hair off a horse.

They looked like a pair of fishwives facing off over the last mackerel, and the image struck him so funny that a laugh puffed past his lips.

*"Warum has du gelacht?"*

He stepped back, the image solidified into a ceramic figurine in his imagination, and he laughed again, this time with real humor. "Look at us," he said. "About to tear into each other because we both did the same thing and we both know it was wrong."

"There was nothing wrong with giving a bag of herbs to Oran Yost."

"And there was nothing wrong with trying to sell my pieces in the gallery. But Sarah, what is wrong is that we both gave up after only one try."

*"You* gave up. I am still selling my herbs. And Simon will get another job."

"Maybe that's true. But if it doesn't matter so much to you, why does it make you angry?"

"I'm not—I'm not—" She turned her back on him, and he saw she had been sitting on something wet, like the grass, or that bucket next to her hoe. There was something very appealing about the thought of a woman who wasn't afraid to get her clothes dirty. Who would sit on the grass as though she belonged to it.

Then she sighed, as if she'd lost an argument with herself. "I suppose I am angry. I tried to help someone, and he rejected my help."

"Worse, he injured your boy."

"I don't think Simon sees it that way, but he certainly injured our income—never mind. That's not the point. My pride was wounded, and it deserved to be."

"I don't think it was pride. I shouldn't have implied that. It was a desire to help. Sarah, are you going to let

Oran Yost get in the way of doing what you believe is right?"

"Is it right?" She turned to face him. "To turn my attention from my family and out to people who might be like him, and not help themselves?"

"What do you think?"

Her face softened, and he found himself staring. He shook himself back into sense just as she glanced up into his face. "I think my mother would have liked to have seen me do it. Caleb thinks I should. And goodness knows my in-laws would be happy."

"Then why not do it?"

She didn't answer right away. "At least your pots wouldn't kill anyone if you made a mistake."

"They might, if I used the wrong chemical in a glaze. But I do my best not to make mistakes like that. All we can do is our best."

"That is all God wants, isn't it?"

He didn't have an answer for that one, so he kept silent. She gazed at her garden. The rising wind shook the maple branches overhead, whispering.

And then she said, "I think there might be room in this crazy quilt of a garden for some comfrey and coneflower, don't you? And maybe some bushier things could go there, along that strip before Jacob's cornfield starts." She looked up. "Any chance you might be going over Whinburg way? If you take me to Ruth Lehman's, I could be back before Simon and Caleb get home. I don't have anything to pay you with, but the roast I have out for supper will feed three men and more."

It was the best offer he'd had all day. Maybe even all week. But still...Paul and Barbara had been pretty firm about the damage to her reputation if she was seen with a man who was not family. On the other hand, she clearly needed a ride, and the Amish folks hired *Englisch* taxis all the time.

That's all he was. And he was fine with that.

He jingled his car keys. "Ready when you are," he said.

# CHAPTER 17

To her credit, Ruth Lehman did not say "I told you so" when Sarah explained why she was there, though the appearance of an *Englisch* car in her lane driven by the much-talked-about Henry Byler might simply have surprised her into silence. Instead, she nodded, said, "I thought you might come to it," and led the way around the farmhouse to the greenhouse that sat to one side of the orchard.

"You might want those boys of yours to build you one of these." She took a flat that could have come from a garden store long ago, and began setting slips in tiny paper pots into it. "Our winters are too long for some of the things you'll need, so we start them early. Some of the fussier ones stay in here all year round. That way, you'll always have fresh leaves on hand if you need them."

When the flat was full, she got a piece of paper and drew a grid, with the names of the plants in the squares, and a word or two about what kind of soil and sun each one liked.

"Ruth, I don't even know where to start."

"It will come. Begin simply and the rest will grow from there. Folks around these parts favor certain complaints, you'll find—burns from the stove, cuts from the lawnmower blades, head colds, stress, flu. These plants are the basics.

Get them going and they'll carry you through most problems you'll run into."

The greenhouse was warm, and perspiration made Sarah's dress cling to her arms and between her shoulder blades. Carrying the flat in both hands, she followed Ruth outside and dragged the fresher air into her lungs with gratitude.

"Give me that," Henry said, reaching for the flat. "I'll put it in the trunk."

"Can we set aside some time to work together?" Ruth asked. "Maybe once a week?"

Sarah had known this path would involve sacrifice, and here it was. "I usually do the sewing on Tuesdays, but I can do that in the evenings instead." There hadn't been a lot of new dresses in recent months, but the boys always needed their pants and shirts mended, and hooks and snaps seemed to escape in handfuls.

Ruth nodded. "Tuesdays would be fine. I usually compile on Thursdays, but I'll do the baking then instead."

"Thursdays are my baking days, too, so that I have lots of cake and pie on hand when the boys are home on the weekend, and we have company on Sundays."

Ruth glanced at Henry, who slammed the trunk closed and ambled back toward them. "Is he going to bring you? It's a fair way for a horse."

"Probably not. Today was more a...spur-of-the-moment thing."

"There's a bus runs between Willow Creek and Whinburg. I don't know when, but I often see it while I'm out. Come into the house and I'll give you some recipes for your book. And if you don't mind, I'll write to some of my patients and tell them you'll be looking after them now."

"Oh, no, don't do that," Sarah exclaimed, apprehension

pooling in her stomach. When Ruth raised her brows, she stammered, "I mean—people might not want—they may be used to you and not want to change."

"I'm not throwing you to the wolves, Sarah," Ruth said quietly. "These are regular patients who live closer to Willow Creek. All you'll need to do is mix up their teas, and in one case, a tincture, and see they get them twice a month. The *Englisch* man with the tincture doesn't pay as regular as the others, but he pays when he can."

Oh. Just mix up a tea with a recipe Ruth used. That didn't sound so bad. She could do that.

"I'm just so afraid I'm going to—to hurt someone," Sarah whispered.

"I won't give you anything that will hurt anybody, unless you pour a gallon of it down their throats." Ruth gave her a sideways smile as they climbed the back steps to her compiling room, which had once been a large, airy sun porch. "You'll need to get over this fear pretty quick. It doesn't inspire confidence—and half the cure is confidence in the healer. The bigger half."

"Right." She swallowed. "Confidence."

"How are your first patients doing?"

For a second Sarah wondered who she meant, but when Henry leaned on the door frame to watch, it came to her in an uncomfortable rush. "Not so well. The man flat refused to take the rue mixture you sent, and his wife doesn't think the Sunshine Tea can do anything for her. Unless each makes the other take their tea, they'll both just stay the same. Plus, he's angry that I told you his personal business even if I've not told you his name."

Another glance at Henry, who smiled. "Mum's the word," he said.

"I'm not even going to ask how you know," Ruth told him in a tone as wry as lemon juice. Then she got busy with powders and leaves, wrapped in the cleverly folded packets and paper boxes that were her signature.

Could Sarah learn to do that, too? Or could she simply deliver a powder in a mailing envelope?

"I will say that there are some folks who resist anything you can do for them. In those cases, there isn't much I can do but pray."

"Don't people want to be well?"

"Most of our folk do. But the man with the tincture, like I said, he's *Englisch*. His daughter does her best, but it's no secret he'd get better if he took the herbs more faithfully. Some people would rather just take a pill because it's easy. But what they don't realize is that their health is worth putting a little effort into."

Ruth wrote out the names and addresses of her patients. While most would come to her place in the future, Sarah felt it would be more neighborly to visit them first, and see them in their own homes. Six people to begin with. Eight, if she counted the Yosts.

No, that was more like a negative number.

As if she had been listening to her thoughts, Ruth said, "An accounts book would be a good idea, to keep track of what folks pay and what they owe. You'll need a record for the tax man at the end of the year."

"I have one for my herbs."

"That's right, you would. Well, this should do you for this week. I'll see you next Tuesday, then, about midmorning?"

She held the door and Sarah and Henry descended the steps carefully, their arms full of papers and bundles.

"See you then. *Denki*, Ruth. I appreciate your helping me."

"You're helping me. That's about thirty dollars' worth of herbs there, but you'll see what I charge is written on the packets. You can pay me back out of what you earn."

She made it sound so ordinary—as though selling herbs with which people could cure themselves was no different than selling them rosemary and thyme to cook with. But both went into the body and helped it to work as God meant it to. It was clear she hadn't been thinking of it in the right way before at all.

And there was one more good thing. Sarah glanced down at the packet on top, and realized that while Ruth's prices were competitive with what she'd seen in the natural foods store in town, they were also enough to give her negative balance in Jacob's notebook a little relief. Maybe more than a little.

Maybe this would really work.

She and Henry filled the backseat with parcels and she buckled herself in with a sense of lightness, as if the burdens she had carried in her hands had been accompanied by a burden of the spirit that she'd been toting around for weeks.

"All right?" Henry started the engine and turned the car around in the yard, then crunched his way up the lane.

She nodded. A curious feeling, this lightness. And then she recognized it.

Peace.

Peace like a glow deep inside her, expanding and warming her. It meant safety. It meant knowledge of the way in which she should go—a way she'd been looking for all these months.

It meant that God the Father approved what she had done—not for her neighbors, not for Ruth or her father-in-law's account book, but for the *Gmee*. For the Kingdom.

Caleb and Simon were washing up just inside the barn door when Henry pulled to a stop in the yard, giving her a tableau of two identical wide-eyed expressions through the window above the sink as she climbed out of his car.

Caleb, predictably, was the first to recover. "Mamm! Henry!" he called, dashing outside. "Where have you been?"

"In Whinburg, at Isaac Lehman's. Henry was kind enough to be a taxi for a day so I could pick up some herbs."

"A taxi, is all?" Simon came out of the barn, wiping his wet hands on his pants.

For a moment, she couldn't think what he meant. She glanced at Henry to see if she could find a clue in his face, just in time to see the tips of his ears redden.

And then what her son meant crashed into her understanding. "Yes, a taxi is all," she said with calm coolness. "Mind your manners, Simon Yoder, and take these plant slips around to the back porch. Mind you put them somewhere high, or the chickens will eat every one and you'll have wasted Henry's time and Ruth's care."

It wasn't very often she needed to take that tone with her boys, but when she did, they jumped to it. And in teaching them, she saved herself from further embarrassment in front of Henry.

How could Simon even think such a thing, much less say it aloud in front of everyone? She hustled into the kitchen with the sheets of recipes, carefully written out in Ruth's black, spiky script, and busied herself with putting them in her accounting book. It was all she had until she got to town and could pick up some kind of binder for them.

When Caleb came in with his hands full of packets, she

waved him over to the counter. "Henry is staying for sup-per as payment for driving me. Just put those there for now."

"So you're really going to be a *Dokterfraa*, Mamm?" He inspected a packet shaped like a little pyramid, and shook it gently. The contents rustled. "What's this?"

"That is a tea for someone, and if it comes open, you'll have a long ride tomorrow to get some more."

"That's okay with me. Maybe Henry would drive me."

"You would be very presumptuous to expect it. You know how the *Englisch* taxis work. You never assume that someone is waiting around just for you."

"He's not a taxi, is he, Mamm?"

"No, he is not. He just did a favor for me. And now you can set the table."

Caleb got the knives and forks out of the drawer. "Is Henry going to sit in Dat's place?"

Sarah looked up just as Henry stepped into the kitchen with an envelope that she must have overlooked—and just in time to hear the question.

Heat prickled up to the roots of her hair. Worse, Henry saw it.

"*Neh*, Henry will sit by Simon so that your brother doesn't eat all the potatoes."

"I'm a big fan of potatoes," Henry said gamely, and Caleb, bless his innocent heart, nodded with shared enthusiasm.

"Mamm makes these roasted ones with onions that are my favorite."

"Can we convince her to make them tonight, do you think?"

Sarah held up her hands and played along, feeling the blush fading from her cheeks. "You don't have to convince me.

Roast potatoes it is. Caleb, I'll need six, and a jar of horseradish from the cellar."

He flung himself across the kitchen, crashing into Simon, who was coming in, and spiraling off down the cellar stairs like a gangly puppy in full cry after a stick.

"Where's he going in such a hurry?" Simon peered after him. "Slow down before you hurt yourself," he called. As he turned back, his gaze settled immediately on the table with its neat place settings.

Should she say something? Because they needed to come to an understanding before her elder son got any more wrong-headed ideas. But before she could do more than pull out a knife for the onions, Henry spoke.

"Simon, I want you to know that I don't mean anything by driving your mother to Whinburg this afternoon. I did it because she needed to go and I had the means, that's all."

Simon hunched his shoulders and rammed both hands into the pockets of his pants. "I just thought—well—how did you know she needed to go?"

What was this? Henry would think she was a terrible mother, allowing her children to question an adult this way— an adult they were only just getting to know, who a month ago had been a stranger.

Though somehow, thinking of Henry Byler as a stranger felt as foreign as thinking of herself as a *Dokterfraa*.

Again, Henry forestalled her. "I came over to tell your mother I wouldn't be able to make pots for her herbs after all. When she told me she needed to go to Whinburg this afternoon, I offered. As any neighbor would."

Sarah could contain herself no longer. "Henry was just being kind, Simon. It is not your place to question. You are not the head of this household."

Her boy straightened, his face flushing even as his hands came out of his pockets. "Someone has to stand in Dat's place, and you've told me often enough that it's me."

"That is true for many things, but not this one."

"I stood up for you this morning with Oran, man to man, the way Dat would have."

Had that been what had prompted that disastrous conversation? That he felt he needed to defend her? She loved him for his protective instincts, even if neither of them had exactly shone in the end.

But Simon was not finished. "At least you've left his place empty at the table."

A silence fell. "What has come over you, Simon? Neither Henry nor I have done wrong, and you are making insinuations that I do not like."

"Well, maybe there are some things I don't like, either." He was not only flushed now, but emotions flashed in his eyes that she had only seen but rarely. Hurt. Challenge. But why?

"Simon," she said gently, putting out a hand. "What is wrong? Did something happen today at the Hex Barn?"

But he only shook his head and pushed past Caleb, his elbow catching the burden his brother carried. Potatoes thudded down the long flight of steps as Simon's boots thumped across the porch.

"Simon?"

But he didn't turn or even slow his pace, and by the time she'd rushed out to call him back, he was gone.

# CHAPTER 18

Only outsiders thought that Amish buggies all looked alike. Well, they were supposed to, of course, Priscilla reflected, but there was still room for individual style, especially among the *Youngie*. Which was why she immediately recognized Simon's buggy in front of the Hex Barn—first, because it was the only one there amid the rows of *Englisch* cars, and second, because of the pattern of orange and red reflectors that he'd added to the back. They formed a distinctive chevron pattern that was similar to the one on the old wreck that Joe and Jake Byler drove before Joe had got his new courting buggy, but with the colors reversed. Pris was pretty sure they'd done it together and on purpose.

She was walking home from the fabric store in Willow Creek, and Mamm was expecting her to help with supper. But only an act of God would keep her out of the Hex Barn if Simon Yoder was in there.

Not that she was interested in him now. But curiosity was a powerful force, and a girl was allowed to be curious about such an unusual sight, wasn't she? Besides, it might not be Simon at all, and if it was Sarah or Caleb who had borrowed his buggy, she could get a ride home. So really, it would be smart to go in and have a look.

She'd never been in the Hex Barn before. The first thing that hit her as the door swung shut behind her was the air-conditioning, cool as wading into a lake. A little premature, seeing as they'd only just got their gardens in. The second thing was the smell. Right in front of her was a table heaped with candles and soap (AMISH MADE! the sign proclaimed), though to her knowledge, no one in ten miles made candles like that. Old Nina King made beautiful beeswax candles, and Ruth Lehman and Mamm both made soap, but the bars they made sure didn't smell like someone had spilled a bottle of perfume on hot plastic.

"Mommy, look! It's an Amish girl." Priscilla turned to see a little girl in pink overalls and pigtails staring at her like she was a horse at the auction. "Are you a real Amish?"

"*Ja,*" she said.

"Can I touch your bonnet?"

"It's called a *Kapp.*" Priscilla dipped low enough for the child to touch her heart-shaped organdy covering, then straightened. "We wear it because the Bible says we should keep our heads covered when we pray."

"Are you praying now?"

"No, right now I'm talking to you."

"Then why do you have to wear it?"

"I don't have to," Priscilla said. "I want to."

The *Maedeli*'s face screwed up in an effort to figure this out, but she was rescued by her mother. "Amy, look, a real Amish girl."

"I know. She has to wear her cap to pray."

"Does she?" The woman eyed Priscilla as if she meant to buy her for her daughter, like a doll. "Do you think she'd pose for a picture with you?"

"We don't do that," Priscilla said hastily, before this got

out of hand. She took a step past the candle display. Another step and she'd be behind it, and then she could dodge between the laden tables toward the back.

"I'll give you five dollars. Come on, just one picture."

"We don't pose," Pris repeated. "It's vanity."

"I won't tell if you won't. Come on, one picture. Can't you see Amy wants one?"

Amy probably wanted one of everything she saw, and if she got all of them, she would be so spoiled no one would want to be around her.

"Excuse me," Priscilla said, and made a break for the back of the store, putting as many displays of jams and jellies (MADE LOCALLY BY AMISH WOMEN!) and aprons (JUST LIKE THE AMISH WEAR!) and potholders and quilts in bright flowered prints (MADE BY AMISH QUILTERS!) as she could between herself and Amy's mother.

From across the store, she heard a disgusted sigh. "They go to all this trouble to make themselves a tourist destination and then they won't let us take a picture?"

A woman in a simple dress and a kitchen apron similar to the one Priscilla herself wore intercepted the woman and she could hear her soothing tones as she explained about the Amish reluctance to be photographed. Her covering was a prairie bonnet in a calico print. But maybe that was a good thing. At least no one could say she was dressing up Amish.

Priscilla ducked through the door at the back of the store and found herself in a barnlike warehouse, where boxes of goods were being unloaded off trucks that were definitely not Amish.

There was only one person in broadfall pants and suspenders, though, and he looked up over a stack of cardboard boxes and saw her as she practically fell out onto the dock.

"Pris!" he said. *"Was duschde hier?"*

"Trying to avoid being sold as a real Amish girl," she said a little breathlessly. "What are *you* doing here?"

"I work here. I just started today."

"You did? At the Hex Barn?" None of their gang would even have thought of working here—it was too crazy, too fake. And behind it all was the thought that if you did, you were somehow supporting the store's fakeness. Lending it credibility when, from what she could see, there probably wasn't a single Amish-made item in it.

"It's a job, and I need one," he said simply. "I'm the only plain man here, and already there's some talk about sending me up front."

"I wouldn't recommend it."

He nodded. "The pay's better back here, but they're all fired up about my 'visibility.'" He gave her a considering look. "I'm making twice what I did working for Oran. You should apply up front." He examined her with a stern eye. "I'm just not sure you look Amish enough."

He was so cute when he was joking. "So I wore my bib apron to town instead of a cape and away bonnet. Mind your own business, Simon Yoder."

"Yoder," called a man from the other side of a pallet of boxes, "gab with the GF on your own time, dude."

"She's not my girlfriend," he called back, and Priscilla schooled her face to show no reaction. There wasn't much she could do about the blush, though. It scalded her face and she wished she could just roll down the loading ramp and disappear into the ground.

"I have to get back to work, Pris. Was there something you wanted?"

She shook her head. It had been foolish of her to come in.

"Come on, I'll walk you out this way." He pointed down the ramp next to where a big truck was backing into a bay. "I'm serious about the job. Do you want me to give them a recommendation?"

She'd never thought about getting a job. And she'd certainly never spent two seconds thinking about working at the Hex Barn. But working for the same outfit as Simon? All day long? Sure, he wasn't interested now, but who was he going to take his lunch with? Who would he ride to work with? Her, that's who. Getting paid for having her dreams come true seemed like a sin for sure.

And yet... "I don't know, Simon. This place is—well, it might give folks the wrong idea."

"How's that?"

How to put this without offending him, since he'd just signed on? "Um...you know, like if we work here, we're saying that what they're doing is all right. The stuff they sell—that it's really Amish."

Under that level gaze she felt the blush heating her cheeks again, her spine wilting, and a sudden urge to smack herself for saying stupid things.

"It's just a job, Pris. Not a statement of faith."

Priscilla sucked in a breath of surprise. "What do you mean?"

"Yoder!" came the holler from inside the warehouse. "Daylight's burning and you still have this truck to unload!"

"I've got to go. Think about it, Pris. Katie and Saranne could help with your chores, couldn't they?"

Cooking, and cleaning, and sewing, and washing...Katie would. She might have to make a trade with Saranne. She wavered.

*The Hex Barn.* Oh, how Rosanne and the rest of their buddy bunch would laugh!

*Simon.* She didn't care about Simon. Yes, she did. She cared enough to bear that laughter, and if he started to see her differently, then she would be the one laughing.

*Money.* It would be real nice to have some of her very own, and Mamm couldn't argue if she gave half of it to her for the household expenses.

"All right, I'll do it," she said, feeling as though she'd just jumped off a tree limb into the Byler pond, and she couldn't feel the bottom.

"Great! Give me fifteen minutes to get this truck emptied, and I'll walk you up to the office to introduce you."

He was as good as his word. Fifteen minutes later, he took her upstairs, and ten minutes after that she had a job offer.

Dazed, a little giddy, holding a bunch of papers that had to be signed by her parents since she wasn't yet eighteen, she walked the rest of the way home.

It took every step of the two miles to figure out how she was going to explain this to Mamm and Dat.

Dat wasted no time on her attempts at persuasion—he merely stuffed the papers in the stove.

Priscilla had known this would be a hard row to hoe, but she hadn't anticipated the extent of her parents' opposition to the very existence of the Hex Barn, much less the possibility of their daughter working there. Fortunately, the woodstove he'd been closest to was the one in the big room downstairs that they used for church, not the kitchen stove that ran all day long and kept the whole house warm. So that night, she tiptoed down the stairs and rescued the papers, which only had a little smudging on the back where some of the black had rubbed off.

She wouldn't give up—and she didn't, not once over the next week and a half. Priscilla was sure that the mention of a wage that was pretty decent would make Mamm come around eventually. It was she who feared for Priscilla's service to God in such a place.

"They'll turn you into a little Amish doll, *Liewi*, all dressed up and standing there ready for photographs," Mamm said on Saturday, when Pris had judged the time might be right to bring out the permission forms again. Mamm only shook her head at the sight of them—she had not missed which stove they'd gone into, either. "Can you tell them with a straight face that yes, those gaudy quilts would go on our beds? And what hours will you have to work? Saturday nights? Sundays? It's a slippery slope and I don't want you to step foot on it. Besides, we've never met those people. Who would you be spending your time with?"

*Simon.*

"Simon Yoder is working there, too. I wouldn't be completely alone," she explained. "We can eat lunch together and—and help each other."

"Simon works at the Hex Barn?" Mamm's eyebrows rose half in disbelief, half in astonishment. "What happened to his apprenticeship? I'm surprised Sarah Yoder allows it."

"It's just a job, Mamm, not a statement of faith."

"Don't be lippy with me, young lady. I am trying to settle my spirit for the Lord's Day."

And that was the end of that conversation.

There was nothing Priscilla could do about it now, and bringing up the subject on Easter Sunday, when they were supposed to be thinking of the resurrection of Jesus, would only make her parents more upset. So she tried to make her mind stop worrying at the edges of it like the chickens nibbling at the edges of the forbidden lettuce leaves poking through the garden fence, and focus on the sermon and the joy of the day.

After the lunch was served and cleaned up, Priscilla went to join Malinda and some of her buddy bunch, who were ostensibly looking at the new lambs in the field, but who had formed a telltale circle, talking, their faces animated over their aprons of Sunday white organdy.

Halfway across the lawn, Priscilla heard a male voice call her name. She turned to see Joe Byler ambling toward her, his black vest open and his hands in the pockets of his black Sunday pants.

"Hallo, Joe. *Wie geht's?*"

"*Gut, gut.* Nice day, ain't it?"

For once, it was. "After the March we had, I'm glad to see April is changing her tune."

"It'll be a nice evening. For our ride home from singing."

"Our—" Oh, goodness. She'd completely forgotten that she was supposed to be going home from singing with him. "*Ja*, I suppose it will." How *could* she?

"You didn't forget, did you?"

"*Neh*," she fibbed. "It's just that all this fuss about the Hex Barn has taken up most of the room in my head."

"*Ja*, Simon told me he got you a job there. Do you think you'll like it?"

"I might not get a chance, if Mamm and Dat forbid it. Which they are, at the moment."

"They'll come around. The supper gang's at Lev Esch's, right? With volleyball before?"

As if he didn't know. As if all of them hadn't known where

and when the first outdoor game of the season would be since the last church Sunday. "*Ja.* I'll see you there, okay?"

He grinned at her in reply, as if she'd said something particularly smart that he welcomed the sound of, and loped off in the direction of the barn, where the men and boys tended to congregate and swap news.

She resisted the urge to go and hide in Nina's old-fashioned outhouse for the rest of the afternoon. Instead, she laughed and chattered with the rest of her friends and, later, caught a ride with three of them over to Lev Esch's place on the outskirts of the settlement. The advantage to his family having a big spread was that they had a wide, flat lawn that accommodated two volleyball courts, so people didn't need to sit out for very long unless they wanted to.

Priscilla loved volleyball, and she had a good enough spike that she could hold her own with the boys her own age. Some of the older ones hit the ball too hard and too fast for her liking—a clock on the head from one of Dan Byler's balls could send you inside for a bag of ice and an aspirin—but in a mixed crowd everyone knew it was all about fun and not about winning.

After three or four games, they went in for the potluck supper, and after sundown, it was time for singing. Some of the boys lingered outside, setting the ball off the tips of their fingers from one to another among themselves. There was always someone who thought he would show off a little—and always someone who was gently chivied in by a father or an uncle like the last of the cows for milking.

Little rebellions. Like being the last in the door for church.

Holding up the singing.

Putting fancy decorations on a buggy.

*Working at the Hex Barn?*

Was that what the two of them were doing, she and Simon? Maybe Simon was. He sure seemed to be having a hard time lately, like every little thing upset him. She was only trying to be near him, but she felt like something to be moved to the side of the road to Colorado—like a cow who'd broken through the pasture fence—unless she managed somehow to get his attention good and proper.

And if she wasn't allowed to work at the Hex Barn, how was she going to manage that?

The songs they sang on Sunday nights started off with choices from the *Ausbund*, the hymnbook the *Gmee* had been using for hundreds of years. It didn't have any written music in it, but they didn't need it. When you heard the slow Amish singing while you were in your mother's womb, you tended to remember it week after week, year after year. The *Youngie* sang from the green book, too, but most popular were the faster songs, like "The Old Rugged Cross" and "*Wo ist Jesus mein Verlangen,*" which they always put to "What a Friend We Have in Jesus." That really sped it up.

Priscilla hardly ever picked a song, because she who chose it had to lead it, and there was no way she was singing even the first few words all by herself before the others joined in. She could carry a tune in a bucket, but not very far.

After a spirited and slightly risky chorus of "Take Me Home Country Roads"—which was really pushing the worldliness factor, but it was so appropriate!—people began to get up and straggle away to find buggies and plastic containers and Igloo carriers. Joe caught her eye as he loped down the steps, and she collected the plate on which she'd brought a few dozen oatmeal chocolate chip cookies, and went out to the lawn to wait.

Dark shapes moved down behind the Esch barn, and the

sound of muffled laughter and the acrid scent of cigarette smoke wafted toward her on the breeze.

Ugh.

She could be glad that both Simon and the Byler boys weren't so fast. The bishop in their district wasn't as strict as some—like Daniel Lapp in Whinburg, for instance—but still, it wouldn't be long before Lev's father smelled it, too, and swept those boys out of there.

With a jingle of harness, Joe brought the courting buggy to a stop in front of her, and Priscilla could swear that every head in the yard turned their way.

"Say, Joe, is that your new buggy?" someone called. "Priscilla, are you breaking it in for him?"

"I hear she's the only girl who's ever ridden in it." Someone else whistled at this very personal detail.

"Drive, Joe," Priscilla said, holding a smile.

"You all are just jealous of this fine rig," he called to his friends, and Priscilla could have curled up under the seat with the battery in embarrassment.

"Aren't you supposed to ask if they're jealous of your girl?" One of the older girls laughed.

"Drive!"

"Don't get a bee in your bonnet," Joe said, unperturbed, flapping the reins over his horse's back. Finally the buggy lurched into motion—not nearly fast enough, in Pris's opinion. "Everybody teases courting couples. I bet you've done it yourself a time or two."

"We are not a courting couple." Her face was going to crack from pretending to go along with all the jokes.

"Maybe not yet."

The voices and laughter faded in the crunch of the wheels in the lane, multiplied as other buggies began to roll out behind them. And under the familiar sounds, she gathered her wits together.

"What do you mean, Joe?"

"I got a new courting buggy and you're the only girl to ride in it, like they said. We could keep that up, if you wanted. Otherwise, why agree to come along?"

"Be…cause…we're friends?"

"I'm friends with all the girls in Willow Creek. Don't see any of them up here tonight, do you?" He gave her a long sideways look while his horse jogged briskly down the side of the road, ignoring the *Englisch* car with New York plates whose occupants all turned to stare out the windows at them as they passed. "I wanted to take you home because I have something to ask you."

She was so mixed up. She'd been a complete idiot to agree to let Joe Byler take her home, when all she wanted to do was be with Simon. Had he even seen her leave with Joe? And had she really sunk so low that she wanted that—wanted to make him jealous?

"Pris? Are you listening?"

She felt like giving herself a good smack. "*Ja*, Joe. What is it?"

"I'd like for you and me to be special friends," he said simply. "What do you think about that?"

*Special friends* was the local term for being boyfriend and girlfriend. *Special friends* meant the boy wanted to court you exclusively, to come by on Saturday nights and talk in the front room, to take you out for an ice cream or ask his parents to give you a seat at the dinner table.

Priscilla could have wept. This was so wrong—and she'd brought it all on herself. If this had been Simon doing the asking, she'd have been so filled with joy she might have just floated off the seat. But it was Joe—good old dependable, handy Joe Byler whom she'd known her whole life, who had probably never done one single crazy thing or made his Dat worry for a moment.

Yet.

Hold on.

"But Joe," she said carefully, "how can we be special friends when you're planning to go out to Colorado? Is that plan off?"

"Nope," he said, pulling on the reins and checking both directions before they crossed the county highway. He flapped the horse into motion and gave half his attention back to her. "Me and Simon, we had to do some figuring after old Oran kicked him out of the shop. We figure we'll do better to stick around and save money. My uncle wrote to my folks, too, and from what Dat says, he might be able to let me go for two weeks, like you said."

She could have hugged him from sheer relief if it wouldn't have given him the wrong idea. "So you're not going to go for good after all?"

"Even if we did, that don't have anything to do with you and me."

"It does, too. Why would a girl date a boy who's just going to leave?"

He chuckled. "You talk like you're going to plant celery for a November wedding. You're only sixteen, ain't you?"

"Well, yes, but—"

"It's a little early yet to get that serious. I've got two more years at the buggy shop to finish my apprenticeship—if old Oran don't find a reason to kick me out, too—and then a couple years to get myself established somewhere. I ain't looking for a wife quite yet, but I would like a special friend. I'm seventeen, and it's time."

She didn't want to be his wife. But being somebody's girl-friend was getting less and less appealing, especially when it sounded like she was merely going to be the first of a string. Not that she wanted to be his one and only. Far from it.

"Do you think that's right, Joe? To date a girl this summer, and another girl next summer—how many special friends do you plan to have before you settle down?"

Another chuckle. "Don't be so old-fashioned. People don't just date one person anymore, you know. How can you know if a girl is right for you if you don't have anyone to compare her to?"

This had to be the most unromantic conversation she'd ever had in her life—and that was saying something.

Was she unreasonable? Expecting too much? Was this how people fell in love—after trying each other on like a pair of winter boots?

He was waiting for an answer, and she needed to give him one, after leading him on this far. "I'd like to be friends, Joe. Good friends. But I'm not sure if I want to be *special* friends."

"You never know until you try."

"My folks think I'm too young."

"Young is what people are in their heads. Got nothing to do with their age."

"*Ja*, well, in Mamm's head, I'm only twelve, believe me."

"She knows you're running around."

"But I'm not. Not really."

"You could start. How about this? Simon says there's going to be a band hop over Stinson way on Wednesday. A bunch of us are going. How about you ride with me? And not in this, either. In the four-seater."

"Alone?"

He shook his head. "Simon was going to go with me, and you can bring your sidekick if you want."

Rosanne would be up for it, no doubt about that. And things had changed from last time. Maybe by then she'd be his coworker. She'd have a bond with him that nobody else shared.

And even if her parents took away her papers again and forbade her to go within a mile of the Hex Barn, she could still go to a band hop. If she did, they'd have to see that she wasn't twelve anymore, that she could make her own decisions.

"All right," she said. "I'll go with you. It'll be fun."

# CHAPTER 19

Before his move, Henry might spend a Sunday morning holed up with a Starbucks espresso and the *Denver Post*, and then in the afternoon give one of his coworkers a call and suggest a hike or a golf game. There were all kinds of ways he had filled in the hole that worship used to occupy—filled it so well, in fact, that before the news of Sadie's death, he'd forgotten that Sunday was anything more than a bonus Saturday.

But when you lived in Amish country, and there was no one to call and nothing to call them with, you could hear the clip-clop of all the hooves heading briskly off to church starting before dawn, and falling off abruptly around eight, when the service started. And then you realized just how deep the hole was, and how vitally necessary it was that it be filled.

He just wasn't willing to fill it with God. Not even at Easter.

Henry sipped his instant coffee and frowned at the view out the kitchen window. The road was empty of buggies at ten thirty, the sounds of hooves conspicuously absent. They'd start up again after the fellowship meal ended, and this sense of tension—the feeling that he should be with them—would dissipate once it was no longer possible to join them.

He had no intention of joining them, blast it.

But his relatives and neighbors would probably rejoice if they knew he felt the pull, like the one the moon exerted on the tides—the combination of guilt and memory and social expectation that demanded he knuckle under and submit to God's will.

Oh, he knew what his cousins and Sarah Yoder were up to. The fact that he no longer believed in God or a heavenly plan for his life wouldn't stop the invitations to supper, the friendly conversation, the willingness to be seen with him in public. It wouldn't stop them from trying to love him back into the Kingdom, because he wasn't shunned. He hadn't joined church, that was all, and that decision was possible at any time without the show of public repentance that shunning would demand. They probably figured that if they seduced him back into their social life with suppers and whoopie pies and pretty widows, he'd sink happily to his knees in front of the bishop without even a struggle and say yes.

After all, they would think, what else does he have to live for?

A fair question. He was working on an answer.

A real breakfast would do for a start. He grabbed his coat and his car keys and drove the two miles into town—a distance he could have and probably should have walked, but the return trip would be fraught with buggies and friendly greetings and the distinct feeling that every family who passed not only knew who he was, but knew of his solitude.

Solitude.

*Allison, nearly invisible under the web of tubing and IV shunts and the oxygen mask—a web that had tried to keep her alive.*

He slammed down the gates of memory before the flood

of emotion roaring behind it could swamp him, and concentrated on the empty county road.

He had grown up believing that God held each person in the palm of His hand, with a unique plan for each individual's life. Now, the thought of it made Henry shudder in horror. If that diesel rig on that particular curve had been God's plan for Allison's life and his instead of the wedding and family that everybody else got, then he could just do without heavenly plans of any kind, thanks.

The sight of Willow Creek was a relief from his own thoughts. He pulled in front of the Dutch Rest Café and shut off the engine. A place manned by *Englisch* folks, it was open on a Sunday like an oasis in the desert. He ordered up a big plate of home-fried potatoes melting in cheese, eggs, and sausage with gravy so thick it made the biscuits disappear like garden shrubs under a snowfall.

When he was about three-quarters done, the waitress came over and refilled his cup, then leaned on the edge of the table.

"You were in here before, weren't you, with Sarah Yoder?"

He nodded, then reached for the coffee to take a gulp before he could speak. "You make a fine meal. I'm surprised there aren't more folks here."

She smiled, revealing front teeth that overlapped just slightly. "It's the calm before the storm. Just wait until next month, on Memorial Day weekend. The line will be out the door by the time the Amish Market closes, and all the B and Bs will be full. Summer is the only thing that keeps us going through the winter."

"I think that's true for more than retail. I used to live in Colorado, and sometimes all that would get us through February was the thought of June."

She topped up his cup again. "So are you visiting?"

"No, I live here now—or maybe I should say *for* now. If I don't find work, this could be the last time you see me in here, even if I could get a table."

"What do you do? There's not a lot going on if you're not in the tourist trade—or Amish."

On the tip of his tongue balanced a confession about being neither, but then he thought better of it. "Not Amish, but I guess you could say I'm in the tourist trade...I'm a potter."

"Like Harry?" She grinned.

Smiling, he shook his head. "Like clay. I make things— you know, bowls, plates, cups." He glanced out the window at the Amish Market, shuttered and closed for the Lord's Day. "I thought about renting a stall in there. Do they let *Englisch* folks sell?"

She looked at him oddly. "That's what the Amish call us."

"I know. It's as good a differentiator as any, I suppose."

"It just sounds funny, coming from a regular guy. Anyhow, yeah, they do, but if an Amish vendor comes in and wants a stall, they might bump you. Considering the name of the market and all. When the tourists come, they want to buy Amish stuff, you know? Unless they don't know any better and they go to the Hex Barn."

He needed a more reliable way to build a business.

"You said you made plates?"

He nodded. "Plates, bowls, matched sets of just about anything." He wouldn't do art pieces again. He'd stick with what was nice and safe, with function more important than design. Nobody would laugh at a simple plate, as long as it did what it was made to do.

"You should try around at the B and Bs. Ginny Hochstetler at the Rose Arbor Inn was in here yesterday in a huge tizzy. Apparently she ordered a bunch of mugs and the delivery guy's forklift failed somehow getting the crate off the truck. Dumped the whole shebang right in the driveway. Made an awful mess."

He could just see it. "I hope she has good insurance."

The waitress shrugged. "Don't know. But I bet she needs a bunch of mugs."

Somehow he'd managed to clean his plate and drink three cups of coffee on top of it. She gave him the check and he left her the kind of tip that would make her remember him.

"Thanks for the tip." She had a nice smile, despite the teeth.

"And thanks for yours. I'm going to head over to the Rose Arbor now." Then he thought of something. "Say—this Ginny Hochstetler, she's not Amish, is she? Would she be home?"

The girl shook her head with a laugh. "Hochstetler's her married name—she kept it after the divorce. Says it's good for business. Good luck."

He waved and got into the car, following the directions the girl had scribbled on a napkin. The Rose Arbor Inn was conveniently close to the covered bridge that appeared in all the tourist brochures about Willow Creek, along with the Amish Market, the farmhouses that displayed quilts on their clotheslines close to the road, the buggy shop, and the Hex Barn. As he got out of the car in the shady little parking lot, he had no doubt that the picturesque quality of the bridge in the background, the sound of the creek, and the scent of the roses that would soon be coming into bloom over the gate would immediately charm the socks off anyone passing by, whether on the physical highway or the information highway.

Behind the parking spaces, he saw chips of white china still lying in the gravel. With any luck, the insurance company's loss would be his gain.

The inn's brass door knocker was in the shape of a rose, and he could hear the sound echo in the hall. In a few minutes, light footsteps came pattering up and the door swung open.

"Hi, you must be Mr. Goldstein." She peered around him. "Is Mrs. Goldstein with you, or did you change your mind about the babymoon?"

Whatever he'd imagined Ginny Hochstetler might have looked like, it wasn't the African-American woman looking so expectantly at him, a wide smile and dancing amber eyes nearly ambushed by an explosion of corkscrew curls.

"I'm sorry," he said. "There weren't any other cars in the lot. The name's Henry Byler—I live just up the road."

She threw back her head and laughed. "Trust me to put my foot in it—and bare ones at that." She stuck out a leg and he got a flash of hot pink toenails that matched her pants exactly. "Come on in and tell me what I can do for you. Wedding? Business meeting? Secret getaway?"

He followed her into a jewel box of a sitting room, which made him take a second look at the place. The inn looked to be over two hundred years old, with wide hickory planking on the floors and a ceiling bearing a medallion in the center from which an iron chandelier hung—neither of which had come from Home Depot.

"Mugs, actually."

With a snort, she poured him a cup of coffee, then tapped the glossy stoneware that looked vaguely historic with a hot pink fingernail. "The story got to town already? It only happened yesterday. A whole crate of busted mugs just like this is going to young Sam Yoder's for some project he's doing. I'm glad it made somebody happy."

"It's a shame." He examined the mug. "Not handmade, are they?"

"Nope, but they look it. I guess that's why they were so expensive."

"What did they cost you?"

When she told him, he did some rapid calculations. It would mean selling his skill for about as much as a farmer made, but considering where he stood, maybe that wasn't a bad thing.

"I can make you a crate of mugs that look pretty close to this for around that price. I'm a potter, and I'm looking to start a business here."

"Is that so? A hundred mugs? You must be a kept man, then. Nobody can hand-make a hundred mugs for that."

He must've been with the Amish too long if her blunt language could startle a laugh out of him. "I keep myself, thanks. But I won't be able to forever unless I get some word of mouth going. I figure an inn like this might be a good place for ground zero."

She nodded. "I get a lot of traffic through here, for which I thank the Lord daily. Tell you what. Make me up a couple of samples, and if I like them, you'll have a deal." She waved an arm to encompass the balloon shades, the branches of early forsythia arranged in a willow-pattern bowl on the coffee table, and the dining room beyond, which appeared to be set for the next morning's breakfast guests with ten places. "I go through a lot of mugs, between people dropping them, stealing them, and actually buying them for souvenirs. It would be nice not to have to wait around for the UPS truck whenever I need a couple more. Shop local, right?" She grinned at him, hands on hips, and only a dead man could have resisted grinning back.

A bell clanged. "Oops, that's got to be my babymooners. Come on and I'll see you out."

"What's a babymoon, if you don't mind my ignorance?" He followed her to the door.

"It's the last-chance vacation you take as a couple before the first baby comes." She pulled a business card out of a silver holder on the hall table and handed it to him. "I get a lot of those, usually stockbrokers and high-stress types with well-groomed wives from New York and Philly. I'm on a lot of the baby websites, you know? There's a method to my madness."

She swung the door open to greet the Goldsteins—the woman so advanced in her pregnancy it looked like she might be having the baby that weekend—and he slipped out with a smile and a handshake.

Babymooners. What next? Then again, as long as they used stoneware, it didn't matter. A hundred mugs. All identical, all functional, all as straightforward and undemanding as—as oatmeal.

Well, oatmeal had its place. Lots of people liked it. Lots of people found it satisfying.

He hoped Ginny Hochstetler did, too, and would tell everyone she spoke with where her oatmeal mugs had come from.

He started the car, turned it in the tight little lot, and crept down the lane toward the covered bridge. She and the waitress at the Dutch Rest were probably the first people he'd met who didn't have designs on his soul's salvation. Well, okay, he could probably include Sarah Yoder in that number, when she wasn't getting in his face.

Wouldn't she be happy that he'd taken her lecture to heart?

Now she wasn't the only one who'd taken a step forward. Granted, it had taken the woman some major guts to go to that scary *Dokterfraa* and agree to be her apprentice. It had taken him some guts, too, to approach Ginny Hochstetler, though dealing with her had been a lot more pleasant than dealing with Ruth Lehman. If he never got to do that again, it would be too soon—he was going to make good and sure he never got sick. Crawling all the way to Whinburg General would be easier than facing that gimlet stare and handing over personal details as though they were little defenseless hostages.

On the other hand, sharing some details with Ginny might be nice, if she ever got any time off.

*Allison would have wanted you to move on*, his almost-mother-in-law's voice whispered in his memory, during a visit a year after it had happened. He had rejected that notion then, and every moment of the ten years since.

But if today was a day for new beginnings…

His stomach swung, sickeningly, and he gripped the wheel with hands that suddenly felt slick with sweat.

Or not.

One thing at a time.

Maybe he should stop by the Yoder place and see if Caleb was available to start work. There was no time like the present, Mamm used to say…and no present like time.

# CHAPTER 20

"People take their herbs a number of ways," Ruth Lehman said, chopping plant matter with energy on the counter of her compiling room, "but the simplest—other than eating them, which sometimes isn't very practical—is in a tea or a tincture."

Sarah felt as though she'd been taking notes for hours, but in reality it had only been one. One more to go. "Why isn't eating a fresh herb practical?"

"Think about stinging nettle."

With Caleb's run-in with the nettles in recent memory, Sarah got a graphic picture of the result. "Oh. But you can make it into a tea? Won't that sting? Or do you have to dry it first?"

"No, indeed. If you pour boiled water over chopped nettles and cleavers—those sticky weeds in your garden—you have a nice refreshing tea that's good for the lymph nodes and can actually help clear up the skin."

"Cleavers," Sarah said on a note of discovery. "Is that what they're called? I've probably pulled up an acre of those things."

"That's a shame—you can make a tincture out of the fresh plants and sell it for ten dollars a bottle. Weeds are only plants that aren't growing in their proper places, Sarah. And sometimes their proper place isn't where we expect it to be. God has put them there for a reason."

"Out behind my chicken coop, for instance?"

"If it's cool and shady and gets a little morning sun, that's exactly where God wants those nettles. Imagine if he wanted them by your back door, and you got stung every time you brushed past."

Sarah nodded in acceptance. "If God wants them there out of the way, that's fine with me—and the chickens."

"They won't hurt you, and if they do, I told you about the yellow dock and crushing up the leaves. Now, here's how we measure and dilute the liquid for the tincture."

To Sarah's surprise, once she actually got her hands dirty, so to speak, and began to chop and pour and measure, the second hour passed much more quickly than the first. There was just so much to know that she despaired of ever approaching Ruth's level of competence. When she said so as they were washing up the bowls and jars afterward, Ruth's gaze held understanding.

"Give yourself time. I've been doing this since Amelia and Christopher were little, and they're in their thirties now. Begin simply and work outward from there."

"*Ja*, but where do I begin?"

"If you get to know just two or three plants in your garden really well in the first year, that's a start. I began with nettles, calendula—those orange, stalky marigolds—and lavender. You might choose something different."

"My mother loved lemon balm and I have a couple of big bushes near the back door."

"With that, nettles, and cleavers, you could do a lot. I can give you some recipes. Try things out on yourself and the boys, and see how they work. You'll do some reading and get some books from the library to learn more and more ways to use them, and you'll gain confidence in your ability." Ruth put the kettle on the stove. "Come outside and we'll see what we can harvest for tea."

Sarah followed her down to the creek at the bottom of the yard behind the barn, before Isaac's fields and pastures began on the rise of the hill beyond.

"Speaking of confidence, I'll be introducing myself to your patients today and taking them their packets."

"They're your patients now. I wrote and told them all to expect you."

"And no one protested?"

"John Casey did, but that's because he's stuck and hates change. You won't get him to come to your house—he's the only one you'll need to deliver to."

"Stuck?" She pictured a wagon mired in March mud. "Stuck how?"

"Stuck in his thinking, stuck in his innards, just stuck. I'm giving him digestive bitters to get things moving, but it will take more than that to change his thinking. Mostly he's stuck in the past. Folks who are afraid tend to hide there because it's safe. You knew what was what in the past."

"Faith makes the present safe."

"Ah, but he's my *Englisch* man, and I'm not sure God has brought him to that reckoning yet."

"So what do you do? You can't treat the mind and the heart, can you? Only the body. But doesn't that create only half a cure?"

Ruth smiled at her, and it changed her whole face. Her eyes twinkled, and one cheek deepened in a dimple, like a dent in cream. Suddenly Sarah saw the woman Isaac Lehman might have fallen in love with decades ago, and her view shifted, the way it did in the eye doctor's office when he put the lenses in the machine.

She had been stuck, too. Stuck in fear and in hanging on to her own way. She and this *Englisch* man might have more to talk about than she'd first thought.

"You're a wise woman in many ways, for one so young," Ruth said.

"Not so young, with a fourteen-year-old."

"Wait until you have grandchildren that age. But you're right. Sometimes the real cure is needed in the heart, and all the herbs in the world can't make a change there."

"Do you find that a lot?"

Cradling a selection of cleavers and chickweed in their hands, they climbed the gentle slope back up to the house, where they found the water boiling. Ruth chopped the plants and poured the water over them, then added in fresh mint and a couple of heads of lavender. A delicious aroma filled the kitchen, like the freshness of a summer day.

Ruth cut two slices of cherry pie and set a small jug of cream on the table. The combination of cherries and the meadow scent of the tea practically made Sarah's eyes roll back in her head with delight.

"I have to make this at Corinne's for sisters' day," she sighed. "They'll never be the same."

"One of my daughter's friends, Emma Weaver, says that God is always giving us little gifts. We just have to recognize them. The plants and flowers in the fields are some of those gifts—the cleavers, the plantain, the dock. Humble, but so useful if you know what God has given them to hold for us."

"I can see the lesson in that," Sarah confessed at last. "To be humble—and useful. It would be *gut* for me to remember it."

Ruth lowered her mouth to her cup and took a sip. And when she smiled, it was hard not to smile with her.

It took Sarah the rest of the day to drive back from Whinburg. On the way, she visited each of her six new patients to deliver their cures and get to know them. Ruth had chosen well. She had two young mothers whose broods were suffering from spring colds and flu, one elderly lady with a skin complaint that required a salve, and two women who were drinking Ruth's Sunshine Tea on a daily basis for a month.

It would be such a help if the women could have a word with Adah Yost the next time they met at church. Maybe later, when she became comfortable enough with them in her new role, she could put her nose in again where it didn't belong, but Oran's reprimand was still too fresh to allow her to take that step now.

The last patient, living in the tiny housing development on the edge of Willow Creek next to the mini-mall that housed the Hex Barn, was John Casey. The Stuck Man, as she was beginning to think of him. The one it was now her responsibility to unstick.

There was nowhere to tie the horse in front of the condominium buildings, which looked like an array of shoeboxes set on end, so she made do with tying Dulcie to a newly planted poplar. Then she climbed the steps to number 31-A.

The door swung open under her knock, and a man in his fifties stared at her in surprise. "You're not Ruth Lehman," he said. His hair had probably been blond in his youth, but now it was gray, cut short like a military man. He leaned on the door frame, both beefy arms raised to grip it on either side.

"No, I am Sarah Yoder. Ruth wrote to you that I would be taking over your case." She sounded so official, like a doctor. She would have to think of another way to put it, or Caleb and Simon would never stop teasing her.

"Did she?" He glanced over his shoulder, where a counter-top held a pile of mail that threatened to slide off and engulf the narrow galley kitchen. "Come on in and I'll tell you all about it."

The condominium was only a little bigger than a shoebox. From where she stood on the mat just inside, she could see living room, kitchen, and bathroom. There were no other doors, but a set of stairs led up to where the bedrooms must be. He had very little furniture—one chair, and not even a ta-ble to eat from, which meant he either ate standing up or in his chair, opposite the television. But for all the barrenness of his furnishings, the walls more than made up for it.

Painted stark white, they were covered in pictures and memorabilia—a football jersey in a frame, certificates, blown-up photographs of a group of men getting progressively younger until, near the bathroom, they were Caleb's age.

"I need to be getting back to my boys," she said, "so I can't stay long."

"I've been stuck on the computer all day, drumming up business. I'm glad of the chance to talk to a real person."

"Is your wife not home?" There wasn't a single feminine touch that would make this house a home.

"No wife. Not anymore. My oldest daughter still lives in town, but the wife took the younger kids and went back to Philly. Guess the carriage business didn't make enough to suit her."

"Carriage business?" Did he make buggies?

"Yep. Restoring old carriages like those ones that take the tourists around in Central Park, or a fancy gold and white rig for a wedding. That's what I do—I make the past work for the present."

Stuck.

"Where is your shop?"

"Over there." He jerked a chin in the direction of the mini-mall and the Hex Barn. "If I need a specialist, I call in one of your folks. Oran Yost knows more about harnesses and hardware than anyone I ever met. Know him?"

"*Ja.* We live in the same district. Until recently, my oldest son was his apprentice."

"Simon, or Joe?"

"Simon."

"Okay, now I've got you placed. Fine boy. He should go far. You can be proud of him."

She said nothing, because to admit to pride was a sin. A woman might say she was happy for her son, or that she was glad he filled a useful place, but that was the extent of it.

Instead, she pulled the packet of herb tea from her handbag. "I have your tea here. That will be ten dollars."

"Get right down to business, don't you?"

She inched a little farther into the house and laid it on the table. "I have dinner to make and a pile of the boys' clothes to mend yet today, and this is my last stop. I'm sorry to have taken so long with my other visits." If she had been in his place, she would have appreciated a little time to get to know the stranger who had appeared on her doorstep. She would have made some tea and dished up a fat slice of cake or pie, and waited to learn a little about the other person.

"That's okay, don't apologize." He picked up the pyramid-shaped packet. "I can't tell if this is doing any good. Did Ruth tell you about me?"

"She said she's treating you for a digestive problem."

"No, I didn't mean that way. I meant about me." He waved a hand at the wall full of…him. "She tell you you're treating a bona fide state football champion?"

"No."

"Yep, the scouts were after me big-time. If it hadn't been for Bobby Schotzkey's tackle during that last game of senior year, you might be treating an NFL quarterback now. Retired, of course, but still."

He might as well have been speaking Latin. Something else that lived in the past.

"That's very nice," she said. "Can you tell me a little about what kinds of foods you eat?"

He waved at the kitchen. "Heck, I don't know. Whatever I can scrounge up. Pizza, hot dogs, the odd hamburger. The kids used to like that macaroni and cheese in a box, so sometimes I have that."

"What about vegetables?"

"What about them? A man's gotta carbo-load, young lady. Carbs and protein, that's the ticket if you want to last all day."

"Maybe when you play sports, but you're not doing that now. Your insides need roughage to—to make the plumbing work properly."

"You sound like my grandma. She died twenty years ago, but I can hear her voice in my head clear as day. 'John, eat your peas. Eat your broccoli.'" He shuddered. "I'm not one of them veggietarians. Stuff'll make you weak in the knees."

"But you're constipated, and you probably have acid reflux, *ja*?"

"That's what the tea's for, isn't it?"

"Asking the tea to make you well is like asking a chicken to lift a wagon. It's the vegetables that will work harder for you. Do the heavy lifting, you might say."

He peered at her. "You're an awful know-it-all, aren't you?"

"I don't know anything," she told him with complete honesty. "But I have boys, and I know boys' innards. Mine eat the kinds of foods I just said, and their plumbing works perfectly."

"But they're young. Everything works perfectly when you're young. Just ask me. You should have seen me back in the day. The head cheerleader asked me to the Sadie Hawkins Day dance, you know—and it wasn't because I was on the team, either."

"That was then, Mr. Casey. This is now."

"I read a book by that name in eleventh grade. You read it?"

"We don't go as far as high school. I went to eighth grade. And now I must be on my way. I hope you'll think about what I said the next time you go to the grocery store."

"Yeah, yeah, maybe. You bring a horse over?"

"Yes, I tied her to the poplar out there."

"Is that what that is? Skinny thing. Might not survive. Guess it ate too many vegetables, huh?"

His laughter followed her out the door and she was aware of him watching her as she untied Dulcie and climbed into the buggy.

The Stuck Man.

Someone else who didn't really want to be helped. She would never have suspected there could be so many in the world.

# CHAPTER 21

*There's a first time for everything.* How many times had Priscilla heard that expression? Folks were always saying the obvious, like there was some kind of wisdom in it that the *Youngie* couldn't figure out on their own.

Well, she'd better figure it out, or her first time sneaking out of the house would be her last. It probably would be anyway. Band hop and Simon notwithstanding, her heart couldn't take much more of this—of knowing her parents didn't approve of such a worldly activity, and going ahead and doing it anyway. Dat had talked it over with her, and as far as he knew, she'd seen reason. But it was only this once.

She'd go one time, no more—and that's what she'd tell them in the morning.

As quietly as she knew how, Priscilla slipped down the stairs, carrying her sneakers. Once out the back door, she rammed her feet into her shoes, took off across the lawn, and headed for the road, avoiding the gravel that would crunch under her soles and give her away.

Jake's old buggy waited on the side of the road with the twins in it, and she climbed in, plopping onto the back bench before she realized Simon was back there, too. "Am I late?"

she asked, breathless from the run . . . and the stress of deceiving her parents.

"Nope." Jake flapped the reins over their horse, and she winced at the sound of hooves on the asphalt. "They'll just be getting started."

The word had gone out that the location had been changed at the last minute to an old fallow field on Sadie Byler's place, right up against the woods where the trees would absorb some of the sound, on a north slope where crops never did very well. But anyone within a mile could tell where they were headed. They could see buggy lamps converging from here.

"Whoever planned this was smart," Simon said. "The sound only carries so far, and the slope forces the sound into the trees, like a theater."

"Did anybody ask Henry Byler for permission?" she said when she saw where they were going. "Isn't this a little close to home?" It was a couple of miles from their place, but still.

"Nobody hardly sees the guy and it ain't likely he's going to stay," Joe said. "Besides, we ain't doing any harm, and I bet he's no stranger to music and beer anyway, being a worldly man and all."

Worldly or not, fallow field or not, it didn't seem right to move in on a man's land and use it for a party. It was really hard to have a good time when you had the chilly feeling you shouldn't be here at all.

But Simon was here, and the twins, so they'd look after her. What could happen to them out in a field?

"Loosen up," Joe said after he'd tied the horse to the fence, nudging her in the side as they tromped toward the circle of cars, some with their engines running, some just sitting there with their headlights on, aimed at the hay wagon being used for a stage.

She smiled at him. "Don't fall asleep in a cow pie tonight, or Jake will tie you under the buggy like a volleyball net to get you home."

He laughed and took her hand. "I promise I won't. Not if I'm looking after you."

Simon spoke up from behind them. "Anybody want a drink?" He had probably seen it, now that they were inside the half circle of lights. She hoped so.

"A beer would be good," Jake said.

"Pris?"

"Just a soda." She'd never drunk beer in her life, and now didn't seem a very good time to start. "What if I need to drive home?"

Jake just laughed and walked off toward the coolers next to the stage, as if she hadn't asked a perfectly serious and reasonable question. Clearly she was not cut out for a life of reckless dissipation.

"Relax," Joe said, tugging her over to a truck, where he gave her a boost up into the bed and plunked himself down on the side to watch the band. "We'll listen to some music, drink a few beers, maybe dance a little, and then go home. There's nothing to worry about."

"Have you done this before?"

"Sure, lots of times."

"Twice," Simon corrected him, heaving himself up over the side of the truck bed the way some guys heaved themselves up over the edge of a swimming pool.

"Well, that's twice more than me," she said, forced to sit a little closer to Joe to give him room. "The band is pretty good, isn't it?"

"They're okay."

At least she could recognize the tune—Lonesome Highway's "Nine Pound Hammer," even if it was a little fast and the harmonies didn't quite match up. In the odd pause in the music, she could hear the putter of a generator somewhere behind the wagon, which she supposed powered the electric guitar and the speakers. She took a sip from the can of soda and tried to do as Joe said and relax. Maybe this wasn't so bad. People were laughing and drinking, sure, but since Simon and Joe wouldn't be getting out of control, she'd be safe with them. Jake seemed to know the boy who owned this pickup truck. He and his friends were horsing around up in front of the headlights, trying to talk a group of girls in dresses and *Kapps* into dancing.

It was a relief to see other Amish girls here. They weren't from her church, but at least she wasn't the only one. Priscilla relaxed a little more, and took another sip of soda. Two songs later, the group at the front of the truck had migrated around to the back and joined them, packing into the truck bed like they were all going on a hayride.

Someone jostled Pris and she lost her soda over the side, a plume of dark liquid fanning out and splashing the shirt of a boy wearing *Englisch* clothes. "Dude! Watch it!" he hollered, before staggering out into the dark, where everyone could hear the sound of retching.

*Wunderbaar.*

"Guess he's been here a while," Joe said. "Want me to get you another one?"

"*Neh*, I'm good," she said. The sound of someone else being sick was making her a little queasy, too. Or maybe it was just her stomach, still tied up in knots.

"Here, have some of my beer." Jake waggled it in her face. There was only a little left in the bottom of the can, from the sound of it.

"*Neh.*" She pushed his hand away.

"Aw, come on, Pris."

On her other side, Joe frowned. "She said no, Jake. Back off."

Jake stood, the beer evidently having taken a layer off his usual good humor. He leaped down and vanished into the crowd, heading in the general direction of the stage...or maybe the coolers.

"Don't worry about him, he can look after himself," Joe told her, following the direction of her gaze. "Want to dance?"

"Yeah!" The two boys behind him let out a whoop and they pulled the three girls off the tailgate, the rest of their friends following and dragging Priscilla, Simon, and Joe along with them. "Let's dance!"

"Joe, I've never danced in my life." Priscilla found herself inside the circle of lights, directly in front of a big speaker. She had to shout to be heard, and when he replied, she got it more from reading his lips than because she heard him.

"It's easy. Just like this." He took both her hands in his, which wasn't as graceful as she'd have thought, considering one of them held a half-full can of beer. Then he started pushing and pulling her, in and out, circling around her and doing it again.

Was this dancing? She tried to follow his movements, but they didn't really make any sense. In and out. Around and around. Clearly dancing wasn't going to be a temptation for her, not the way second helpings of dessert and gossip with her buddy bunch were.

"Joe, I'm just not very good at this," she said at last. "Can we go sit down now?"

"It's okay," he said soothingly, as if she were a horse. "Listen, they're playing a slow one now. Come here."

And there she was, pressed up against him in a very forward way, with his strong arms around her back. She had no choice but to put her arms around his neck—which was far, far closer to Joe Byler than she had ever imagined she'd be.

Oh, if only this were Simon!

Joe seemed to be more comfortable simply swaying from foot to foot, rather than adding all the complicated arm stuff. Maybe she could do this without looking like a complete idiot. Her nose was pressed up against his Woodpecker-red shirt, which smelled clean, as opposed to the faint whiffs of beer she got every time he took a sip of the can in one hand.

How long did songs last? And what was she going to do if he didn't release her after this one?

All around them, couples swayed to the music—it sounded like "The Yellow Rose of Texas," but she couldn't be sure. Maybe she was going deaf.

"Joe, couldn't we—"

Somewhere behind the stage, there was a flash of light and a girl screamed. Priscilla cried out, twisting out of Joe's grip and trying to see past the other couples. The stage went dark and silent, and a discordant sound that was the lead singer's guitar twanged into the sudden absence of noise.

"What the—" someone shouted, and then, "Fire! Look out! Fire!"

Joe said a word that he sure never heard in church. "Them fools blew up the generator and caught the grass. Find Simon and Jake and send them back there. I'm going to go help put it out."

The sunny, windy week they'd had, which she had thought was such a blessing after all the rain, had dried last year's grass just enough that it caught. Faster than she would have thought possible, it ate its way out from behind the stage, where the band was having fits trying to get cables and equipment out of the way.

"Start up the tractor and pull it over there!" Joe shouted, and the big diesel tractor still hitched to the wagon roared into life. The musicians were still up there, and as the stage jerked into motion, they were yanked off their feet and fell in a furious tangle of cables and instruments and bodies.

Priscilla ran for the pickup, but it was gone, its taillights bumping over the field and heading for the road. "Simon!" she screamed.

"Here!" A figure waved, illuminated by the creeping flames at his feet as he stamped and beat at them with his jacket. "Find something to put it out with before it gets to the trees!"

She would never have believed that an April field could catch fire, but here was the proof of her own eyes. She grabbed the arms of two girls standing next to the coolers, gaping at the band as it tried to get its footing on a moving platform.

Ice. The coolers were full of ice.

"Come on! Get the ice in here out to the fire!"

It was almost as though the girls woke up out of a trance, and welcomed someone telling them what to do. It took four of them, two on each end of the big coolers, to run them out to the forward edge of the flames, which were almost at the trees. Simon, Jake, and the boys with them grabbed the coolers and dumped the ice water, ice cubes, and cold drinks straight onto the flames, which went out with an angry hiss.

"Good thinking, Pris!" Simon shouted, beating back the last of them while the girls rolled cold, wet cans into the remaining flames with their feet. One of the girls started pulling tabs off and emptying beer into the burning grass.

The fire gave up, having run out of dry fuel, and Priscilla's knees began to wobble as she realized that they'd won. Simon grinned at her, teeth white in his sooty face—or what she could see of it in the headlights that had been turned toward them. His shirt was torn, his coat smoldering, and the hem of one of his pant legs was burned to the knee. All around them lay cans of soda and beer in the soggy mess.

One minute he was standing at the burn line. The next minute, he was hugging her, filling her nose with the smell of smoke and sweat.

"You all right?"

"*Ja,*" she said, breathless from running and from the shock of his hug. "I'm just glad the ice did the trick."

"It was close. Another minute and—" He lifted his head, his attention suddenly riveted to the east. "Uh-oh."

Away in the distance, she heard the wail of a siren.

# CHAPTER 22

Henry's mother used to call them *white nights*—nights when you couldn't sleep, when your mind was as alert as if it were daytime and nothing could convince it to shut off and rest. To Henry, there was nothing white about sleeplessness, unless you lived in Alaska or somewhere in the far north, where the sun never set. No, sleeplessness was a black void where grief waited for you like a hungry monster, where if you closed your eyes even for an instant, it would jump you, chew you up, and swallow you.

As the years passed, he'd found ways to dodge the monster. Night school. Art classes. And finally, his own studio, where he could work for twenty-four hours straight if he wanted to, and when the gray light of day filled the windows, steal a few hours of rest out of the jaws of the night.

It would be a long time before the light touched the windows up there at the top of Uncle Jeremiah's barn.

Henry sat under the Coleman pole lamp, its light so merciless and glaring that this would qualify as a white night on that basis alone. Until he got county power in here, he was stuck with the Amish way of doing things. Luckily for him, no one had thought to borrow the old Honda ten-K generator that still squatted under the workbench, so there was a chance that he'd be able to use his kiln for Ginny Hochstetler's mugs. If the draw from the kiln blew out the poor old thing, he'd need to rent some time in someone else's kiln.

But first he needed clay.

He opened a box labeled TOOLS and dug around until he found his cutting wire—a piece of strong wire with a wood post knotted into either end. Then he knelt next to the carton of clay that Caleb the Curious had opened "by accident," and sliced off a chunk of it, much the way a hostess might slice a piece of cheese.

He began to wedge it, slapping it down on the clean workbench over and over, softening it, making all the microscopic platelets line up so that the mass would become smooth and malleable. When that one was soft, he wrapped it in plastic and cut another, and another, feeling his shoulders seize up and his muscles begin that bone-deep ache that told him just how long it had been since he'd performed the physical art of working clay.

Bang, bang, turn. Bang, bang, roll. Pound after pound, pounding after pounding.

He'd beaten the royal stuffing out of hundreds of pounds of clay after Allison's funeral, taking out his grief and rage on it, pounding the drivers of that diesel rig into his worktable time and time again. It was no wonder his pieces had received no praise. There had been so much anger beaten into and out of that clay that it was a wonder it could hold its shape at all, much less show the viewer any beauty.

Ginny's mugs would be different. One after another, he'd mold and shape them with the hand of a craftsman, and they'd march obediently out of his kiln and into her bed-and-breakfast, eager to please and sure to find approval. No one could laugh at a nice, plain mug. Instead, they'd be glad to use it, more concerned about the coffee or hot chocolate than what held it.

Yes, they'd see their hot drink. Not him. Not the artist who had made the vessel. They'd be visible, but he would not, and no one could write a review on an art blog and say that they were ubiquitous but not unique. Unique was a liability with mugs, so he'd focus on ubiquitous.

That was his goal, wasn't it? To sell his mugs, his plates, his bowls, into the homes and kitchens of folks in this township. That was it. Ubiquity had a bad rap. From where he stood, it looked pretty good. It looked like a living.

An hour passed, punctuated by the slap and thunk of clay, until far away, he heard a sound.

Sirens.

From the exhaustion in his arms and belly, it felt like three or four in the morning, which meant it might be safe to go to bed. Clearly, though, someone out there wasn't having quite so productive a night.

Henry wrapped the last lump of clay in plastic, ready for the next step in the process, and calculated he'd wedged well over a hundred pounds. The possibility of fifty mugs, give or take, sat there waiting to be made reality. He'd done some sketches and had a good idea of the shape he'd give them— a hint of a potbelly, like an old-fashioned tankard of ale, but with a wide mouth so a person could savor the scent of what they were drinking. A nice open loop on the handle, and—

The sirens were getting closer. Clearer.

Downright loud.

Because—good grief—one of them was coming up his lane.

Henry dropped the cutter on the workbench and ran outside, heedless of the bits and streaks of clay on his hands. A sheriff's black-and-white with its lights revolving, bouncing blue and red off the house and barn, ground to a halt in the yard, skidding and crunching on the gravel.

A man in khakis and boots climbed out, wearing a dark nylon jacket with a star embroidered on the chest. "Are you a member of Sadie Byler's family?" he said without any pretense at a greeting.

"I am. Henry Byler. She passed on and left this property to me." Sheriff's deputies didn't come screeching in with sirens going to talk about property lines. "Deputy, is something wrong? How can I help?"

The man's eyes raked him stem to stern, but if he saw anything weird in a fellow coming out of a barn fully dressed in the middle of the night, he said nothing. Probably thought he was pulling lambs or something.

"We had a report of a hoedown that devolved into a grass fire. We understand you're the owner of the field that backs onto the woods over there?" He hooked his thumb over his shoulder.

"Hoedown? Fire?" Plainspoken words. Countrymen's words.

Words that made no sense whatsoever.

"Are you the owner of the field, Mr. Byler?"

"If it belongs to this farm, I am."

"Would you come with me, please?"

Henry's jaw dropped. "Am I under arrest?"

The deputy looked at him as if that were the last thing on his mind. "Of course not, sir. But there's been some property damage and some injuries on your land, so I need you to come with me to survey the damage."

Wordlessly, Henry got into the cruiser. Had he fallen asleep after wedging all that clay? Was he having a nightmare?

But no, the cruiser had a metal cage between him and the deputy, and there was a shotgun in a rack under the dashboard. The radio emitted static and the occasional bullet-like sentence. Having never been in a police car in his life, how could he dream up details like that?

Half a mile down the road, an open gate loomed up on the left, the ground scored with the wheels of buggies and the wider, softer tracks of *Englisch* vehicles. The plot plan hadn't delineated fields; this one, he realized as the cruiser bumped and jounced over it, had been left fallow the previous year and was probably going to be left the same way this year, to give the ground a chance to rest and to allow any fungi in the soil to die off.

In the east, the sky had begun to lighten to gray. It was later than his body thought.

"Looks like they had the band up on that flatbed," the deputy said, pulling the car to a rocking stop. "Whose tractor is that?"

"I don't own a tractor—not with tires on it, at least." Henry climbed out. "This was an Amish farm."

If his cousins were going to use a tractor, they'd have had to remove the rubber from the tires and come up with some other means of moving it. Some farmers pulled their machinery with their plow horses. Some just made do and rolled around on the rims. But this tractor had fairly new tires on it, and it was hitched to the flatbed, so the whole rig had come from somewhere else.

The county fire engine sat some distance away, and as the light strengthened, he saw a huddle of Amish kids being given a talking-to by one of the firemen. So some of them had stuck around to take the consequences, had they? He was pretty certain he would have hightailed it into the woods, had he been in their shoes.

The deputy guided him over to where one of the firemen was walking the fringes of a scorch, scattered with cans of beer and soda. A couple of upended coolers lay in the mud. The fireman looked up at their approach. "You the landowner?"

"Yes."

"From what the kids say, they were having a hoedown and quote, there was a flash of light and then the grass caught fire, unquote. Probably the generator shorted out."

"They empty the coolers on the fire?" the deputy asked.

"Quick thinking." Henry looked over at the little group wilting under the lecture of the fireman, and blinked in surprise. "Hey. I know those kids."

"Great. Maybe you can help us with an ID."

Henry strode over to the rear of the engine, and Jake Byler met his gaze with an echo of his own surprise. Then shame and regret surged in and he hung his head. "Cousin Henry. Sorry about this. It was an accident."

The fireman looked between them. "You folks are related? Did you give permission for this event, sir?"

"No," Henry said, "but if I'd known about it, I would have." He studied the boy he had thought was Jake Byler, and realized now it must be his twin. "Joe, do your folks know you're here?"

The kid shook his head, and Henry looked beyond him to the boy and girl behind him.

"Simon? You okay? Who's this with you?"

"Priscilla. Her parents farm the place next to ours."

"We came together." The girl was pretty, even if her face and clothes were blackened with soot, her narrow glasses splashed and dirty. Her *Kapp* was gone and the bun at the back of her head had begun to unwind out of its coil. "I don't know what happened. I'm sorry."

"I don't think it was you getting a band together and hauling in a stage," he said, surveying the abandoned vehicle. "Any idea who did?"

They shook their heads, and the other Amish kids, whom he didn't recognize, stayed mute.

The deputy cleared his throat. "Are you going to press charges? Trespassing, for a start, and malicious mischief. Vandalism. Holding a public event without a permit."

With every word, the kids flinched. Okay, so he got that the guy was trying to make a point, but he was preaching to the wrong choir. The Amish kept themselves to themselves, and rarely met a policeman except under duress, like an accident.

"We got the fire out," Joe offered.

"There's been no real harm done," Henry said. "Deputy, I won't be pressing charges. The responsible parties seem to be long gone, though you might track down the owner of that tractor." He could see it had a plate, though he couldn't read it from here, in the poor light.

The cop leveled him a glance that said, *Don't tell me how to do my job*, as clearly as if he'd spoken aloud.

"Are you sure, Mr. Byler?"

Henry nodded. "I don't think there'll be too many more raves happening in this field." He glanced at the miserable bunch shivering in the cold dawn. "I'll take my friends here down to the house and give them something hot to drink, if you're done with them."

The deputy shrugged. "We're done if you are."

"Thanks for responding. It could have been a lot worse, all the way around."

"I'm glad it wasn't. Want a ride back to the house?"

Five kids and two adults weren't going to fit in that cruiser legally, and if he accepted a ride himself, Henry had a feeling the deputy would leave the kids standing on the road without a second thought.

"No, thanks. We'll walk across lots. It's about time I had a look at the lay of the land anyway."

He left the firemen to take photos and finish up, and gathered his bedraggled little flock for the walk back to the house. "I hope you know where you're going, because I don't."

"We can go in the buggy," Joe said. "I never unhitched."

So for the first time in a couple of decades, Henry found himself crammed into an Amish buggy, with a girl on the floor with her feet hanging out, and a kid clinging to the back like a monkey. When Joe pulled into the yard and everyone climbed out, Henry felt himself expand as if he'd been packed into a Volkswagen with a dozen college kids on a dare.

In the kitchen, he got down some cans of soup and dumped them into a saucepan. The girls—Priscilla and the other one whose name he hadn't caught—took out milk and coffee and bread and he realized with a shock that they were making breakfast without being told. French toast and soup. Well, he'd had stranger meals lately.

In less time than he would have believed, the kitchen had warmed up with the fresh wood Joe had put in the stove, and they were sitting down to eat.

His first company—stained, torn, and smelling of smoke. He allowed himself a smile. It was just so apropos.

"So, you guys are sure you're okay?" he asked. "I can run you in to the clinic if you need it. Simon, your leg looks a little sketchy."

The boy shrugged. "I'll just put B and W on it. That's what Mamm does for burns."

"What's B and W?"

"Burn and wound salve," Priscilla put in. "Everybody uses it. You should have some on hand, just in case. The Esches on Herschfield Road sell it at the store in their shed."

The Amish had a network of stores, from fabric to groceries to used equipment, completely independent of the usual chains in small towns. All you had to do was find them.

"I'll remember that. But what I'd really like to know is how you're going to explain this to your mother, Simon."

He hunched over his plate defensively. "I'll think of something."

"Like maybe the truth?" he suggested.

Joe shook his head. "I ain't saying anything at all. I'm just putting Merc away in the barn and going out to the field, and by the time I get back for supper, it won't matter. All Pop cares about is getting the oats planted anyhow."

"I'll just go to work," Simon muttered. "They probably have some B and W in the first aid kit."

"You can't work with your pant leg burned to the knee," Priscilla told him. "You have to go home first."

"Your Mamm will be so glad you're all right that she won't care about what time it is," the other girl offered.

"You don't know her," Simon muttered.

"I know parents," the girl said with what Henry thought was a lot of good sense.

"If you kids are done, I'll take you all home in the car. Except Joe."

To his surprise, every one of them shook their heads. "The only thing worse than not coming home is coming home in an *Englisch* car," said the third boy. "Thanks, Henry, but me and Silvia will just walk."

Silvia, that was her name. So many names. He was definitely going to start on that chart so he could keep track of
where everyone belonged.

"I'll see Pris home," Simon said.

"She came with me," Joe Byler objected. "I'll take her
home."

"She's right next door to us, and you're all the way over
here. You take Silvia and Aaron."

Before fisticuffs broke out in his kitchen over the girl, who
was so red-faced that it was a wonder he didn't have to put her
out with a cooler of ice, Henry spoke up. "I will drive Simon
and Priscilla around to their folks. If I have to drop you at the
end of your driveway, I will, but I expect you to be truthful
with your parents about where you've been."

"Maybe he's right," Priscilla said softly. "Maybe Dat will
think working at the Hex Barn isn't so bad after this."

"He'll ground you for a year, more like," Silvia said with
more wisdom.

In another ten minutes, the girls had his dishes done.
When they finished, Joe went with Silvia and the other boy,
the rattletrap of a buggy disappearing into a dip in the road
before Henry could say thank you.

He knew Simon could just have followed his little brother's
track up the hill and got home in a few minutes. But he had
to admire the kid for going with Priscilla. He let them out of
the car in the Mast yard, in front of the house, where already
he could see heads bobbing in the windows.

"Thanks, you guys, for helping to put out the fire. I
owe you."

Priscilla shook her head. "You can't owe us for getting into
trouble. Thanks for the ride. You better go. Here comes Dat."

He couldn't just leave these two ragged kids smelling of

smoke on their own. He respected their willingness to stand up and take the heat—unlike the rest of the kids who had congregated in his field and left them to take the consequences they all should have borne together. He wasn't going to head off up the lane and leave them here. He got out of the car and leaned against the hood as a big Amish man came down the steps and took in the scene in one incredulous glance—a glance in which fear and love were equally mixed.

Henry felt himself relax.

Where there was love, anger wouldn't survive long. And neither would fear.

# CHAPTER 23

The Bylers' kitchen table was much bigger than her own, Sarah reflected, but then again, if she had five children and in-laws with big families and was hosting Christmas dinner, she'd want one this big, too. They'd all been invited over for supper—she and Simon and Caleb, Henry Byler, and the Masts—to talk over the events of the night before.

As they settled over huge, puffy pieces of lemon meringue pie, Sarah could see the *Youngie* exchanging anxious glances, as though the dinner conversation up until now had been an agonizing exercise in suspense. She knew how they felt. She hadn't yet got over the shock of hearing the car tires crunching to a stop in the yard—and knowing in her bones that it was the police, there to tell her she'd lost Simon, too.

Fortunately, her bones had been wrong. For the most part.

"So," Paul Byler said at last after a particularly speaking glance from Barbara, "why don't you tell us about what happened in Henry's fallow field last night."

Joe stopped chewing. Simon's ears reddened. Priscilla stared at her untouched pie as if the answer were written in the meringue.

Finally, Henry spoke up. "It seems there was a hoedown, with the band playing up on a flatbed trailer. From what the firemen tell me, the generator's exhaust manifold failed and a spark caught the grass. These kids here put it out with ice and water from the drink coolers."

"Is that true?" Paul asked his son.

"*Ja*," Joe said. "Me and Simon were trying to beat it out with our coats but it wasn't working. It was Pris thought of the ice."

The eyebrows of Priscilla's younger sister Katie rose in admiration.

Henry said, "The deputy came by this afternoon to tell me that the tractor and trailer belong to Hiram Fisher, who has a place on the other side of Willow Creek. He hadn't reported it stolen and didn't even know the rig was missing."

Isaiah Mast said, "Does he have so much equipment, then?"

"Turns out his boy is in this band. So that solves that mystery. But since no real damage was done, and they came and got their tractor just before I left to come here, I let the matter rest with an apology."

Paul shifted in his chair and pushed his pie away. "So everything ends happily for everyone, does it? Our children go to a hoedown without our knowledge, a tractor is stolen, a field catches fire, and people get burned, and we let the matter rest?"

"I would not say that," Isaiah Mast told him. "While Henry has clearly not forgotten the teachings of his youth in his willingness not to take the vengeful course, there still must be consequences. Priscilla clearly has too much time on her hands. She will be starting work as a *Maud*, cleaning bedrooms and bathrooms at the Rose Arbor Inn here in town."

Priscilla looked up with a start.

"When she comes home, she will do everything she used to

do to help her mother in the home and garden, and by the time she goes to bed, she'll have no energy to run around at night getting into trouble."

Throughout this sentence, Priscilla's face had gone paler and paler until finally she looked almost green. "But Dat—"

"I have already spoken with Ginny Hochstetler at the motel. My cousin's daughter Karen worked there, and Ginny has been looking for reliable help since she got married in February. You start on Monday."

"But I want to work at the Hex B—"

"No child of mine will work in that place, which I thought I already made very clear."

"I work in that place," Simon said, so quietly that it took Sarah a few seconds to realize who had spoken.

"It's nothing to be proud of," she reminded her son. If her pocketbook hadn't been starving to death for want of something to put in it, she would never have agreed to his working there. But beggars couldn't be choosers, and Simon had gone out and got the job all on his own.

*And it's not in Colorado. Count your blessings.*

"It's nothing to despise, either," he said steadily, in a tone that gave information but not offense. "They wanted me up front in the sales room, but the money's better in the back, so I suggested Priscilla. They hired her on the spot."

"They could not have hired her, because I did not sign the papers," Isaiah told him. "She will go to the Rose Arbor, which at least doesn't pretend to be Amish. She can make an honest day's wages there."

"We can spend the Hex Barn's money as easily as the Inn's." Simon pushed away his empty pie plate.

If he'd been within reach, Sarah would have given him a nudge with her foot under the table. "We didn't come together to talk about jobs. We're meeting with Henry to see what you three can do to make this up to him."

"Us!" Joe said. "We were the ones who put out the fire, not the ones who started it."

"They don't owe me anything, Sarah," Henry said, backing them up. "I might not be a member of the church, but even I can see that punishing them for being there misses the point. If I could find the kids who organized it and had the bright idea to hold the shindig in my field, that would be different. But coming down hard on these kids for doing me a good turn doesn't sit well with me."

"Being deceived about my daughter's whereabouts doesn't sit well with me," Isaiah said, and Priscilla seemed to shrink in her chair. "After we talked and I thought the matter was settled, she still went out and your boys met her on the road." His gaze moved from Sarah to Barbara. "They deceived you just as thoroughly, and deception has its consequences."

Now it was Paul's turn to frown. "*Ja*, they did, but that is what young men do when they're running around. They act stupid and get into scrapes. I remember a thing or two about you in those years, Isaiah Mast."

"You and Timothy Yost," Barbara said, and then covered her mouth with her hand, as if too many words had escaped.

"Who?" Sarah couldn't remember ever hearing that name before. "Yost? Is he related to Oran and Adah?"

Now it was Isaiah's turn to redden, and to Sarah's surprise, he got up from the table and put his hand on his wife's shoulder. She rose, too, as he said, "I thank you for a good dinner, Barbara, and we'll see you on Sunday. Priscilla, go and get your coat and your mother's, and see to the young ones."

"But—"

"Now, Priscilla. I believe our conversation here is concluded. Good night."

And before Sarah could do much more than push back her chair, the Masts were shaking hands all around and streaming out into the yard to their buggy. Simon and Joe picked the same moment to vanish into the dark, leaving Sarah, Caleb, and Henry in the kitchen with Barbara as she gave the two-year-old to her eldest daughter and bade her take him up to bed.

"What just happened?" Sarah said to no one in particular.

"It was stupid of me." Barbara shook her head at herself. "Isaiah Mast is making a mountain out of a molehill, and I was just so frustrated with him that it slipped out."

"What slipped out?"

"Is Timothy Yost the one who was shunned?" Caleb wanted to know.

Sarah stared at him. "Caleb Yoder, what on earth..."

"We do not gossip about such things in this house." Paul Byler came in from seeing his guests off. "Sarah, your horse is ready if you have everything."

*I have nothing*, she felt like replying. Just the feeling that she had missed something important. If only she knew what.

"*Denki*, Paul. The dinner was *gut*, Barbara. You must come to us next time. My peas are up, so we'll have fresh vegetables from the garden soon."

And then at last she and Caleb were climbing into their buggy and setting Dulcie's nose for home.

❁

Dear sister Sarah,

With my wife's encouragement I have been taking your tea (or maybe I should say Ruth's tea). I am sorry to say that it does not seem to be doing any good. I'm enclosing the rest in case someone else can use it.

Oran Yost

"Well, if that doesn't ice the cake." Sarah dropped Oran's letter on the table and Corinne picked it up, scanned it, and handed it to Amanda.

"No one ever said Oran Yost was an easy man to get on with," Corinne said, taking Sarah's coffee cup and getting up to refill it. "And he's not the first man who didn't have the patience for being doctored."

"Ruth warned me," Sarah said, "but it still hurts—like offering someone a hand to help and having it slapped away."

"I've seen many a toddler do it," Amanda put in. "I bet Oran Yost was a trial to his mother."

Sarah couldn't imagine him as a toddler no matter how much she tried to stretch her mind around it. But it was as good an opening as any to the topic that had been uppermost in her mind since Thursday night.

"Speaking of mothers and sons, a strange thing happened when we were over at Paul Byler's."

"How did that go?" The cups filled, Corinne put the coffee back on the stove and sat, reaching for another slice of orange cake. "People are pretty surprised about Henry Byler. I have a hard time believing that a man who's practically a recluse could be hosting wild parties on his land."

By now, of course, the entire settlement knew about the fire. But clearly the details had gotten a bit muddled in transit.

"He didn't host it. At least, that he knew about. The *Youngie* were looking for a place to have a party, and that field was close to the road, had a screen of woods and a gate with no chain, and was handy. That's all they needed to pull right in. I'm just glad it didn't get more serious. But that wasn't the strangeness I meant."

She had their attention now.

"The men were talking about the scrapes they'd gotten into, and how with the *Youngie* there's nothing really new under the sun, and Barbara said something about what Isaiah Mast and Timothy Yost had done."

Amanda looked puzzled. "That doesn't sound very strange."

"The strange part was that the moment that name came out of Barbara's mouth, Isaiah Mast decided it was time to go home, and in less than a minute the whole family was out the door."

"You're right." Amanda nodded thoughtfully. "That is strange. Mamm, who's Timothy Yost?"

Corinne sighed. "He was Oran and Adah's son, and it would hurt Adah terribly if she knew we were talking about them."

Oran had a horror of people getting into his business. Was this the reason? "Are both of them so private because of something to do with Timothy? Did he die under unusual circumstances—no, wait. Caleb thinks he was shunned— the only person I've heard of in our district that has been. Though of course a person can be shunned and then taken by the Lord."

"Are you going to let me tell this story—or would you rather play the guessing game and see how long it takes?" Corinne's gentle smile made Sarah close her mouth. Corinne had the sweetest way of making you see where you'd gone wrong...and not holding it against you in the least.

Not for the first time, she wished that her mother and her mother-in-law could have met. Sarah was sure that the two of them would have become fast friends. It was God's will that they hadn't, of course, but she still thanked Him daily that He had brought her into this family.

She could have folks like the Yosts for in-laws, for instance. God indeed was good, and His mercy endured forever.

"I suppose it's twenty-five or thirty years ago now," Corinne mused, "but for some of us—Isaiah Mast, I'm thinking—it could have happened just last week." She glanced at Sarah, and then her gaze lingered on Amanda. "Are you sure you want to hear this? I would hate for you to think of certain of your brothers and sisters in Christ any differently because I opened a book that should have stayed closed."

Amanda's face sobered, and some of the light went out of it. "Is that likely?"

"I'm telling Sarah because she's attempting to help a patient. If you would rather not hear, then maybe you might work on the quilt a little while in the other room."

Amanda nodded, and took her coffee with her. For a moment, Sarah was tempted to follow her sister-in-law out. What ugly can of worms was she about to open, if Corinne could encourage someone *not* to listen?

Her mother-in-law sighed. "She's a wise old soul in a young woman's body. I'm looking forward to seeing what kind of man God has in mind for her."

Sarah hoped the *gut Gott* would get around to that sooner

rather than later. Amanda was twenty-four, and eligible young men were scarce on the ground in Willow Creek. But there was no hurrying the God of Heaven. He would reveal His will to Amanda in His own time, as He had done with Sarah—and that would be the very best time of all.

Corinne took up the story again. "I was a young mother when all this happened. Michael was weaned and toddling around the house, and Jason not even a twinkle in his father's eye. It was a busy time, but not so busy that I didn't see what was happening between Isaiah Mast and Timothy Yost...and Ruthanne Gingrich. She was the prettiest young woman you ever saw—tall and slender, with skin like porcelain china and dark hair that reached her knees when it was down. The boys were crazy for her, but by the end of that summer, it boiled down to Isaiah and Timothy. She'd go to singing with one and come home with the other, and didn't seem to care that people said she was fast. Those two boys didn't care, either— all they wanted was whatever she would give them, even if it was only five minutes and a smile."

"Does her family still live here?"

"They never lived here—not her parents anyway. She was working in Willow Creek and boarding with Sadie and Jeremiah. So I suppose with no mother to guide her, and Sadie busy with her own family, it wasn't surprising."

"What wasn't?" Sarah's stomach began to churn, never mind the fact that she didn't even know these people.

"Isaiah joined church the following spring, and everyone thought that Ruthanne would, too, and by fall we'd be hearing them published in church. But everyone was wrong. She just went on doing what she was doing, even when Isaiah asked her to marry him."

"Was she baptized?"

"She went to one or two classes, as did Timothy, but then they started missing, and our bishop—not Dan Troyer, it was before his time—told them they would have to wait until the next series began. Then the next thing you know, Ruthanne began attending classes like they were going to save her life, and she was baptized that spring along with Isaiah and several others."

Sarah sat back in her chair. "God must have changed her heart, then."

"I'm sure He did—and the fact that she began gaining weight helped speed that along."

"Gaining—" Sarah stopped. "Oh."

"Needless to say, she had to make a full confession before the church before the baby came, which she did. And then we all waited to see what Timothy Yost would do."

"It was his."

"So she said." Corinne sighed and watched her coffee cool.

"Well, what did he do?"

"He refused to join church—and refused to marry her. He said he couldn't be sure it wasn't Isaiah's, and he wasn't even sure he was cut out to be Amish. At this point she was about eight months along."

"What did Isaiah do?"

"I think he honestly loved her, but it takes a certain kind of man to go into marriage knowing he's going to have to raise another man's child—another man he might suspect already holds the woman's heart."

"Oh, how sad." Clearly, Isaiah had not chosen this path, because it was not Ruthanne living next door on the Mast farm.

"Well, Ruthanne was distraught, and Isaiah told her he would have to pray on the matter—until he received an answer, he could not make a decision. But Ruthanne took the choice out of his hands. No one knows for sure, but it appears she had a final meeting with Timothy, and..."

Corinne's lips trembled, and she couldn't seem to finish. Sarah found herself holding her breath.

"And the next morning, they couldn't find her anywhere. It wasn't until that afternoon that some boys who had gone fishing found her poor body under the weir, churning around and around in the water."

Sarah's breath rushed out of her lungs, and she pressed her fingers to her mouth in an echo of Barbara's action a few nights before. "She did it—on purpose—but the baby—?"

Tears trembled on Corinne's lashes as she shook her head. "They tried to save it, but it was already too late. Maybe she went walking after talking to Timothy, and missed her footing on the top of the weir. It was a shortcut back then, before the county fenced it off. Maybe she was so distraught she no longer cared about the sixth commandment. All anyone knew was that same day, Oran Yost disowned his son and sent him out of his house."

"He was shunned?"

"No, no. He had never been baptized, remember? Only Isaiah and Ruthanne were. But Oran was set against him in punishment, and if it was possible for a single person to shun another, he did it."

"But—but—how could he know for certain that Timothy had had anything to do with it?"

"From what I understand, he said that a man can be the cause of death without laying a finger on another. Timothy made a few attempts to hire on with men in the district for board and room, but his father made it impossible for him to stay long. It took four or five months for Timothy to get worn down and finally leave town. No one has seen him since, and after all these years, no one has a reason or a desire to speak his name. Certainly not in the Yosts' hearing."

Sarah felt a little winded. Thirty years to live with such knowledge. After the righteous wrath faded, what would be left? Doubt, perhaps, that you had been right in sending away your only son—that you hadn't believed him when he might have been telling the truth. Regret that you didn't know what kind of man he had become—and if he had turned out bad, wondering if you could have prevented it.

And Adah, too—how had she felt? Was it any wonder that, as she said, there was a dark cloud pressing on her that she couldn't seem to shake? Even if she had obeyed her husband and stood by him to watch her son walk out the door, what would it have done to her heart?

Sarah was all too familiar with the dark clouds of grief. But it was one thing to grieve the loss of someone, knowing that God had taken him to Himself and that he was in Heaven, rejoicing in the presence and the love of his Savior. It would be another thing completely to know that the husband you sat across from at breakfast every day had cast out the boy you both loved. A woman would be worried, fearful for his soul, maybe even in despair of the husband who had done this...and there would be no acceptable outlet for those feelings. She could never speak them aloud. They would turn inward, never to be released.

Oran had sought to punish his son for setting Ruthanne on her dreadful path. But it seemed to Sarah that this case went further than that.

After all this time, could Oran still be punishing himself?

# CHAPTER 24

Early the next morning, Sarah found that even though she had prayed for peace, a release from the knowledge that she had asked for about Oran and his family was more difficult to come by.

In fact, she was having a hard time finding peace at all.

Simon had volunteered to take double shifts at the Hex Barn—out front in the store from ten until two, and then back in the loading dock from two until six. He had worked an eight-hour shift at the buggy shop, too, but somehow this new schedule seemed longer and the end result was that she never knew whether he'd be home for dinner or not.

On this bright morning, it seemed that April was going to go out like a lamb. Sarah took her gloves and trowel out to the garden, determined to plant and pull weeds and breathe and let her fingers sink into the soil. And the only way you could do that comfortably was to kneel.

Was it part of God's plan that when you worked in the garden, you usually found yourself in a position to pray?

*Father, thank You for giving us soil and plants and a reminder that Your grace is sufficient for us. Help me to know what to do for poor Oran and Adah, because it's clear that Your sheep are suffering. You have put me on this path to help the members of the flock, and I need Your guidance now. Breathe Your spirit on me, Lord, as I work among the herbs and vegetables. Help me to grow the way You help these plants to grow.*

Prayer took discipline to quiet the voices in her head, the demands of self, and practice *Uffgeva*, that giving up of one-self to God. When Sarah opened her eyes again, she was grateful to feel an easing of her spirit, as though God had given her a promise. Her chest felt a little less tight as she bent with her plastic tray of tomato seedlings and got to work.

Now that the last frost was behind them, it was safe to plant the more delicate things, like the tomatoes, and corn, summer squash, and cucumbers. Her strawberries were up and getting ready to bloom, and all around the edges of her crazy quilt garden, the calendula were pushing vigorously toward the sun. Soon the marigold petals would open and all their little sunny faces would reflect that larger light, each one faithful in giving her a lesson that such was her place, too—to reflect the light of Heaven to others.

Which brought her back to Oran and Adah. With this new knowledge, uncomfortable as it made her, she had a choice to make. Sarah lifted the tomato seedlings and planted each one carefully, thinking her way through this puzzle. She could try again to treat the couple's symptoms on a purely physical level, trying to get them to drink their tea and probably frustrating both them and herself when they found reasons not to do it. Or she could go straight to the heart of the matter and talk with them about what seemed to be the real problem.

A breeze made her *Kapp* strings brush the side of her neck, and she shivered. She could see the reaction in the Yost kitchen when she brought *that* subject up. She'd probably find herself out on the back porch with her coffee cup still in one hand.

There must be some other way. If Oran had a horror of people knowing about his stomach troubles, maybe it stemmed from his horror of people knowing any more than they already thought they did about his family troubles. Any reminder that something had gone badly wrong all those years ago might bring the subject back to people's minds, and he would not be able to bear it.

Fine, then. There must be another way—another direction by which to approach this and come in the back door of the barn, as it were. She just needed to think what it might be.

Up on the road at the top of the bank, she heard a burst of laughter as a couple of girls walked past, heading toward Willow Creek. Something twittered repeatedly and a girl's voice said, "*Ja?* Hello?"

Many of the *Youngie* had cell phones, even though Bishop Troyer frowned on it, as did most of the parents. Probably Simon had one, too, though she'd never caught him talking into it. There had to be some way for all the kids to have known about the hoedown, and Sarah suspected cell phones were behind it.

What if she tried to find Timothy Yost? But if she did and she succeeded, what would she do with him? Bring him home and engineer a reunion and hope that father and son would forgive each other? Who on earth did she think she was— God? For surely that was His place, working in lives in His time, bringing people together and holding them apart according to His will.

She wanted to help Oran and Adah. But would this be help, or would it simply be interference? Would the cure she undertook so clumsily be more painful than the original wound?

But at the same time, clumsy or not, it seemed awfully

clear to her that if nothing was done, the couple's symptoms might turn into something more serious. Oran could develop cancer of the stomach. It had happened before, if her conversations with Ruth could be believed. Adah's depression could progress to the point where she might struggle with the temptation to harm herself.

No, it was not her place to bring Timothy home. It was the Lord's. But surely it wouldn't hurt to at least know where he was? Maybe even to let him know that his parents weren't well? Wouldn't any son want to know that, even if he were estranged from them? Then, if he chose not to respond, that would be on his own head, and she would have done everything her conscience and her sense of responsibility had urged her to do.

She didn't know how one went about finding someone who had disappeared into the *Englisch* world as completely as had Timothy Yost. But she knew someone who might.

When you wanted to find some dill seed, you went to a dill plant. And when you wanted to find an *Englisch* man, you went to another *Englisch* man.

Sarah felt in her pocket for the mini-flashlight that usually sat on the kitchen windowsill for emergencies. The silvery twilight was fading after the sunset, but there was still enough light to see by as she followed the trail Caleb had made up the hill and over its shoulder to the back of Henry Byler's barn. It was the first time she had gone there without her boy, and she hoped it would be worth the firm words she'd had to use to keep Caleb from coming with her. In the end, it was only her teaching him that when it came to a patient, she was not going to be able to share details with him, and he was not to ask, that made him stay behind.

She wasn't sure that her boy was convinced any case was important enough to miss out on visiting Henry, though.

Holding up the *Schnitz* pie like an offering, she knocked on the kitchen door. Through the window, she could see that a lamp stood burning on the kitchen table, but she could feel no vibration in the boards of the porch that told her someone was coming to the door. She pushed it open just wide enough to put her head in.

"Hallo? Henry, are you here? It's Sarah Yoder."

The kerosene lamp sputtered in the silence.

Had he gone for a walk? She closed the door and went down the steps, undecided whether to call out or give it up and walk home.

And then she saw that the lights were on in the front part of the barn, where Sadie had kept her buggy. Quickly, she retraced her steps and put the pie on the dining table, then pulled her felted-wool jacket around her and headed back along the way she'd come, detouring up the gravel ramp to the barn doors, which stood pulled open a couple of feet.

And there he was, hunched over an apparatus that consisted of an arrangement of pulleys and a big, heavy wheel. A cord ran across the planks of the floor, which had been swept and even scrubbed clean—a job that made her realize exactly why Caleb had been able to give her twenty dollars the previous Saturday. The cord led to a generator that was grumbling and humming like an enormous bee, drowning out her steps as she crossed the floor.

"Henry?"

He jumped, and the cylinder of wet clay around which his

entire body had been focused wobbled, flared under his hand, and slumped, defeated, to the surface of the wheel.

"Oh, dear. I'm so sorry. Is it supposed to look like that?" The thing looked dead—like a flower that had wilted.

Henry stretched out his back and shoulders and flapped his hands as if they pained him, then took a piece of wire, cut the clay from the surface of the wheel, and carried it, dripping with chalky liquid, over to a bench above which several pot-bellied cylinders seemed to be drying on a clean board.

"It's all right. It had a bubble in it anyway, which kept throwing it off center. I thought I could save it, but maybe it's just as well that I start over."

"Can you do that?"

He began to roll the flared, bent cylinder back into a ball, hitting it on the bench and pressing it with both hands. "Oh, sure. Clay is pretty forgiving, but one bubble will mess up the whole thing, especially when the walls of the vessel are thin."

"What are you making?"

"Mugs for the Rose Arbor Inn."

"Ah." She knew Ginny Hochstetler by sight—which wasn't difficult, since she was the only black woman in Willow Creek—but had never really spoken to her other than to say hello in the market or smile as they passed on the sidewalk. And now she was Priscilla's boss. "My sister-in-law told me about the crate of smashed mugs."

"Ginny's hired me to make some to replace them." He indicated the row of pale shapes on the board. "These are almost ready to have their handles put on. They dry slowly because the air is pretty damp, but that's a good thing. It means they won't crack."

"They look very nice."

"Here's a finished one. I experimented a little with the glaze to get the color she wanted. I hope she likes it."

"I'm sure she will." The gray-blue mug sat cool and glossy in her hand, its lines clean and the curved shape pleasing—she could well imagine someone taking a sip of coffee from such a mug and enjoying what they held in their hands as much as what they held in their mouth.

*What could he have done with your ginger jars? You could have had the pleasure of seeing what he could make for you.*

No, she'd made her decision, and besides, she couldn't give people their teas and tinctures in ginger jars, could she? She needed plastic baggies and medicine bottles with child-proof lids for that. The ginger jar idea had been for the tourists, but she had no idea yet which side of her work would come uppermost. She might not have time to collect the herbs for the tourists as she had done before.

Henry seemed to notice the silence that had fallen as she came back to herself.

"What can I—"

"I left a—"

Smiling, feeling a little foolish, she motioned for him to go ahead.

"I just wondered what I could do for you," he said. "Do you need the car?"

"What?" She shook her head. "No, no. I left a pie on your kitchen table. *Schnitz.* I hope you like it."

"I do, as it happens. One of my best memories from the home place was Mamm's *Schnitz* pie. But..." He eyed her, puzzled. "What did I do to deserve that?"

"It—nothing. Well, nothing yet. I mean, I hope that you might do something. For me." Oh goodness, she sounded like a fifteen-year-old talking to a boy for the first time. Worse, a blush was rising in her face and she could do absolutely nothing about it.

"Did you change your mind about the ginger jars? Because I'm sorry to say that this commission will take pretty much all the clay I have on hand."

"No, it's nothing to do with that. I—I wondered, do you have the Internet?"

It was a good thing he wasn't still holding the poor wilted mug, because he would surely have dropped it.

"The...Internet?" he said carefully. "No, not here. You need electricity to make a modem work, which is what would make Wi-Fi work. To say nothing of charging up my laptop in the first place."

"I don't know what all that means, I'm sorry. So you could not look something up for me?"

"Not here. I could go to the library and use the public computer. Wiring this place is on my list as soon as I get some money coming in, and Wi-Fi will be right behind it."

He really meant to stay *Englisch*, then. The still, small voice of the Spirit was not strong enough to win out over the song of the world.

He was still gazing at her like a lock for which he didn't have the key. "What do you need looked up?"

"It's to do with a case. One of my—my patients. I want to find someone."

"Oh? Who?"

She'd have to give him the name when they were at the library, so she supposed there was no use in trying to keep it confidential now. Besides, he'd already heard it. "Timothy Yost. Oran and Adah's boy."

"Ah." He turned and splashed some water on the wheel, cleaning its surface, and then turned off the generator. The silence fell as suddenly as a shout in the old barn. "Come into the kitchen and let's have some of that pie. You can bring that mug. I'll make some coffee and you can test-drive it for me while we talk."

So much for the way she thought this would go—ask a question, get an answer, be on her way. Talking alone in his kitchen as night fell and the kerosene lamp made shadows in the corners, enclosing them in a glow of intimacy, was not what she had expected at all.

Half of her wanted to run away down the path and take refuge in her own house. But the other half—the half that concerned itself for her patients—made her follow him out of the barn.

# CHAPTER 25

Henry slid a glance toward Sarah in the passenger seat as she shifted under the seat belt, tugging at it as if it interfered with her breathing. "Too tight?"

"Hm? No. I'm just fidgety. I still don't know if I'm doing the right thing."

"We can turn around."

"I've dragged you away from your work. The least I can do is go through with it. Besides, I might learn something—more than where Timothy Yost is now, I mean."

He slowed for the stop sign at the county highway and waited for a number of buggies to pass, then a bread truck trying to get by them. A busy Monday morning in Willow Creek, Pennsylvania, and what was he doing?

Cyber-stalking a stranger for an Amish woman.

Right. There was one for the Twitter feed.

Henry still wasn't sure why he'd agreed to this. When she'd told him the story Friday night over a piece of pie so good his eyes had practically rolled up in his head, he couldn't quite believe her guts. Henry had seen himself the odd behavior of Isaiah Mast, to say nothing of Oran's hunched-over walk and irascible temper. When Sarah had told him what she suspected, that Yost's guilt and sorrow were making him sick, he'd realized that an inexperienced herbalist with just enough knowledge to be dangerous might actually be onto something. In the lamplight, with her eyes shining as she explained the situation to him, it had made sense.

So did gazing into those eyes and wondering how they would look across from him in the morning, over breakfast—a thought that he had slapped out of his mind the way he'd swat a fly.

Now, in the prosaic light of a Monday morning, he was having second thoughts about more than just her eyes. And clearly she was, too.

The closest library in the township was in Whinburg, which sent out the bookmobiles to various towns, including Willow Creek. But bookmobiles didn't have public computers on them. Whinburg meant planning a day's trip for a buggy, but in his car it was only a matter of minutes before they were pulling into the postage stamp–sized parking lot.

The library had just opened, so the public computers weren't yet occupied by retired folks checking their Facebook news feeds and the price of gold. He pulled up a second wooden chair for Sarah, and settled in front of the screen.

"I'll check Facebook first. If he's there, it might give us a town to start with."

There were four Timothy Yosts. What were the odds?

"I guess I should be grateful his name isn't something common, like Samuel Yoder. Do you know what he looks like?"

Sarah shook her head, gazing anxiously at the list of possibilities. "He's in his mid-fifties, though, I would think, if he was running around when my husband was a toddler."

Henry felt a jolt in his solar plexus at the mention of her husband, as if she were still married and the man might object to this outing with his wife. Then he shook his head at himself. Guilt was a habit. And habits could be broken with as much determination as thoughts could be swatted away.

"This one looks about right." He pointed to the picture associated with the third listing. "What do you think?"

"He could be. But he doesn't really look like either Oran or Adah."

"He could be a throwback, and look like a grandparent. He lives in Philly—that's not so far away, but it's an easy place to get lost in if that's what a man wanted."

"So lost that we couldn't find him?"

"Let's try something else." Google Images yielded a host of pictures, a few of which even looked like Timothy Yost number three. "This must be from a photo studio." Henry pointed at a family portrait. "Looks like this was taken a while ago, when the kids were young." Maybe ten years before. The studio had used it for advertising, if the copy across the bottom was any indication.

Sarah was staring at the children, so Henry clicked on the image to make it larger. "Look at his little girl," she said, pointing. "Don't those look like Adah's eyebrows? See how they go up, like birds' wings? The boy has them, too."

"Timothy doesn't."

"Maybe it's like you said. Things skip a generation."

Good enough for him. "All right. Let's assume this is our Timothy, and dig a little deeper." He searched on Timothy's name and the suburb where the photography studio was located, and up popped a listing from a charity fund-raising committee of some kind that included a phone number. He ran it through 411.com and bingo.

"Here's his address. Want to write it down?" After that, it was easy to find the names of his wife and children, what schools they'd graduated from, how much their house was worth, when it had been built, and what it looked like from the sidewalk.

Sarah sat back. "My goodness. The *Englisch* certainly like to tell each other all about themselves."

"Oh, I doubt he did it voluntarily. This is public information."

"There is no such information about me."

"I bet there is. What's your street address?"

She frowned at the results and got up abruptly. "Make it go away."

He closed the browser, shut down the computer, and yielded the chair to the silver-haired guy in the golf shirt loitering behind the paperback carousel. "So now what? You're going to write to him?"

"If that's the man we want, then Oran and Adah have grandchildren they don't even know—and who don't know them," she said as he followed her out the glass doors and into the soft morning. "I wish I knew what the Lord wanted me to do."

Henry wasn't going to touch that one. Bringing the Lord into the equation always complicated it, filling it with the variables of other people's needs and desires and messy moral questions about one's own motives.

He leaned on the fender of his car and crossed his arms. "Don't you think that if Timothy had wanted to reconcile with his father and introduce him to his grandkids, he would have done it by now?"

"Would that take more courage than one man has?" she asked in return. "Knowing Oran Yost, that might be so. On the other hand, if I were estranged from Simon and someone wrote to tell me that he was ill, ancient history might not matter so much. I would forget it all in my rush to go to him."

"I believe you would," he agreed. He opened the door for her and went around the hood to slide under the steering wheel. "I guess you need to decide whether—as you put it on Saturday—sticking your nose into someone else's business serves the truth or will just cause more offense."

She sighed, and her shoulders sagged. The sunlight coming in the passenger window touched the side of her face, turning her *Kapp* transparent and gilding her downcast lashes. When she looked up at him, the light made her gray eyes luminous.

"You sound exactly like my own thoughts." When she looked away to take in the sights of downtown Whinburg as they drove past, he felt a pang of disappointment, as though despite his attempts to avoid it, someone had taken a picture he wanted to study and turned it to face the wall.

What he needed to be wary of here was the fact that if he sounded exactly like her own thoughts, it meant he was thinking like an Amish person again.

"That's your errand taken care of," he said. "Mind if we stop by the Rose Arbor Inn on the way back? I want to show these mug samples to Ginny Hochstetler."

She straightened. "Of course. It's your car and you're doing me a favor. Run as many errands as you need to."

Ginny's pleasure at his coffee mugs was a balm to his lacerated self-confidence. If the Denver art critics had been even a little like this, how different might his life have been? If Allison had waited five minutes to get into her car . . . if he'd gone to California instead of coming out here to Sadie's farm . . .

*If.* He could just imagine what Sarah would have to say on the subject of *if* . . . and that was a fine reason to enjoy what Ginny had to say instead.

"I don't know if I can choose a style—they're all so nice."

She turned the potbellied one in her hand. "How could you resist anything served in this?"

"I liked that one best, too," Sarah said from where she stood near the door, holding her handbag by its strap in front of her.

Before Ginny could get the wrong idea, Henry put in, "I was helping Sarah out on a project this morning, so I asked her opinion, too. I figured I should do my market research while I could, if I had a built-in focus group."

"Can't have enough." Ginny turned the mug on her palm. "Can you do a split order? Half of this and half of the straight ones that have the painting on the side?"

Sarah's gaze sharpened on the second style of mug. "Is that a branch of rosemary?"

"No, it's a wild rose. I thought I'd do a line of roses to go with the 'rose arbor' theme."

"What a mind you've got." Ginny's eyes held such twinkling delight he thought she just might hug him. "What about we combine the two ideas? Instead of the stamp with the inn's name on the side, can we put it on the bottom, and have the roses be the main focus?"

"It'll take me longer to make each one."

"That's okay. I just have to figure out how to keep people from breaking them. They're too pretty to waste."

"Have them buy them when they come," Sarah suggested. "It could be included in the room rate. They'd get a discount if they didn't want one, but if they did, people tend to be more careful about things they've paid for."

"Now we're talking," Ginny said slowly, nodding at her in appreciation. "It would be a perk—you get your own mug to use while you're here, and you can take it away with you as a souvenir of your stay."

"You'll be washing the various people's mugs a lot," Henry put in.

"I wash dishes anyway. But my new chambermaid started today, so I'll have someone to take that over. Thanks, you guys."

He didn't want Ginny bracketing him with Sarah in her mind, even in the most casual of expressions. "Great—I'll get started on the combined style right away. I can do about thirty a week, give or take. And if it's all right with you, maybe we might celebrate sometime, say in the next couple of days?"

"I'd like that." He could really get used to that twinkle and that smile. "Give me a call."

His own smile was a little rusty from disuse, but she didn't seem to have a problem with it. And when he turned to go, he found that Sarah had already slipped out the door and was waiting next to the car, gazing at the creek as if it weren't the very same one that wound between his place and hers.

"Ready to go?"

"*Ja*, but I can wait if you'd rather spend more time here."

"Ginny's busy, and now I'm going to be, too." He thumbed the door release on the key fob. "Door's open."

As he pulled out of the small gravel lot, he was pleased that not only did Ginny like his ideas—*See? It is possible to create something unique, ubiquitous, and useful, all at once*—but she seemed to like him, as well. If every day turned out to be as good as this one, he might just—

"So, it seems you're interested in Ginny Hochstetler."

He turned from his contemplation of one woman to answer the other. "She's a nice woman."

"She is."

"Then why do you sound like my oldest sister?"

This time, instead of looking out the window, she fiddled with the flap on her purse. "I'm not your sister, so it's not my place to say anything. Forgive me. I shouldn't have brought it up."

"But you did, which means that whether I answer or not, you have an opinion."

"Who you go out to celebrate with is none of my business. I'm just glad there's something to celebrate." She paused, and added softly, "But..."

"I knew it. Spit it out."

He shouldn't encourage her when he knew that she struggled with what she saw as a failing—this inability to stay out of other people's business. But maybe that was just the Amish for you—it wasn't that a woman was a busy-body, it was that she was so involved with those around her. Family, neighbors, friends—hers was a life knit into those of others.

He was the anomaly in this community. His life here wasn't knit into that of anyone, except maybe for his cousins' and once in a while with young Caleb's.

Well, if Ginny's smile meant anything, he was about to step out and try to change that pattern.

Sarah took a breath as they left the edge of town. "I feel I must ask you... if this interest deepens into anything more, what then?"

He glanced at her, puzzled, then back at the road, which was wide open and took you in one direction without getting ambivalent about it. "What do you mean, what then? I think you're getting ahead of me."

Another breath, as though she needed courage. "What I mean to say is, if in time you both decide to spend your lives together—"

"Now you're so far ahead of me you're in the next county."

"How will that affect your relationship with God?"

If there had been a place to pull over and get to the bottom of this without distraction, he would have done so. But there wasn't, unless he wanted to run over all the little shoots of corn coming up in the field beside the road.

"My relationship with God—or not—is my business, Sarah. I don't see what that has to do with it."

"I think you do. I think you might be allowing this—this possibility with Ginny to grow so that you can close yourself off from the church for good."

Henry braked to a stop at the mouth of someone's lane and turned in his seat to stare at her. "Are you kidding me?"

She gazed at him, then away at the gravel drive, as if she hoped the farmer would come out and rescue her.

"I show my appreciation for an attractive woman and suggest dinner, and it's because I'm running away from being Amish?"

"Isn't it?"

She was as aggravating as her kid, but once again, a part of him had to admire her guts. Not everyone would have sliced right down to the heart of the matter like this.

"No, it isn't!"

"What if you married her, and you decided in a few years that you wanted to join church after all?"

"I hate to break it to you, but that's not going to happen, whether I get married or not."

"But if you did, and God spoke to your heart, and you decided to come back to Him. You know, don't you, that you would have to put her away, and if you were baptized, be alone for the rest of your life?"

"Yes, I know that. It's a harsh, cruel standard that doesn't make sense in this day and age. And don't quote Matthew at me. I know those verses as well as you do."

She was silent, and he started up the car again.

"Sarah, I like and respect you. But I have to lay down some boundaries here. My personal life is off-limits, if all you're going to do is lecture me about an *Ordnung* that means nothing to me anymore. It will only cause offense between us, and I don't want that. We're neighbors and friends, and I'd like to keep it that way."

Still silence. Either she'd taken his words to heart and was doing as he'd asked, or she had a whole lot more to say on the subject and was just marshaling the words into order.

He had a feeling it was probably the latter.

"I'm sorry."

He dropped the shift lever into gear and eased out onto the road again to give himself time to regroup. Nothing like getting all revved up for a fight and then not getting one. He should have known better, though. His sparring partner was Amish.

"I hope you know I spoke up out of concern. Both for you and for Ginny, who probably doesn't know our ways."

"She was married to a Mennonite man."

"It's not the same. There may be a time when you will need to tell her, Henry."

"I can safely promise you that time will never come. For right now, if any discussion happens, it'll be over a nice steak at the River House and probably won't get any more complicated than which bottle of wine to choose."

"You'll be glad you have a commission if you're going to eat there. I hear it's expensive."

"Boundaries, Sarah."

He saw the point at which she gave it up and, all the way

back to Willow Creek, simply watched in silence as the green hillsides and the early flowers in the people's gardens went past her window.

Henry had never silenced a woman before.

He found he didn't like it much.

# CHAPTER 26

L ook, that's Henry Byler's car."

Priscilla pointed down the road as Simon turned the buggy into the Yoder drive, and by the time they'd gone halfway down, the car had turned in as well, crunching along the gravel at a respectful distance that merely made Dulcie swivel her ears rather than dance nervously to the side.

Instead of hopping out to slide the barn door open so Simon could back the buggy in, she and Joe Byler got out in the yard when he brought it to a stop. They'd walked over to the Hex Barn for something to do—not a date, just two friends going for a late-afternoon walk once Joe and Jake had finished planting the last field—and Simon had given them a ride back when he got off work. And now she could practically see the question marks flying around in the air as Henry Byler got out of one side of the car . . . and Simon's mother got out of the other.

"Mamm?" Simon hung on to Dulcie's harness, his fingers tight. "Where have you been?"

"I had an errand to run in connection with a patient, and Henry gave me a ride." Her voice was measured, cool—a tone Priscilla had rarely heard Sarah use.

"And you're still not a taxi?" Simon asked Henry.

"Only to my friends."

"Mamm, are you going to pay him?"

"Simon, don't be rude. Dulcie needs to be put up; look after her, please."

Simon turned and led Dulcie closer to the barn while Joe wasted no time in getting there ahead of him so he could push open the heavy door. It didn't take two of them to unhitch the horse, but Priscilla could already hear Simon's voice, pitched low, as the door rolled shut behind them.

"Oh, dear," Sarah said on a sigh. "Henry, I know I'm overstepping again, but if I could just tell him that you're interested in Ginny Hochstetler and not—er, anyone else around here, it would really help."

Priscilla pricked up her ears. Henry and Ginny, her new boss? Really? But if he got involved with her, then that meant he was never coming back to church.

"I'd rather you didn't," Henry said. "The last thing I need is people telling her who she's seeing."

For the first time, both of them seemed to notice Priscilla. She hadn't been hiding, but just standing there wondering what on earth was going to happen next.

"I—I just started work at the Rose Arbor Inn," she blurted out.

"See what I mean?" Henry asked nobody in particular.

Sarah smiled for Pris alone. "Do you think you'll like it? Ginny seems as though she'd be good to work for."

"Well, so far I haven't done much but make beds and clean bathrooms, but at least I've had plenty of practice at that. And if a person has to have a job, I could do a lot worse."

"I'm glad you feel that way," Sarah said. "It will make obeying your father easier if you actually like it."

But that reminded Priscilla of what she'd been trying to

forget all week. The more she tried to get closer to Simon, the farther away he seemed to be, like one of those mirages in the desert that she'd read about. And now he and everybody else were convinced that she and Joe were dating, which meant her clever plan to make him notice her was a total flop.

"Well, good night, Sarah," Henry said, swinging into the driver's seat. "And good luck with your project."

"*Denki*, Henry. I appreciate your help today."

"The wages of sin are a good *Schnitz* pie," he said, which made Priscilla wonder if he hadn't been standing out in the sun too long.

What was taking those boys so long? Unhitching a horse didn't take that long—maybe they were giving Dulcie a bath and shampoo while they were at it. Pris smiled at Sarah, who was already on her way into the house, and headed into the barn through the tack room door.

At which point she realized she'd stepped into the middle of a nor'easter.

Joe had his hands on Simon's shoulders as if to hold him down, and as Simon pushed him away, Priscilla saw there were tears leaking from the corners of his eyes. "I don't understand it!" he said, trying to keep his voice down and failing utterly. "She tells me I can't do what I want to do for no reason at all, and yet she's carrying on with an *Englisch!*"

"Would you calm down?" Joe demanded. "He gave her a ride to town. That's it. Why are you so stuck on this?"

"She's not *carrying on* with him," Priscilla informed them both. "He's seeing Ginny Hochstetler, that divorced lady at the Inn." Well, no one had told her specifically to keep quiet, had they? And it wasn't like any of the three of them were going to go out and start talking about Henry's love life. "Simon, did you hear me?"

"I don't believe you. He brought her home and she wouldn't tell me what they were doing."

"Yes, she did. You just don't want to believe the truth because it's boring and innocent." Priscilla lost patience. "Honestly, can we cut the drama? It's not all about you, Simon. Other people have lives, too—and some of us would rather have a mother that would let us work where we want, like yours does. You aren't suffering, believe me."

She'd done it now. The easygoing Simon she used to know seemed to have taken a vacation and she wanted him back.

"Thanks for the vote of confidence, Priscilla. When I get to Colorado, maybe I'll send you a postcard."

"By the time you get to Colorado, I'll be twenty-one and sending you postcards from all my travels," she shot back.

"No, you won't."

*"Neh?"*

"Simon," Joe said, as though he knew what was coming and was trying to stop it.

Simon sucked in a lungful of air and held it. When he turned red in the face, he let it out and picked up a brush to curry Dulcie.

"Come on, Pris, I'll walk you home." Joe took her elbow and practically hustled her out the door.

"What on earth is the matter with him?" she wanted to know as they walked through the orchard toward the Mast place. "What a way to talk about his mother. He should be ashamed for even thinking what he's thinking, never mind saying it out loud."

"He's just mad."

"That's no excuse. I get mad, too, and I don't say mean things about my family."

"Simon's been *kitzlich* lately. He don't mean no harm."

"That's no excuse, either."

"He looks all easygoing and like he doesn't care about things, but he does. He has his heart set on seeing some of the world, and he feels trapped here."

"So? Maybe I do, too."

"Yeah, but you don't have a one-way ticket to—" He stopped dead and rolled his top lip between his teeth.

Priscilla stared at him. "What did you say?"

"Nothing."

"You said 'one-way ticket.' Joe Byler, are the two of you coming back? Is that what you tried to stop Simon from saying?"

He stubbed the toe of his boot in the crumbly soil on the edge of the field. "Me and Jake are going to get the second planting of corn done for my uncle."

To anyone but her, that wouldn't have made a lick of sense. "To get it all done a couple of days ahead of schedule? So you can leave with a clean conscience? What does Jake think about all this?"

"He thinks I'm crazy for leaving my apprenticeship, but at the same time, if it goes right out there, he's thinking of coming, too."

"You told your folks it's a vacation?"

"Nope, it's for the whole summer. And maybe longer. Especially if—"

"If what?"

He was silent. Then he seemed to give in, as if it were a relief to share his news with someone. "We're not going to my uncle's at all. Simon's got a smart phone. This dude ranch up in the mountains out of Buena Vista has a page on Facebook so we sent them video of us working with the horses and tack, and another of me and him driving the six-mule hitch. We

*Adina Senft*

had jobs the next morning." He grinned at her. "I ain't never had such an easy time with anything in my life—and it pays maybe three times what we would make farming for Onkel Elias."

"Oh, Joe." Her voice had the falling tone of despair, but she couldn't help it.

"What's that, Pris? You think you might miss me?"

"Of course I'll miss you. I'll miss both of you. But I still don't think it's right to tell your parents one thing and do another—especially when you're going to work for a worldly outfit you've never even seen. Is that why Simon's mad? Because he's feeling guilty about deceiving Sarah?"

"It ain't that. Maybe part of him doesn't want to leave Sarah when that Henry is buzzing around. Maybe that's trapping him, too—that he thinks he should stay because he's the man of the house."

"Then he should." She started walking again, and he ambled after her, keeping up even though he didn't seem to be moving that fast.

"Tickets are for next Tuesday's train," he said. "We bought 'em just as soon as he got his check, but we could only afford the one way." He stopped her with a hand on her arm as they crossed the ditch onto the Mast lawn. "Think you can drive us into Whinburg to catch the ten o'clock bus? Simon will take his buggy like he's going to work and meet me at the pizza place instead."

With her hands on her hips, she gazed at him. "What are you going to do if I say no?"

"Ask Henry."

"Good luck with that."

"Does that mean no?"

"*Ja*, it means no." Her heart felt like it was going to crack.

Simon was leaving on Tuesday. All her dreams and hopes for the summer—for the next year—wavered, crumbled, and came crashing down around her.

In the deafening noise, she barely heard Joe say, "You ain't going to blab on us, are you, Pris?"

That was a very good question. "I should."

"But you won't. There's no harm in earning good money."

"Deceiving your parents isn't right, and you know it."

"They wouldn't let us go at all if they knew we were going to the ranch. But our folks will be so glad when we write and tell them how well we're doing that it'll all blow over."

Priscilla wasn't so sure that a hurt like that would just blow over. But the last thing she needed was for Paul and Barbara and Sarah to think she'd had any hand in this.

"No, I won't tell. But I won't give you a ride to the bus station, either. I don't want either of you thinking I'm in favor of this."

"We would've known that even if you did give us a ride." He paused under the cherry tree that stood outside her window. Its bloom had come and gone, and now it was thinking about bearing fruit. Above her head, in its branches, two wrens argued about the best place to build a nest.

"I know you don't like what we're doing, but do you think you might kiss me good-bye?"

Ten minutes ago her heart would have cried for Simon. But since then, he'd revealed himself to be...not quite the boy she'd thought he was. But in front of her stood Joe, dependable Joe, probably the only one who could keep Simon from flying off the handle and give them both half a chance at succeeding out there on this dude ranch. "When are you coming back?"

He shrugged his shoulders, broad and muscled from managing the six-mule hitch. "Could be late fall. Could be next week. Won't know until we try it out. Well?"

She had dreamed about her first kiss for a year now. And the boy asking had always been Simon. *Time to give up a little girl's dreams. Simon isn't looking at you, he's looking at the horizon out there past you. And right now, you have Joe's whole attention.* "All right," she whispered, and tilted up her face.

His mouth was soft and yet firm, and clung just long enough for her to smell sandalwood and clean, healthy sweat before he straightened and she opened her eyes.

"Something to remember you by," he said. "I'll write, if that's okay?"

Her first kiss. It hadn't been a bit like her dreams of it. It had been shorter. Nicer.

"Pris?"

"Okay," she said, before his question caught up to her wondering brain. "*Ja.* Okay." He loped off across the lawn and was nearly to the ditch before she opened her mouth. "Good-bye, Joe. Be safe."

He lifted a hand and was gone.

*Keep them safe, Lord. Watch over and protect them, and turn their thoughts toward home so that they'll come back again. Keep him safe. Please keep him safe.*

But this time, she didn't know which *him* she was praying for most.

# CHAPTER 27

Dear Timothy,

My name is Sarah Yoder, and I live in Willow Creek, where you used to live. At least, I hope I'm writing to the man who used to live there. If I have the wrong person, please let me know.

If you are the right person, then what I'm about to tell you will make sense. I am learning to be an herbalist, and I have been treating your father and mother. Your father suffers from digestive problems and chronic stomach complaints that cause him great pain, and your mother is depressed. God has led me to the conclusion that both conditions are caused by one thing, and that is their anguish over your absence from their lives.

Please believe me when I say that no one holds you responsible for that. But I think both your parents would have a much better chance of returning to health if you were to come for a visit and reconcile with them. I realize how much pain there has been in the past, but the cure for that kind of pain is repentance, forgiveness, and the love and grace of God.

If I do not hear from you, I will take that as an answer and continue to try to treat their bodies as best I can.

But some hurts go soul deep, and can only be healed by love. I hope you will understand.

Yours sincerely,
Sarah Yoder

Sarah put down her pen with a sigh. She could only hope that God's grace would make up for the bluntness of the words. Expressing what she felt to a lifeless piece of paper felt like talking to someone through a window of thick glass, where the recipient might be able to see her mouth move, but couldn't get to the truth of what she was saying.

Dealing with Simon earlier today had been a little like that. If ever she had congratulated herself on escaping the moods and mistakes of adolescence with him, she was paying for it now.

His behavior this afternoon with Henry had gone beyond the protectiveness of the elder son into downright disrespect. He'd stayed in the barn and not come in for supper, and when she'd sent Caleb out to get him, her poor younger boy had looked so downcast that she'd been half tempted to go and get her hairbrush and use it on Simon's stubborn backside, the way she had when he was small.

But that wouldn't solve a thing. Besides, he was taller than she was now, and he'd probably just shake his head and take it away from her.

She folded the letter into an envelope and wrote out the address on it. The lamp sputtered, reminding her that it was nearly eleven and Simon had not yet come in from the barn. She pulled a shawl off the peg on the back of her bedroom door, pushed her feet into a pair of sneakers with no laces, and went outside.

Light glowed in the cracks between the boards. She pushed open the rolling door and slipped inside. Patience was the key, and love. She could hardly encourage Timothy Yost to love and forgive and not do the same, could she?

Sarah had taken a breath to tell her son how much she loved him, when she realized that it was far too quiet in the barn. "Simon? Are you in here?" Had he gone out? But no, there was Dulcie, blinking at her unexpected visit, and the buggies sitting in their usual places, their rails tilted down on the cement floor.

She walked back to the house. Maybe he'd gone to bed and she'd been so preoccupied with her letter that she hadn't heard him.

Hadn't heard a young man's weight on the stairs, or in the bathroom? Not very likely. She poked her head into his room to see his bed, smooth and flat, and no one at the desk.

He'd been upset. Who would he go to talk to? He might go and see Jacob. Maybe at this moment they were making wheat dollies or whittling the walking sticks that Jacob had taken to making for the Amish Market. Maybe she'd just walk over there to her in-laws' and check.

But when she stepped through Corinne's garden and went around the house, it was silent and dark. The family had all gone to bed, and what was she doing out here, wandering around the countryside in the middle of the night?

Shaking her head at herself, Sarah walked home across the field. Maybe—maybe he hadn't gone somewhere to be consoled. Maybe he'd gone to the source of what he saw as the problem.

Maybe he'd gone to have it out once and for all with Henry.

The fact that there was nothing to "have out" wouldn't

matter to a young man who had become touchy and morose over the past couple of weeks. She should have seen it sooner. Sarah lifted the lantern to better see the trail over the shoulder of the hill. She should have talked to Simon when his anger was small and easily cooled, and poured love on the flame so that he would feel forgiveness instead of defensiveness.

She could still try.

This time she made sure that no one was in the barn before she crossed the dark yard to the house. A lamp was lit in the kitchen. Half of her wanted Henry to be alone. The other half desperately wanted Simon to be there so that she would know he was safe, and not walking off his feelings somewhere like the middle of a deserted road or the dark edge of a pond, where an accident might happen because he wasn't watching where he was going.

Henry came into the kitchen and got a mug down from the cupboard—not one of the ones he'd made, but a store-bought one with a picture on it. Through the window in the kitchen door, Sarah watched him fill the kettle and put it on the stove, his movements smoother than she'd seen them before. He'd become familiar with Sadie's kitchen, though she'd never kept mugs and cups in the cupboard next to the sink like that. It seemed strange to see a man all alone in a woman's space—someone should come in and bump him out of the way, put some cookies on a plate for him, offer him bread and jam if he wanted a snack with his tea or coffee.

He looked as painfully alone in his kitchen as she had felt in the vast echoing space of his barn.

*What are you thinking, spying on the poor man like this?*

She knocked on the pane of glass, and he turned, searching the dark of the porch for the identity of his visitor. Sarah lifted her lamp so that her face was illuminated, and his expression of surprise settled into polite lines.

Polite. Not welcoming, as a friend's might be, but pleasant and noncommittal. Which was exactly as it should be, after this afternoon.

But it was a little disappointing.

He opened the door. "Sarah? Is everything all right?"

"I—well, I hope so. Is my Simon here?"

His eyebrows rose as he motioned her inside, toward the kitchen table. "Why would he be here?"

"I thought he might have come to talk things over with you."

He pulled out a chair for her and got down another mug. "I'm sorry, but he hasn't—or if he did, I didn't know. I just came in from the barn. I was getting things ready for a firing tomorrow. I just hope I don't burn the place down—or blow up that old generator."

"Goodness. I didn't know kilns were so dangerous."

"They aren't, on a normal hundred-and-twenty-volt city grid. Wish me luck."

"I don't believe in luck. Whatever happens will be God's will."

His gaze caught hers the way the cleavers in the garden caught at her clothes as she passed. "Then why are you so worried about your boy? Whatever happens to him will be God's will, right?"

She was onto him now. Sometimes he said things just to get a rise out of her, not because he actually thought that way. "*Ja*, but I'm still his mother. I'm still concerned, especially after this afternoon."

He nodded, and got up to wait by the kettle, as if he meant to hurry it along. "I'm concerned about that myself."

"He'll simmer down. Simon has a quick temper, but it blows out just as quickly."

"I don't mind a man's temper. I do mind that he's got something in his head that shouldn't be there. That maybe I did something to make him think things that aren't true."

"You haven't. You've acted like a *gut* neighbor. Maybe he's got courting on his mind and he sees it even where it doesn't exist."

"We're certainly not courting," he agreed.

Certainly not. "I'll be glad when you take Ginny Hochstetler out for that celebration dinner. Maybe you could find a way for everyone in the district to notice."

"Maybe I could find a way to tie in blowing up the barn when I switch on that kiln."

"That's it!" She clapped in feigned delight. "You could invite her over to watch, and then save her life by pulling her from the flames."

"Hm. Sounds a bit extreme. Maybe I'll just settle for dinner and a bouquet of flowers. A fiery rescue just doesn't scream romance, you know?"

"Romance doesn't scream."

"You sound very firm about that." He pulled the kettle off the flame and reached up to the shelf above the mugs, where a box of tea bags sat. It appeared to be the only thing on that shelf. "What does romance do?"

*"Charity suffereth long, and is kind."*

"That's charity. Brotherly love. We're talking about romance...though I have to say, it can produce its share of suffering."

Something—a shadow, a memory—passed through his eyes and he turned away to dunk a tea bag in her cup. When he handed it to her, he'd ironed the bleakness from his face.

"But it is kind," she said softly. "Kind, and caring, and puts the other person first. The way I imagine you treating Ginny."

"I would hope so, if it gets that far." But his tone sounded stiff, as if he were talking about someone else. "Is that how Michael was with you?"

"Oh, yes. It was so easy to submit with him, because I knew he put me first—sometimes even when he shouldn't have." Her face crumpled before she could stop it, and she struggled for control.

"Are you all right?"

She nodded, but she couldn't quite get her lips to take a sip of tea, and her teeth clinked on the rim of the mug. Best to put it down. "He kept it to himself, you see—the cancer. He didn't tell me, because he didn't want to worry me. And by the time he did, and we got to the doctor, it was already so advanced that he—" *Breathe. In and out.* "The doctor said he couldn't imagine anyone could live with that kind of pain and still keep going. It was in stage four by then. Three weeks later, he was gone."

"Sarah," he breathed, and she realized that he had reached across the table to take both her hands in his big, warm ones. "If you need to cry, don't be brave. Just let it go."

It had been five years. She was all cried out. But that didn't seem to matter as the dam broke and she wept—wept for Michael and his love for her . . . for his son Simon, who, like his father, kept his upsets buried deep inside until they all came out at the same moment . . . at Henry himself, who simply wouldn't see that he belonged among them, and would rather waste his life and jeopardize his soul on purpose than admit it.

It was this final thought that gave her the strength to pull her hands out of his gentle grasp. "Henry."

"Sorry, I just—I—"

"You mustn't touch me in this way."

"You were crying and I—it was natural to reach out."

"But what is natural is often wrong." What was she saying? Hadn't she let herself stay there and sink into the warmth of a man's touch? Wasn't she as much at fault as he?

She got up from the table and pulled her sweater together tightly across her chest. "Thank you for the tea. I need to be going. Maybe Simon has come home while I've been combing the county for him."

*Stop babbling.*

She got her hand on the doorknob and let herself out, and it wasn't until she was all the way over the hill that she realized she'd left the lantern on his kitchen table, still burning.

There was nothing more she could do tonight. Simon was nearly eighteen, and she was being unfair to him by worrying so much. But still, when she heard the kitchen door open as she was braiding her hair, Sarah's whole body relaxed in relief. Because it was not his safety she was concerned about—not really. It was his state of mind.

And it was in her hands to do something about that.

She snapped the elastic around the end of the braid and put on a bathrobe over her nightgown. She waited until she heard him come out of the bathroom and then went into his room.

It was dark, but she knew the contours of this house by feel and from having scrubbed every inch of it numerous times over the years. Simon's bed creaked as he sat on it, and creaked again as she sat beside him.

"Mamm? What are you doing up so late?"

"Thanking the *gut Gott* that you're home safely."

"I only went to Joe's."

Ah, of course he had. And here she'd been roaming around the countryside, off on the wrong trail altogether. In the dark, she shook her head at herself.

"You went away with a bad spirit, so I was worried."

"I got over it. Joe and I had a long talk, and then Paul saw the light in the barn, and he came in, too."

"And what did you talk over?"

"The soybeans, and the second planting of corn, and eventually, Colorado."

Her voice calm, gentle, the kind she used for baby creatures, she asked, "I'm glad to hear it."

"He and Joe have been talking a lot. We both know it's going to be a burden on Jake and Paul to do the work without him, but on their side, they know how much Joe really wants to do some traveling and see some of our country before he settles down."

"Settles down? It's a little early to be thinking of that."

"Maybe I should have said 'joins church.'"

"Ah. It's *gut* he's thinking of these things, then. And what about you?"

"Mostly I'm wishing that you felt better about it all, Mamm." He moved a little, gazing out the window as if he were checking the position of the moon. "It would only be for two weeks, and maybe, if it works out with Joe's uncle, for longer."

"How much longer?"

"It could be for the whole summer. And I'd send you half my wages, like before. Nothing would change."

This was the Simon she was used to. She leaned enough to

bump his shoulder with hers. "Nothing but that we wouldn't have your smiling face and terrible jokes at the table. And maybe Caleb would win a game or two of Scrabble. That's his lifelong ambition, you know."

"I know. I feel I should give him a chance, *neh?*" She rejoiced at the sound of the smile in his voice. A little silence fell. Then, "I'm sorry I've been such a bear lately, Mamm."

"I'm sorry I didn't take you more seriously. If I hadn't just been looking at that empty chair at the table, I might have seen a young man who wants to spread his wings a little and begin to make his way. There's no harm in that, and goodness knows you'll be in safe hands with Joe's uncle and his family."

Another little silence fell, and she felt Simon move again restlessly. "So I can go, then, with your blessing?"

She laid her head on his shoulder, which was losing the boniness of adolescence and with hard work and maturity was firming into the reliable shoulder of the man he would become. "*Ja*, with my blessing. And if you hear of any interesting plants out there that I might be able to use, I hope you'll send me some seeds."

"I'll keep my eyes open. Maybe I'll see an Indian medicine man and ask him."

She chuckled, careful not to make too much noise and wake Caleb in his bed across the room. "Good night, son."

And to her surprise, he wrapped his strong young arms around her and gave her a bear hug—something he hadn't done since he was Caleb's age. It was almost as if he had already begun to say good-bye.

She hugged him to her. And in that motherly embrace was everything he would have to come back home to.

# CHAPTER 28

Sarah received no notice, though it had been a week since she'd sent her letter to the person who might or might not be the right Timothy Yost. She was in the garden at the tail end of the following Monday afternoon, pulling weeds and estimating how many baby lettuce leaves it would take to make a salad, when she heard the crunch of tires in the lane.

Henry? Pulling off her gloves, she crossed the lawn to see a strange car roll to a stop, and a man and a woman get out.

Strangers—whose faces gave her a shock of recognition. They were older now than they had been in the photograph, but unmistakably the same. He wore a white shirt and a pair of suit pants with black suspenders. The woman's dress was pale blue with tiny white flowers strewn across it, the cape sewn into the waistband for modesty. On her faded blond hair, which was braided into a bun, was an abbreviated covering, more of a crescent of fabric that made a statement rather than performing a function.

So they belonged to a more liberal church now—a Mennonite church, by the look of it, that allowed cars. He had not left God, as everyone had assumed. He had found a less rigid, less expectation-ridden way to worship than the one found in his father's house.

"Hallo," she called, and they turned in her direction. "Timothy Yost, is that you?"

"It is." He gazed around the yard, as if looking for familiar landmarks from before the farm had been subdivided. "If I have the address right, you must be Sarah Yoder."

"*Ja.*" Up closer, she could see that his neatly trimmed beard was streaked with gray, and that his wife must be a very good cook, since the fabric across his belly strained between the suspenders. "I can hardly believe it's you." Or that he had come here instead of going to his parents' home. Was that not strange?

Maybe he had been and gone already. Maybe Oran had run him off the place, and he was coming here to tell her.

"Believe it's me now, and not what you might have heard about me before. That's all I ask. Sarah, this is my wife, Helen."

She shook hands, glad that for once she'd remembered to wear her gloves and so her hands were relatively clean. "Please come in. I have coffee on the stove, and I made a *Blaum Kuche* this morning that should be cool enough to eat."

They followed her in, quiet as lambs, and she filled the space between them with inconsequential chatter as she tried to figure out whether or not they had seen Oran and Adah. Finally, as she cut the plum cake and served them, she decided she was just going to have to ask.

"Have you seen your father and mother yet?"

Timothy shook his head. "When we got your letter, I hardly knew what to do. I know how my father is. When he makes up his mind to a thing, it doesn't get unmade."

"But it sounds as though it needs to be unmade," his wife said to him softly. "If not knowing you is making them both ill, then we need to do what we can to fix it."

Sarah couldn't agree more. "Did you have a long drive down?"

"It's only a couple of hours in the car," Timothy said. "It took a lot longer back then, when I walked in between thumbing rides."

"He was determined to get to Philadelphia and make something of himself," Helen put in. Clearly she knew the story from the moment of Timothy's departure from his home district. But did she know what had precipitated it?

"How much of what happened do you know?" Timothy asked Sarah, startling her. "I mean, you must know about Ruthanne, if you know that I left."

Wordlessly, she nodded. If she didn't have to hear the details from the horse's mouth, she'd rather not. And there was her answer about how much Helen knew, too. Which meant she could speak freely.

"I don't think we should bring up sad memories," she said. "It doesn't profit anyone to look back. It would be best to look ahead—and since the Lord is the only one who knows what lies in the future, maybe we should pray about it...and then go and see your folks."

"I don't aim to bring up the past, either," he said. "That's all buried in the sea of forgetfulness and I've found forgiveness for the part I played. But you're right." He pushed his empty plate aside and folded his hands on the table. And to Sarah's surprise, he began to pray aloud, humbling her by including her in this intimate moment as he addressed the God of Heaven.

"Father, I thank Thee for bringing Helen and me back to Willow Creek safely, and I thank Thee for moving this woman Sarah to intercede between my earthly father and me. I should have heeded the promptings of Thy spirit years ago and come back sooner, but in Thy wisdom Thou hast held open the door this long. I pray that Thou wouldst go with us to my father's house, sending peace and forgiveness with us. Give me the courage to face him without anger, and give Helen and Sarah the strength to stand beside me."

What? He expected her to go, too? Sarah's hands, clasped on the table, tightened involuntarily.

"I ask Thy blessing on our efforts today, Lord, and thank Thee for Thy care. We ask it in the name of Jesus."

"Amen," Helen murmured, and opened her eyes, catching Sarah in the act of shaking her head.

"You don't mean for me to intrude on a private family moment," she said. "Oran wouldn't like that at all."

"You're the reason we're even here." Timothy smiled. "Have a little courage. He won't eat us."

"He might eat me."

The smile grew wider. "After thirtysome-odd years of being away from him, I've had plenty of time to think about what I might do differently if I got a chance to speak to him. And if I'm not successful, the Lord will bear me up."

Sarah needed to remember that. The Lord would bear her up—and Oran and Adah as well. She hurried into the bedroom to change her dress and put on a cape and apron. As she pinned on a fresh organdy *Kapp*, thankfulness flooded her at the thought that no matter what happened, this wasn't about her and she would be able to pray her way through it.

And then they were in the car, heading over to the Yost place. She opened her mouth to give directions, and closed it again when it became obvious that Timothy hadn't forgotten the way. Maybe he'd even driven past it, spying out the land, as it were, before they'd come to her place.

They drove slowly past the buggy shop, where a couple of

heads popped out of the door at the foreign sound of rubber tires on the gravel. One...two...three....

On the count of four, Oran Yost strode out the door in the back of the shop, following the car down the lane to the house at a pace that told her he didn't yet know who the driver was, and meant to find out. All he'd be able to see was her own white *Kapp* in the rear window, so he'd think it was an *Englisch* taxi, bringing unexpected visitors when Adah was alone in the house.

Sarah took a breath as the car slowed to a stop outside the farmhouse, and sent up a quick *Help us all, Lord,* as she got out and slammed the door.

Oran was still halfway between the shop and the house when Adah opened the kitchen door and came out onto the porch, wiping her hands on her apron and gazing at Sarah, clearly puzzled.

"Sarah? Are you doing errands today in the taxi? I thought we had said we didn't need any more of your—" She stopped. Looked from Sarah, to Timothy in his beard and suspenders, to Helen in her modest dress and covering.

Back to Timothy, who, it was becoming clear, was not an *Englisch* driver.

Like a wounded bird, one hand fluttered to her mouth.

Oran had finally made it into the yard. "Sarah Yoder, I must say that you are very persistent in your efforts to get a person to—Adah, *was ischt?* Adah?"

His gaze had gone past Timothy and Helen as if they did not exist—he did not yet know they weren't merely drivers.

Sarah came around the front of the car with Helen in time to see Timothy smile at his mother.

Adah made a sound halfway between a cry and a laugh, and tottered down the porch steps. But something seemed to hold her back from going farther—some compulsion of obedience that would not let her close the last few feet between herself and her son.

"Mamm," Timothy said, and in two steps he had gathered her into his arms.

Adah, quiet, stoic Adah, who, to the best of Sarah's knowledge, had never showed her emotions in public, burst into tears and threw her arms around her boy's neck in a paroxysm of grief and joy. In the cedar tree next to the porch, a bird trilled, but that, Timothy's soft words of comfort, and the sobs being torn from Adah's chest were all that could be heard in the yard.

Sarah dared a look at Oran Yost.

He stood as if he'd been turned into a pillar of salt. Stiff, upright, unbending, he was as frozen in place in the grass as Adah had been on the steps. Frozen with surprise and disbelief? Or frozen by the power of a vow uttered decades ago?

*Lord, help him to forgive. Help him to forget that they said words to each other hard enough to drive his only son away. Help him to bend and soften and let in Your peace and healing at last.*

Helen was the first to move. She crossed the grass and held out her hand. "*Guder mariye*, Father Oran. I am Helen, Timothy's wife."

His head turned toward her stiffly, like that of a wooden puppet, and it took a moment for him to focus on her. "How...Why..."

"We were married twenty-five years ago this December, and we have a boy and two girls, just as you and Mother Adah did. Your grandchildren—Rafe, Cecily, and Ada Lynn."

"Ada..."

"Yes, Timothy wanted his youngest to have his mother's name." Helen's voice was as warm as if they'd been sitting across the table from one another for every family holiday during those twenty-five years. "She's just told us she's expecting her fourth at Christmas. Rafe has two boys in high school, and Cecily lives in Iowa with her husband and three girls. So you see, you have quite a number of great-grandchildren from us as well as Timothy's sisters."

Oran dragged his eyes from his daughter-in-law to gaze in anguish at Adah and Timothy, still locked in a hug. "I can't speak to him."

Sarah would have given in to tears if she hadn't heard Oran's voice—cracked, hopeless, trapped in a vow he had made in anger and kept in an iron resolve that resembled pride all too much.

"Maybe not," Helen said softly, "but he has waited a long time to speak to you."

With infinite gentleness, Timothy released his mother with a murmured word. She clasped both hands in front of her lips, as though she were praying, as she watched him cross the yard to stand next to his wife.

"Dat," he said. "Will you forgive me?"

Such simple words, blunt and plain...and the hardest that a man or a woman could say.

Oran's face cracked. Crumpled. All the pain he had been carrying in his body all this time seemed to flow into his face. "How can you?"

How can he come like this? Sarah wondered. How can he stand there and speak? What did Oran mean?

"I forgave you years ago, Dat...when I held my own son for the first time and realized the weight of responsibility that a father holds. You did what you thought was right—even though for me, it was wrong."

"So many years."

"I know. But we will make up for them now, if you are willing."

Moisture glistened in the corners of Oran Yost's eyes, like the rivulets running down the solid face of concrete when a dam is about to burst. "Son. Forgive me. I must hear the words, here, to my face."

"I forgive you...if you forgive me for not coming sooner. For wanting you to make the first move. That was my pride and I should have prayed to have it taken from me."

Oran nodded. "I do. I forgive you. Oh, my son." The drops became a rivulet, and then Sarah turned away as the impossible happened. Oran Yost began to weep in earnest as he took his son into his arms.

Though they sat at the big family table in the dining room, no one could seem to settle to something as ordinary as eating. In fact, Sarah was quite sure that the sight of Timothy's face was feeding Adah's very soul. She couldn't stop herself from touching him—a pat on his sleeve, a brush of the hair, an adjustment of his collar—as if to assure herself that he was real, there in the chair next to her.

Sarah somehow found herself next to Oran, with Helen on her other side, and the daughter and son-in-law who still lived in town on their way to join the reunion.

Oran had not yet recovered from his utter breakdown outside. He could hardly speak, and Sarah thought she might just escape without having to explain her own presence, when Adah finally asked her son, "But how did it all come about? I still cannot wrap my mind around it."

Timothy smiled at Sarah. "I got a letter from a friend."

"What friend?" Adah asked. "Surely you have not been in touch with Isaiah Mast or one of the others from so long ago?" She followed the smile to Sarah's face, which only made her more confused.

"Sarah, why don't you tell this part?" Timothy suggested. "Since I'm curious myself as to how that letter got into our mailbox."

Oh, dear. So much for trying to lie low. Well, the truth was better out in the open than hidden in the heart.

"I was worried about your parents," she said to Timothy. "As I said, I had been trying to help them with herbal remedies, but they didn't really have any faith in it. And I wondered if the real problem went beyond a sore stomach or the blues—deeper, into the soul, where only God can work."

She felt Oran's gaze on her the way a hand feels the heat from the top of the stove.

"I wondered if both complaints stemmed from the same cause—the loss of a son. We know that the lost can be found, so I called on a friend to help. One who could work the Internet."

Timothy choked on the piece of date cake he'd just put in his mouth—swallowed violently, and laughed. "The Internet?"

"We—Henry Byler and I—went to the library and he did a search on you. I wasn't expecting there to be so many Timothy Yosts in the world, but we picked the one who seemed to be the most likely, looked up the address, and then I sent the letter."

"You did this thing?" Oran finally got out.

"I could only write. But if Henry ever stops making things out of clay, he could be a detective."

Oran didn't follow this handy side trail out of the spotlight. "You took it upon yourself to find Timothy?"

Time to confess. "I did. I heard the story. About what happened. I didn't hear all the details, because no one knows what passed between the two of you then, and I don't think anyone wants to know now. All I know is that I felt responsible."

"For what?" Adah asked. "How could you be responsible?"

"You had trusted me to help you, and I couldn't," Sarah explained. "But there is One who always can. I'm sorry to have put my nose so deep in your business. But I couldn't leave it. Not if there was something I could do—something God could do with these hands of mine if I just had the courage to let Him."

"And what of my hands?" Oran whispered, pushing his plate away untouched and gazing at the strong fingers that could make a buggy to carry a family. "I pushed my own son away—said some unforgivable things—"

"That have been forgiven," Timothy reminded him. "Dat, that is all past and gone. The mystery is solved, and for my part, I'm glad Sarah allowed God to do His work." He folded his own hand, hardened by toil, around those of his father, and took his mother's hand in the other. "No more pushing away, by either of us. Hands are meant for holding fast, and that's what Helen and I and the children plan to do."

The sound of a horse's hooves coming at a fast clip down the lane filtered through the window, open to the May day.

"There is your sister and brother-in-law," Adah said, craning to look out the big window in the front room. "They have all the *Kinner* with them, and every one of them with a spring cold."

Timothy's glance twinkled at Sarah. "More customers for your cures?"

"These Yosts," she said, smiling back, "they're a stubborn bunch. I have a hard time treating them."

And then she got the surprise of her life as Oran released his son's hand and gripped her shoulder when he got up to open the door. "Maybe," he said. "Sometimes we don't know what's good for us. But I am thankful today that we have a God and *die guten Freind* who do."

And then he opened the door wide and let his family in.

# Chapter 29

Dear Mamm,

It is after breakfast as I write this, but by the time you find it, I will be on the 2 P.M. train for Pittsburgh, where we change for Chicago, heading for Denver.

Like I said the other night, I'm sorry I've been hard to live with lately. It's not your fault—I was just mad at the world, I guess. I know you will be disappointed and afraid for me, but I hope that in time you will see that leaving is the right thing for me to do. We are not going to Joe's uncle in Monte Vista. Joe and I have got ourselves jobs at a dude ranch in Colorado near Buena Vista, 100 miles north, with board and room included. So I won't be sleeping on a construction site or putting somebody out of their bed. I'm sorry I didn't tell you the whole truth the other night. I couldn't. But I am now.

As soon as we're settled, I'll send you the address. I hope you will forgive me. I didn't want to fight but I need to do this. I'll see you in November (there aren't too many dudes coming then, so I expect we'll be laid off).

It's not likely Paul will let Joe come home. Maybe he can stay with us? He's a hard worker.

I'll send money when I can.


Love,
Simon


The sound that tore from Sarah's throat brought Caleb in from the back porch at a dead run. "Mamm? Are you all right? Should I get Mammi?"

She crumpled the letter, gasping for breath.

*"Mamm?"*

Only the terror in his voice could have brought her out of the terrible visions of her elder son alone on a train—on a ranch somewhere in the West surrounded by worldly people—tempted—

*"Mamm!"*

She thrust the letter at him, and pulled herself up to sit on Simon's bed while he read it. "Did you know about this?"

*"Neh!"* Caleb's shocked face as he met her gaze told her the truth. "He was working at the Hex Barn. I thought he forgot all about that crazy plan."

"Looks like it got even crazier. Caleb, run and hitch up Dulcie. We've got to stop them."

He gaped at her like she was the crazy one. "Stop them how? We don't even know what train. There's no train here."

"It's the one in Lancaster. He must have thought I was going to Ruth's today, or I'd never have found this so early. Thank goodness those little Yost children needed some herbs! Go on, quick. I'll meet you at the barn."

"But Mamm, you can't drive a buggy all the way to Lancaster!"

That stopped her dead in the doorway. Of course she couldn't. "Then run to the phone shanty and call an *Englisch* taxi. It will cost a fortune, but we don't have a choice." She was going to save those boys from their own foolishness if it was the last thing she did.

Caleb lit out of the room like a rabbit, and she threw on a coat and her away bonnet, then ran downstairs to pack some food for the journey. It was only noon. They could get to the station before two, and she would have something to feed them for the journey home—because she'd eat her bonnet if she found out they'd thought to take anything with them but their own recklessness and a change of socks.

Basket over her arm, she slammed the door behind her and looked around the yard for Caleb. Not back yet. Maybe he'd had trouble finding a taxi. Sometimes the Mortensens, who charged the least, got busy, and she'd have to go down the list that was posted on the wall of the shanty. She'd just walk up the lane and wait out on the road, then, to save the minute it would take to drive down and get her. A couple of hundred feet closer to the Lancaster train station was still a couple of hundred feet, wasn't it?

But when she got to the shanty, it was empty. "Caleb?" Had she missed him somehow? "Caleb!" But nothing moved except the breeze in the grass, and a red-winged blackbird balancing on a reed in the ditch across the road, singing its heart out for joy that summer was almost here.

And then she heard an engine, coming at speed down the road. Oh, those *Englisch*—thinking that because the road had no cars on it that it was empty. What if Caleb—

Henry Byler's silver car topped the rise and she could swear its front tires actually lifted off the blacktop. He closed the quarter mile in the amount of time it took her to gasp in recognition, and pulled to a halt in a cloud of dust at the end of her lane, where the gravel gave out onto the asphalt.

"Mamm! Get in!" Caleb hollered from the backseat.

Why, that little rascal! "You didn't even come out here! Henry, you don't have to—"

"Clearly someone does," he said tersely. "Sarah, for once in your life, stop finding all the reasons I shouldn't do something, and get in!"

She'd barely got the door closed and her basket on the floor between her feet when he took off like a spooked racehorse. Willow Creek flew by, and then Gap, and Strasburg, and they were on the outskirts of Lancaster navigating through traffic before she could even catch her breath.

"I didn't know you could drive that fast," Caleb said with admiration. "Wow!"

"Neither did I—but look at this mess. It can't be the lunch rush—there must be an accident up here."

All around them, a river of humanity sat in their cars, waiting at lights, waiting for snarls of people turning or trying to go another way to untangle. Sarah was quite sure she could get out and walk faster than they were able to creep down this road—and it was supposed to be a highway. The little blue numbers on the dashboard clicked past one o'clock...one fifteen...one thirty...

"How much farther?"

"One mile less than the last time you asked me. We'll get there, Sarah. Just breathe and try to relax."

Breathing was not a problem. But she wouldn't be able to relax until Simon was safe in this car, strapped down by as many seat belts as she could get around him.

One forty-five, and the cars seemed to be spaced out more.

"There. It was an accident." Henry navigated over to the right. "And there's the sign for the station."

They dove off the highway and he pressed the pedal down as far as he dared, glancing in the mirror every few seconds for a sign of a police car.

One fifty.

He braked to a stop in front of the old-fashioned red brick station. "Go, while I find a place to park."

Sarah left the basket where it was and she and Caleb leaped out and dashed into the building and up the stairs. Where—where—aha!

She ran past the sign that said TO TRAINS and skidded to a stop as a policewoman stepped in front of the swinging doors and held up a hand. "You can't go past this point without a ticket, ma'am. We had a situation and we're on alert here."

She had no idea what that meant. "I don't have a ticket. I'm trying to stop my son from getting on the train."

"I'm sorry, ma'am, only passengers on the bridge beyond this point."

Sarah craned her neck to see past the woman's pleasant but immovable bulk. "Caleb, can you see them?"

He ran to the windows and looked out. "He's not there, Mamm."

"All passengers for the one fifty-six have already boarded," the woman informed them.

"Please," Sarah begged. "I don't want to go on the train, I just want to get my boy off it. Can you send someone down there? He's seventeen, dark hair ... and Amish."

But was he? Oh no, what if he'd dressed *Englisch* for the journey? She knew he had jeans and a T-shirt stashed in his dresser. Had he worn them to blend into the crowd?

Outside, on the other side of every barrier the *Englisch*

world seemed determined to erect to keep her from her son, a long whistle sounded.

"Ma'am, it's too late. The train's departing."

"Noooo," Sarah moaned, and covered her face with her hands.

Caleb dragged her to the window. The silver train rolled out of the station, picking up speed with every second. The windows flashed past, but in none of them could she see a familiar dark head, a much-loved profile, his father's straight nose...

The outlines of the train wavered and blurred, and when Henry joined them five minutes later, breathing as though he'd run a mile, the track was empty...and so were her hands...and so was her heart.

Sarah watched Caleb run through the knee-high corn toward Jacob and Corinne's to tell them what Simon had done. He'd enjoy the telling of it, being the only one in the family who wasn't feeling betrayed and bereaved. He saw the whole thing as an adventure...but wait until he saw the effects of it. The sorrow and worry of those left behind. The consequences of taking one's own way, even when one didn't mean to harm.

When she turned back, it was to see Henry watching not Caleb, but her. Did he think she was going to fall apart again? Not that she could blame him. How many times had she done it already?

"I'll be all right." She patted his arm, the way she would reassure a child or Michael's old dog. "It's not fair that you always get stuck coming to my rescue in a crisis."

"I'm glad I'm here. It's nice to be needed, even if it's only for my car."

Now, that wasn't fair—or true. "I hope you don't really think that." She took off her away bonnet and laid it and the basket on the porch railing, then slowly walked across the lawn in the direction of the garden.

She couldn't go in the house. If she did, she'd only wind up in Simon's room on the quilt Corinne had made for his bed, her face in his pillow. And what would Henry think of that?

He fell in beside her. "No, I suppose I don't, really. Neighbors help each other out, whether it's pitching in with the harvest or lending tools or—what did Caleb call it? Going on a high-speed chase through town."

"Low speed, it seemed to me. If it hadn't been for that accident, we would have got there in time." She bent to inspect the tomato starts, and found that life had stirred when she was busy with other things. In the section she'd seeded, the borage was coming up.

She knelt for a closer look. "Borage for courage, Ruth says. To replenish the adrenal glands and raise the spirits." She touched a little leaf and straightened. "I hope they grow quickly."

"Feeling in need of courage?" His blue eyes held kindness, his face softening with what must be pity.

"Today I do. I fear for him, Henry. He'll be in a worldly place surrounded by rough men who don't know our ways."

"He has Joe Byler with him. Between the two of them, they'll look after each other and muddle through."

Something Michael used to say seemed more than appropriate now. "Fear is what leaks in to fill a heart where there isn't enough faith, *nichts*?"

"I don't think you have a shortage of faith. It's natural to worry. You're a mother. It's what they do."

"*Ja*, but if I had the courage to leave it in God's hands, I wouldn't worry." She sighed. "I wish I was like Corinne. She has the loveliest spirit. Nothing seems to bother her—and I know it's because she's left her worries in God's hands."

The calendula was thriving. If she wanted it to stay that way, she'd better spend a little time out here weeding.

But Henry wouldn't let her avoid the view inside her own heart. "Sarah, quit beating yourself up. I know you're upset, but the way to find the bright side is to think of all the things that are good about your life, not all the ways you fall short."

Easier said than done. "And what is good, do you think?"

"You are," he said simply. "You're a good mother, you take great care of your boys, you take good care of the folks in the district—"

"Timothy Yost came home yesterday. Did you hear?"

His train of thought had jumped the track for sure, from the way he gawked at her. "Did he? We found the right one?"

"*Ja.* He and his father reconciled."

"Now, see? That just proves my point." She had not done such a good job of derailing him, after all. "You helped a family start to heal itself. And I know for a fact that took some pretty major courage."

"You did most of it. With the Internet and—"

He closed the distance she'd put between them in one long step, and wrapped his hands around her upper arms. "You're doing it again. It's not humility, Sarah. This is selling yourself short."

She gazed up into his face, perplexed at why anything she said should have this kind of effect on him. For a moment, the breeze stilled in the trees.

Her breath caught as she met his eyes, where hunger and doubt and honest concern fought all at once. It was the hunger that made her sway toward him—that made him slip his arms around her—solid, tight—as tightly as though she might be torn away from him at any second.

Torn away.

Common sense flooded in like a bath of cold water.

Oh yes, he must be torn away, because he was an outsider and she was flirting with danger and what if Caleb came upon them right now?

"This is wrong," she said, her voice a breath instead of a sound as she stepped back.

"I know."

"Then why..."

"Because I needed to hold you. And you needed to be held." He raked both hands through his hair, leaving it standing straight up from his scalp in a way that an Amish man's would not.

*He is not Amish. He chose not to be. Therefore he cannot choose you—and you cannot choose him.*

"We can't do this, Henry."

"I know. In my head I know. But the rest of me? Not so much." One step back. Then another. "And you know what? I was supposed to have lunch with Ginny today and this is the first I've thought of it."

He'd held her as a man holds the only woman in his heart, and it made him think of Ginny Hochstetler? Oh yes, the Lord had a sense of humor indeed. You couldn't get a much clearer reminder than that, could you?

"Then maybe you should go over there and apologize for being late. The lilac is blooming—you could take her a bouquet."

The lines around his mouth, etched there by pain, seemed to groove a little deeper. "Sarah, don't do this. It won't happen again, I promise. I told you I valued your friendship, and I meant it."

And she valued his. Which had nothing to do with how the last few seconds had changed her—changed the way she saw him.

"Go to Ginny," she whispered. "There is nothing for you here but a friend who is grateful to have you as a neighbor."

He must believe it or she was lost.

Another step back. He turned. And then he was striding across the lawn to his car, climbing into it, slamming the door.

When she heard the engine accelerate away down the road, heading toward Willow Creek, she actually made it to the back steps before her knees gave out. The sun lay warm on her hands as she covered her face. "*Ach*, what have I done? I can't afford these feelings, Lord. I can't have any feelings at all for a man who does not choose You. Help me. Please help me to overcome this craziness and set my heart on You, where it should be."

The breeze touched her face in passing, cooling her hot cheeks and bringing with it the scent of lemon balm, warm in the sun.

Lemon balm, her mother's favorite. For lifting spirits and healing wounds.

Something touched her foot, and she lowered her hands to see that two of her hens had come over to the steps, one of them stretching out for a sun bath against her feet. They only did that when they felt completely safe, when they took time from the business of hunting and eating and laying, to rest.

She should follow their example. For once, to just be still and let the scent of grass and balm fill her senses.

*And the leaves of the tree were for the healing of the nations.*

Not only for the nations. For individuals, too. God was faithful in this very moment in giving her another reminder, bringing back to her remembrance the thing that He wanted her to do. She was learning to bring the healing leaves, and roots, and flowers, as well as the peace and sense of safety that it brought, to others. That was the task God had set for her, and she mustn't lose sight of it.

With a gentle hand, she stroked the hen's feathers and moved her off her foot. She got up and collected some leaves of lemon balm, and a few of mint. The lavender had just begun to bloom, so she took a few heads of it, too.

It was nearly five o'clock, and if she left now, she could make tea for Corinne and Amanda and help them with dinner. She would pour out her heart to them, and they would wrap her in their love that didn't judge, only healed.

Because that was the real healer, wasn't it? Love. It healed all things, and hoped all things, and never failed. And it waited patiently for sons to return.

Sarah collected her basket off the porch rail, put the herbs in it, and set off, her feet sure on the path that love had worn into the earth, the scent of balm gentle on her hands.

# READING GROUP GUIDE

1. Sarah Yoder belongs to an Old Order Amish community, where women are expected to work in the home. Do you think that her being an herbal healer fits in with this view?

2. Sarah's attempts to help Oran Yost don't seem hopeful at first. Do you think she was right to pursue it?

3. What would you do if it was in your power to help someone, and he or she didn't want to be helped?

4. What themes do you see in the book along with the theme of healing the body and the spirit?

5. Have you ever tried home remedies or teas that involve plants from the garden or roadside?

6. Have you ever seen a quilt garden? Would you like to plant one?

7. Henry Byler left the church before he was baptized, so he is not shunned by the Willow Creek community. Do you think Sarah is right to tell Caleb that, while they can be friendly, they can't have real fellowship with someone outside the church?

8. Do you think Henry is fighting the call of God back to the Amish community? Is this why he is pursuing Ginny Hochstetler?

9. Why is Sarah afraid of being alone when she has friends and family all around her? Is this why she is so upset when Simon leaves? Or is there more to it?

10. When you feel "alone in a crowd," what do you do to find peace again?

# GLOSSARY

*Aendi:* Auntie
*Ausbund:* Amish hymnbook
*bidde:* please
*Blaum Kuche:* plum cake
*Bobblin:* babies
*Bohnesupp:* bean soup, often served at lunch after church
*Daadi Haus:* "Grandfather house," a separate home for the older folks
*Daadi:* Grandpa
*Dat:* Dad, Father
*Deitsch:* Pennsylvania Dutch language
*Denki:* thank you
*Deschperaat:* desperate
*Dokterfraa:* female healer
*Druwwel:* trouble
*Duchly:* headscarf
*Englisch:* non-Amish people
*Fraa:* woman, wife
*Freind, die guten:* the good friends
*Gelassenheit:* humility, submission
*Gott:* God
*Gmee:* church community in a district
*Grossdaadi:* Great-grandfather
*Grossmammi:* Great-grandmother
*guder mariye:* Good morning

*gut:* good

*gut, denki:* good (or well), thank you

*ja:* yes

*Kapp:* prayer covering worn by plain women

*Kinner:* children

*kitzlich:* touchy

*Kranken, die:* the sick

*Kumme mit:* Come with me

*Leppli:* vestigial peplum on an Amish woman's dress; now a small triangular flap

*Liewi:* dear, darling

*Maedel:* girl over 12

*Maedeli:* girl under 12

*Mamm:* Mother, Mom

*Mammi:* Grandma

*Mann:* husband, man

*Maud:* maid, household helper

*Meinding, die:* shunning, the

*neh:* no

*nichts?:* Is it not so?

*Onkel:* Uncle

*Ordnung:* discipline, or standard of behavior and dress unique to each community

*Plappermaul:* blabbermouth

*Rumspringe:* "running around," the season of freedom for Amish youth between sixteen and the time they marry

*Schweschder:* sister

*Schnitz:* sliced, dried apples

*Schnitz-und-Gnepp:* apple and dumpling

*sehr gut:* very good

*Sich getempert:* Calm down (Lit. "Be temperate")

*Uffgeva:* giving up of one's will, submission

*verhuddelt:* confused, mixed up

*Warum has du gelacht?:* Why did you laugh? (Colloq. "What's so funny?")

*Warum nichts?:* Why not?

*Was duschde hier?:* What are you doing here?

*Was ischt?:* What is it?

*Was sagst du?:* What are you saying?

*Wie geht's?:* How goes it?

*"Wo ist Jesus mein Verlangen":* "Where Is Jesus My Desire" (hymn title)

*Wunderbaar:* wonderful

*Wunnerschee:* very beautiful

*Youngie:* young people who are running around

For the Lord shall comfort Zion: he will comfort all her waste places; and he will make her wilderness like Eden, and her desert like the garden of the Lord; joy and gladness shall be found therein, thanksgiving, and the voice of melody.

—Isaiah 51:3, KJV

# CHAPTER 1

The young mother in the crisp organdy prayer covering, mint-green dress, and black bib apron looked at Sarah Yoder a little doubtfully. "Chickweed?"

The June sun shone through the sparkling clean windows of the guest room on the first floor of the farmhouse, which Sarah had begun to use as her dispensary. Gripping his mother's hand and trying manfully not to cry was her little patient—a boy of four so sunburned that his skin had already begun to peel.

Briskly, Sarah took the big bunch of chickweed that she'd pulled from the bank near her garden, and demonstrated as she talked. "It's a humble little plant, but it's *wunderbaar*, truly. You scrunch it up and rub it between your hands, like this, *ja?*" The plants began to break down, their juicy stems and leaves forming a wet mass (*mucilaginous*, her herb book said, when *goopy* would have done as well). When it was good and ready, Sarah gently applied it to the little boy's arms and shoulders. "Were you working in the field with your Dat, Aaron?"

He gulped and shook his head, flinching in spite of himself. "We went swimming in the pond. *Mei bruder* and the boys from the next farm."

"Ah, I see. And when you're swimming, you don't feel the sun working on you, do you? Does this feel better?" She dabbed the juicy mass on his cheeks and forehead, and he nodded.

"It feels cool."

She stepped back and smiled at him. "You look like a duck who just came up out of the pond, all covered in weed. What does a duck say?"

Instead of saying "quack-quack," the boy gave a perfect imitation of a mallard's call.

"I see a hunter in the making." She brushed his fine blond hair from his eyes and tried to ignore the pang in her heart.

*Simon. Caleb.* No longer little boys whom she could cuddle and sing to. And now, Simon was gone.

He and his best friend Joe Byler had done a bait-and-switch a few weeks ago, making them all think they were going to an Amish community in Colorado for a working vacation, and all the time they'd secured jobs at a dude ranch, wrangling horses. They were working among worldly people and all the temptations to a young man that living outside the circle of their people would bring.

*Oh Lord, be with him and keep him safe.*

"How long should I leave the chickweed on him?" Aaron's mother asked.

"Not long," Sarah assured her, coming back to herself. This was work she could do, a difference she could make right here with another woman's child. Worrying about Simon profited her nothing. The Lord had him cupped in His hand, didn't He? There was no reason to worry. "Rinse it off when you get home, and if you can, squish up some more and put it on when he goes to bed. He might need to sleep on a towel, to save the sheets."

"*Denki*, Sarah. I'm so glad you knew what to do. Sun screen is no good after the damage is done, and vinegar didn't seem to help him."

Sarah accepted a payment that still seemed to her to be too much for such a simple solution, but the young mother seemed happy with both the treatment and the new knowledge she'd gained. When they clopped away down the drive in the gray-sided buggy the churches used here in Lancaster County, Sarah could already hear Aaron begging to take the reins, just the way Caleb, her younger son, always had when he was that age.

Boys and ponds. Boys and horses. Boys and dirt. You could count on the magnetic attraction between them the way you counted on the turn of the seasons.

She turned and walked across the lawn to her garden—or, as her sister-in-law Amanda was fond of saying, "that crazy quilt patch you planted." The patterns she had seen in her mind's eye back in the muddy days of spring had come to full fruition, the way a complicated star-and-flying-geese pattern materialized out of fabric when Sarah's mother-in-law Corinne Yoder made a quilt.

First there was nothing, and then there was something, patterns emerging to create beauty where there had been none before. Was this how women reflected God as they went about the act of creation in small ways and large?

Sarah knelt to inspect the progress of the peas climbing up their teepees of string. Was she being prideful to even think such things? Because baking, gardening, and sewing were all small acts of creation, when you got right down to it. Leaving out the miracle of conception itself, what about bringing up children? There was no creation as beautiful as a child who worshipped God and learned to love Him at an early age.

"Hallo, Sarah!"

And speaking of . . .

She stood and shaded her eyes against the sun. "Hallo, Priscilla. *Wie geht's?*"

"I'm well, *denki.*" She waved an envelope and Sarah felt a leap in her heart. "I have a letter from Joe. I thought you might like to read it."

From Joe. Not Simon.

As the pretty blond sixteen-year-old crossed the grass, Sarah took a deep breath to settle herself and made her way between the squares of culinary and medicinal herbs to join her under the maple trees. "You're lucky. Joe is a much better letter-writer than Simon, as it turns out. My boy has never been away from home this long—never had to write me letters. The things we find out, even when we think we know someone so well."

"That's why I thought you might want to share it with me."

"Come back to the house. Do you have time for a root beer? I made some on Saturday."

"I do. It's my day off from the Inn—Ginny doesn't have anyone come in on Mondays, and her other helper is working today. I can't stay long, though. Mamm is doing the washing."

Nearly all the women in their district did on Mondays. Sarah had just finished hers before the sunburn patient had arrived.

When they were settled with cold root beer fizzing in tall glasses, Sarah opened Priscilla's letter from Joe.

Dear Pris,

Well, we've been here a month now. Seems hard to believe. Yesterday was officially the longest I've ever been gone from home, including that time we went to

Holmes County when my two cousins married twin sisters and there was a tornado during the wedding.

Simon sends his regards.

We been real busy. Like I told you in my last letter, this ain't no fly-by-night outfit. The ranch house alone must have cost a couple million to build, even if it is just a real big, fancy log cabin, and don't even get me started on the barns and bunkhouses. Everything is first class. Guess that's why they hired us, ha ha.

We just got back from a week-long trail ride. Me and Simon went along to tend to the horses, because a herd of Japanese businessmen don't know much about 'em except which end to put the bridle on.

They treated us real good, and I have to say, I never seen such pretty country as I have here. You really see what God was about when He made the earth. We saw two bears and a mountain lion and a bald eagle. I took a picture of the she-bear with my phone because I didn't think any of the boys would believe I really saw one.

We worked with the guests to teach them about their horses, and by the time we got back, all but one of the Japanese men could saddle and curry his own horse. The one who I guess is the boss of them was real happy with what he called the "team building exercise"—he gave us a nice tip. A hundred dollars is pretty nice, I'd say! I sent it home to Dat.

I've had a letter from Mamm. I think Dat is still pretty mad at me, but he'll come around.

Okay, it's time for supper.

Yours,

Joe

Sarah folded up the letter and handed it back. "Do you think it's true about Paul?"

Priscilla shrugged one shoulder under her deep rose dress and matching cape, and pushed her glasses up with one finger. "I don't know. I think he'd have been less mad if the boys had been honest. It wasn't the ranch he objected to, so much as the lie."

Sarah could well imagine Paul's feelings of betrayal. She'd struggled with the same. On top of it, she didn't have a big farm to run with one fewer pair of hands.

After a moment, Priscilla said, "Do you think they're coming back?"

"It's only for the summer." Sarah wanted to encourage her, but it was hard, when she wondered the same thing. "Lancaster County is their home. I'm sure they'll be back when the snow flies and they're laid off, even if they're not in time to help with harvest."

Priscilla nodded, and as though this had reminded her of something, she changed the subject. "Is Caleb over at Henry's?"

"*Ja*. Henry needed help no matter how he fought against it—did you hear that he got an order from some big kitchen-store chain in New York to make jugs and batter bowls?"

"I did, and I know why, too. One of the men who works for the company in New York spent the weekend at the Inn with his girlfriend. He got Henry's name from Ginny and spent the whole Saturday in the barn with him. His girlfriend didn't mind, though. You should see the quilts she bought— one of them was Evie Troyer's 'Rondelay'—her most expensive one. Mamm worked on it last winter. She said Evie was delighted—and so was her husband the bishop."

Good for Henry, to find such a good commission so soon

after moving here. Sarah wished him well—and as for any other feelings....

After Henry had tried to help her stop Simon from leaving, things had been...different between them. Oh, they were cordial and neighborly and Sarah still sent over a plate of baking with Caleb when she could, but under it all was the faint sound of an alarm bell ringing.

An Amish woman could be neighborly with an *Englisch* man. The Amish were friendly to everyone. But Henry was more than *Englisch*. He had grown up Amish and chosen to leave rather than join the church. He and Sarah might share a fence line, but between them there was a great gulf fixed...and any feelings that might have gone beyond friendship could never cross that gulf.

After Priscilla went home, Sarah spent the afternoon weeding the herb beds next to the house where she grew the plants closest to her heart. The fragrance of lemon balm, rosemary, thyme, and lavender rose up around her the way prayer must rise to God. The Bible called it a "sweet-smelling savor." Maybe it smelled something like this, too.

Her chickens, interested in the disturbed soil, came to investigate, yanking out worms and chasing butterflies. The way they threw themselves wholeheartedly into whatever they did made her smile. People thought chickens were stupid, but she was beginning to learn that wasn't so. She and Carrie Miller over in Whinburg had got to talking when they'd run into each other at the discount barn, both of them looking for shoes for their *Kinner*. When Carrie explained that the birds could learn their own names and understand phrases, Sarah hadn't believed her—until she'd tried it herself.

One of the Red Stars was nipping at the leaves of the sage. "Here, you," she said. "Not for chickens. You go eat the grass." The hen ignored her, so she said it again, and gently moved the bird toward the lawn. The hen made one final attempt, and when Sarah repeated, "Not for chickens," at last she turned away and pulled up a few blades of grass instead.

Sometimes it took a few reminders to do the right thing. Content with her garden and her flock, Sarah found herself giving thanks for her blessings.

She didn't need to look over that fence where forbidden things grew.

*Visit the neighboring community of Whinburg, Pennsylvania
in the Amish Quilt Series*

### The Wounded Heart
Widowed with two young children, Amelia Beiler struggles to run her late husband's business until Eli Fischer buys it. Eli has a personal interest in her, but when she's diagnosed with multiple sclerosis, Amelia feels she must keep her distance from him in order to protect him.

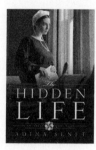

### The Hidden Life
Thirty-year-old Emma Stolzfus cares for her elderly mother by day and secretly writes stories by night, her hidden life shared only among close friends. But when a New York literary agent approaches her about her work, it will change her life in unexpected ways.

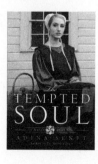

### The Tempted Soul
After years of marriage, Carrie and Melvin Miller fear they'll never be blessed with children. Carrie is intrigued by the medical options available to the *Englisch* in the same situation, but her husband objects. Is God revealing a different path to motherhood, or is Carrie's longing for a child tempting her to stray from her Amish beliefs?

**Available now from FaithWords wherever books are sold.**